PRAISE FOR FOX HUNT

Action-packed with a dry sense of humor and a few good one-liners that eases the intensity, this story is easy to get caught up in.

"Crowned Heart" distinction, – InD'Tale *Magazine*.

"A high octane, pedal-to-the-metal, adrenaline-fueled read."
– Jill, GoodReads reviewer

PRAISE FOR UNDERTOW
(THE UNDERCITY CHRONICLES #1)

The writing duo of S. M. Stelmack have mashed their creative talents and imaginative minds together to create this sci-fi, romantic suspense which has the ability to appeal to horror and paranormal fans alike." – *InD'Tale Magazine.*

"...well-written and atmospheric, incorporating a steamy romance between Jack and Lindsay. The underground cultures are interesting and well thought-out. ...a very enjoyable and thoroughly entertaining read with some nice touches of humour to lighten the often dark tone and setting."
– *Jill, GoodReads reviewer*

FOX HUNT

THE FEMME VENDETTAS

S.M. STELMACK

Copyright © 2013 by S.M. Stelmack
Editing by Alyssa Palmer
Cover Art by CrocoDesigns

http://www.smstelmackauthor.com

Printed in the United States of America

First Edition: September 2013
Library of Congress Cataloging-in-Publication Data

Stelmack, S.M.
    Fox Hunt / S.M. Stelmack – 1st ed
    ISBN-13: 978-0991869855

    1.Fox Hunt—Fiction. 2.Fiction—Romantic Suspense
    3.Fiction—Action & Adventure

To The Woozle and Dr. Maven

(Authors Moira and Serge Stelmack)
http://www.smstelmackauthor.com

A NOTE FROM MOIRA

Dear Reader,

Life is difficult. It's work, it's strife, it's not fair, if fair means things go your way. No life is charmed forever. We all face black moments. We can only hope that we don't have to go through our trials alone, that someone has our back.

For Delta, that someone turns out to be Brian. She pegs him for an adrenaline junkie. His own worst enemy. Then again, isn't that the case for us all?

Don't we all self-sabotage ourselves at least once, and probably, repeatedly? Don't we all have inner fears that hold us back from claiming what we want, maybe even what we deserve? I know I do. Ordinary fears—for my kids, security, health—and the more private ones, too. But for the past sixteen years, I've not faced my fears alone. I have Serge. My husband, the father of my kids and the most honest friend anyone could hope to have. "The best writing I've ever read came from you," he once said and then frowned. "Some of the worst, too."

The fear-mongering part of me wanted to focus on his last words, to justify why I should just give up. But I needed to accept the whole truth Serge was offering me. Things were rotten, but they could become brilliant, even the best ever. It was—and still is—a daunting task but it has allowed me to put one word after another, one event after another.

May we all have the guts to deal with the troubles that inevitably come, may we all—like me with Serge and Delta with Brian—find the one that can help us through those dark times. And if you've found that special person, may you keep them for as long as you both shall live.

Best,
Moira

PROLOGUE

AKENO SAVORED THE sweet metallic purr of the antique safe as he smoothly spun its dial first right, then back. With the ocean of blood money Matsuda possessed, he could've had something more modern protecting his cash, but Akeno appreciated the crime lord's old-world style. The Swiss precision of the mechanism, the Italian polish of its fittings—he was so glad he didn't have to violate the artistry with the usual drills and picks and pliers, yet part of him also felt denied its deflowering on this, his final take.

So far, everything tonight had gone like clockwork. The mansion's formidable security system had been deactivated with the codes provided, and the key to the old man's office had been hanging right where it was supposed to be. It was shaping up to be a classic inside job—quick, easy and relatively low-risk. The real test was going to be getting away with it afterwards, especially considering who Matsuda was.

The last number reached, Akeno drew in a long, slow breath, and exhaled on a three-count. In a moment, he'd discover if his love really knew her employer's secrets as intimately as his own. Pressing down on the safe's handle, he heard a quiet but distinct click, then slowly swung it open to reveal the prize.

Although he'd paid many uninvited visits to wealthy L. A. estates in his career what Akeno saw before him now made his heart kick like never more: stacks of hundred dollar bills almost filled the safe to capacity. Without a doubt, the biggest single haul of his life sat right before him—even after splitting it with his accomplice.

Well, she'd certainly earned her money. He pulled a large microfiber bag from his pocket and swept the cash into it. Now, to make his escape. So long as there was nothing suspicious to tip off the old gangster, days, perhaps even weeks, might pass before the robbery was detected. By that time, they would be on the other side of the country, sipping margaritas in the Miami sun and living out their fantasies.

As Akeno eased the safe door shut, however, his sensitive ears caught the almost imperceptible turning of the office door handle. He ducked behind the nearby desk, an instant before the door swung open, a dim arc of moonlight spilling in from the hallway.

He rested his head against the hardwood floor to peer under the desk. There was a single pair of feet in black running shoes, and from the shape of the shadow that stretched behind, his visitor was a woman. She slipped inside, shut the door, and a familiar voice spoke in the quietest whisper. "Akeno? Are you here?"

Anger and relief flooded through him as he rose to his feet.

"Susan," he hissed, "what the hell are you doing here?"

She turned towards him in the darkness, and though her face was concealed by a balaclava, he knew she was smiling that devilish grin of hers. She sauntered towards him. "Now is

2

that any way to talk to your Mistress?"

Akeno had no idea how to respond to that. Was she here out of her insatiable need for danger? From the past two months of sex he could believe it. The woman was a handful, two handfuls, actually. And she had a way of mixing pleasure and pain into a cocktail more potent than either.

"What's the matter?" she breathed. "Aren't you happy to see me?"

No, he wasn't, because it meant she didn't trust him, understandable given his profession, but the lack of faith still stung. "You know how dangerous you being here is? This isn't one of your games, Susan."

She gave an amused shrug, slinking around the desk to him. "I like risk, Akeno. I thought you did, too." Her body rubbed against his as she eased up her hood to reveal her mouth, with its hot red lips and perfect white teeth.

He gave her what she wanted because he was powerless to do, otherwise. He yanked up his mask, crushing his lips against hers. To say he was being unprofessional was an understatement, but as her tongue slid into his mouth he had a hard time thinking about anything else. He ran his free hand over the silky fabric of her midnight bodysuit, enjoying the curves sheathed within.

It was she, as usual, who broke off the kiss, tugging her mask down to blank out her face again. Her fingers trailed down his arm to where his hand held the bag. "How much did we get?"

He covered his face. "About a million. Maybe a bit more."

Her dark eyes glinted. "Mmm…with that, we could do a lot of things for a long time." Akeno knew what she meant, and he couldn't help but reach for her, again.

Suddenly, the room was again bathed in dim light, the office door opening to reveal a young man standing in the hallway. Akeno froze. The youth squinted into the darkness. "Jeanelle?"

Akeno spun about, his eyes darting in search of an escape route, but then a gunshot blasted through the room and the boy collapsed like a rag doll. Before Akeno could react, Susan seized him by the arm. "Come on! Run!"

The whole house was awake now, and in a rich neighborhood like this, they had only a couple of minutes before the cops would be on them. There was no time to argue. Leaping over the crumpled body, Akeno felt a spike of sickness drive right through his heart.

The kid couldn't have been older than sixteen, dressed in his robe and pajamas, completely unarmed. There was a neat little bullet hole in his forehead, and from the way he'd fallen, he was clearly dead. Oh God, he thought, sprinting after his lover down the curving stairwell to the front entrance. Oh God, Susan, what have you done…?

CHAPTER ONE

BRIAN CHANSE WANTED to notch up the speed of his wipers, but they were already going full out. The rain was so fierce they didn't sweep off the water before the windshield was covered again, and the blackness of the New Mexican night didn't help.

"Might as well be driving underwater," he muttered to himself.

He glanced at the GPS. Should have stopped when he had the chance. Santa Rosa wasn't for another twenty miles, though it was still closer than turning around. He rubbed his eyes wearily. There was nothing to do but press on.

At the rate he was going, it was almost one in the morning when up ahead he spotted someone walking the shoulder of the road. He blinked a few times, but sure enough, there was some poor soul slogging through the downpour.

He crawled past to reduce the spray from his wheels, getting a a better look. A kid. He pulled his Mustang over and checked his rearview mirror. Yep, it was a kid coming up to his door. A runaway? A druggie? Didn't really matter—he wasn't about to pass anyone by in a storm like this. He lowered his window.

Rain splattered his jacket and cut into his face. It was a teenage girl. She was in hiking boots, jeans and a hoodie, all of which were absolutely soaked, and she swayed before steadying herself against his car.

"Bad night for a walk. Need a lift?"

She studied him, her eyes a shocking blue against the pallor of her skin. Definitely pretty and most definitely not well. She nodded after a moment and circled the hood of his car, while he gathered up the empty fast-food wrappers from the passenger seat and fired them into the back.

She slid in, her short blonde hair matted to her head, her arms wrapped about her in a futile attempt to retain some warmth. He took an extra look where the arms were wrapped, then searched her face. She wasn't quite as young as he'd taken her for, just petite. Probably in her twenties and harmless enough. She didn't seem to have any gear.

"Thanks," she mumbled.

Her face was dead white, even her lips were a dark shade of pale. The desert was a cold place at night, and who knew how long she'd been out there. "I know how this is going to sound, but I think you really ought to get out of those wet clothes. I can get some dry stuff out of the back if you want to change. I'll wait outside."

She stared straight ahead at the rain battering the windshield and shook her head. "I'm fine. I just need to get to the next town."

Stubborn woman. Stubborn and stupid. She was going to catch her death, but what could he do about it? He'd warned her, and he wasn't interested in arguing with any more people that insisted on putting themselves in harm's way. He'd already had enough of *that* for a lifetime.

Still, he cranked the heat to max, then reached into the backseat and rooted through the mess until he found a beach towel, handing it to her. She took it gingerly, as if it was diseased.

Stubborn and stupid and ungrateful.

He shrugged. "Suit yourself." He shifted the car into gear and continued down the highway, trying to ignore the sound of her chattering teeth.

By the time he parked at a Santa Rosa motel, she was asleep, her chin on her chest. The place was a dump, and by the looks of the peeling paint and flickering neon sign, it was many a year since it'd been anything else. He sprinted inside and rang the night buzzer several times before an elderly clerk came to the grubby counter, watery gray eyes huge behind thick glasses.

"A room, please."

The man took the last key from the board behind him, sliding it over to Brian along with a coffee-stained registry. "That'll be sixty-five dollars. Check-out time is noon. No pets."

As if a dog would want to stay here.

Leaky ballpoint in hand, he scribbled in his name and address, only realizing as he finished that he didn't live there anymore. Then again, he didn't live anywhere anymore. He doled out the money, then picked up the key and headed back to the car. All he had to do now was wake the woman, settle in for a good night's sleep and spend the next day driving to Los Angeles.

Cold rain drumming on him, he opened the passenger door and tapped her on the shoulder. "Miss. We're here. Get up."

She stirred briefly, before slumping back against the seat.

No good deed goes unpunished.

"Come on, miss." He shook her, but she had all the get up and go of a sack of potatoes. He placed his hand on her forehead. Her clammy skin was ice cold.

"Dammit. Why can't people ever just listen?" Unsnapping her seatbelt, he scooped her limp body into his arms. God, not a sack of potatoes but a feather pillow. He hurried up a slick flight of stairs, and managed to juggle keys and her into his room, kicking the door shut and flicking on the light with his elbow.

He laid her on the bed. Her lips had turned bluish-gray and she was shivering harder than a lost kitten. A check found her pulse still strong. She was hypothermic, but not in any immediate peril. The first thing was to get her warm so she didn't get any worse, then call an ambulance.

Brian grimaced at what he had to do next. Him alone in a hotel room taking clothes off a stranger. Wasn't this just a lawsuit in the making? Then again, a dead woman in his room wouldn't look so good, either.

Peeling off the wet hoodie, his eyes met with a thin white T-shirt, her nipples hard buttons beneath the wet fabric. He reminded himself of the first-aid course he'd taken every year since he was sixteen. This next step was required, that's all.

As he tugged off her t-shirt and sports bra, he tried to keep his eyes to himself, but, oh yeah…she was well-built. He hurried down to unlace her boots. It was then she became conscious. "Don't…please…don't…" she slurred.

"You're hypothermic," he explained, as he slid off her socks and boots. "I'm not going to hurt you, but I have to take off your wet clothes. And then I'll get you some help."

"Don't call…don't call a doctor…please…"

Victims of exposure often made odd requests or even

hallucinated, but she seemed lucid.

"Don't call…" she pleaded. "They'll find…me…please… don't…."

"Who's going to find you?" he asked, but she'd already passed out. He shook his head, then peeled the wet pants over her hips and down her slim, athletic legs. Her panties had come down with the jeans and turning her to her belly, he averted his eyes from her ass. Her firm, squeezable ass. He lost no time in turning down the bedcovers and tucking them snugly around her body. With a bathroom towel, Brian dried her hair as thoroughly as possible. When he was done, it spiked out from her head, and without thinking, he smoothed down its short silkiness. Catching himself, he withdrew his hand. *That* wasn't in any first-aid course.

He pondered getting his suitcase of dry clothes from the trunk, but the rain pounding on the roof and windows settled the matter for him. He next pondered the uncomfortable-looking armchair in the corner of the room, and then the woman's wet mound of clothes. Sighing, he picked them up and hung them over the shower rod in the bathroom.

On his way to the chair, he checked on her. She didn't look good. Her lips still had a bluish tinge and her shivering hadn't ceased. He cursed, shot back into the bathroom and returned with all the towels, right down to the washcloths for her head. He spread them and his leather jacket over her, then flipped the remainder of the duvet on top for good measure, but she kept shaking so badly the coverings trembled.

He hesitated, then took off his shirt and slid beside her. "This had better work," Brian muttered in her ear, "or you're going to the hospital, whether you like it or not." He wrapped his arms around her, pressed his body close, and shared his warmth. Her shivering gradually subsided, her lips flushed a pale pink and her breath blew calmly against his neck. Brian became acutely aware of her soft body against his, and eased himself away before any embarrassing reaction could occur. He'd lie here until she was completely out of the danger zone and then retreat to the chair. He'd just rest for a moment... close his eyes for a while...

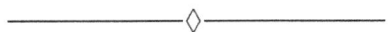

Delta Fox slowly woke, weak, feverish, hungry and... naked. She snapped upright in bed, and when her head stopped spinning, woozily took in her surroundings. The light slanting in told her it was morning, she was in bed, and—oh, shit!— with a man. She recoiled, horrified, but then her leg rubbed against the roughness of his jeans. Reaching down, she tentatively checked herself. Okay, he might've copped a feel but that was all.

She was under a heap of laundry—sheets, blankets, towels, and a man's leather jacket. Her eye on him, she slipped her fingers into the jacket pocket, finding his wallet as she had hoped. She flipped it open, and inside found a respectable amount of cash and platinum credit cards, as well as his California driver's license and a number of other pieces of identification.

The name was Brian Chanse, born thirty-five years ago and a resident of Hollywood. He was a member of the Screen Actors Guild, had a first aid certificate and an organ donor card. She could've fallen into worse hands, but not by much.

Returning the wallet, she laid back, trying to let memories of the previous night solidify in her fevered mind. She'd been hitch-hiking ever since she'd run out of money in Little Rock, and been dumped by a surly trucker out in the middle of nowhere when she'd refused to "pay" him for the ride. Given her luck, it had started raining, and without any real options, she'd been forced to endure the storm. From what she remembered, Brian had been a gentleman and decent enough to respect her request not to call anyone.

She considered taking his cash and car, and heading for the hills. He'd be insured. Except then she'd have the local police on her tail as well. How far could she get sick, exhausted and with an APB on her? Not far enough to avoid either prison or a bullet to the brain.

Okay, first things first. Find clothes.

Her body aching, she draped her legs over the edge of the bed and wrapped a towel around herself. With a steadying hand on the end table, she stood and took a step.

Her legs gave out and she collapsed to the floor with a yelp. From her belly-down perspective, she saw the bed give a bounce, the yank of a sheet and then Chanse was standing above her. Crap, he was hot, all smooth muscles and lean lines. Probably knew it, too. His gaze skittered to her naked backside and Delta grabbed at her towel, doing what she could to salvage her dignity.

He didn't say a word. He bent down, that muscled chest and stubbly jaw up close, and suddenly she was in his arms, the towel twisted between them, and then just as quick, she was back in bed with the covers over her. His hand cupped her forehead.

"You've got a high fever. I'll take you to a doctor."

No, no, no. "No doctors," she said as strongly as she could, but even at that, it came out mewling.

"Look, you were hypothermic last night. You could have died. You really need to at least go to a clinic or something."

"No. I'll be okay. I'll just sleep some more."

His lips in that stubble thinned. "Yeah, but checkout is at noon. I have places to be."

"Listen, I have to get to Los Angeles...I can pay my way..."

"That's nice, but I'm not looking for a traveling companion."

Delta clenched her fists. She needed him. She hated that, hated needing anyone, much less a stranger, much less a gorgeous stranger who probably thought she was some homeless skank. Fighting a wave of dizziness, she forced herself to say, "Then I'll hire you, okay? Get me to L.A. and I'll pay whatever you think is fair."

He snorted. "Sure, and it's because you're rich that you were out hitch-hiking last night. All I want is to get going. If you want to stay here that's fine, but...."

Delta heard his voice fading, his athletic form blurring before her eyes. No, no. She couldn't black out, she had to persuade him somehow. What could she give him...?

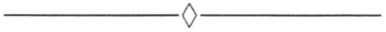

Great. The chick passed out while he was talking. Again. He should up and leave, before he got stuck looking after another train wreck. Hard and recent experience had taught him that people in a mess were usually there for a reason.

She was tiny, and white as the sheets. Dammit. He could go and then he'd spend the rest of the day—hell, the rest of his life—wondering how she'd made out. In the end, he was a soft-hearted sucker. This was going to be Marcia all over again.

She needed rest, lots of liquids and some decent food, and something for her fever as well. The sooner she was on her feet, the sooner he could get back to what constituted his life in L.A.

He pulled on some clothes, then headed outside to ask the motel clerk where the nearest grocery store and pharmacy were. It was ten-thirty in the morning, and already the blazing sun and thirsty earth had almost erased any sign of the night's downpour. The parking lot was empty save for his Mustang and an expensive Acura sports coupe, and as he approached the office he saw a pair of hard-faced Asian men emerge. Both were wearing dark suits despite the summer heat, their shoes flecked with mud.

He made room for them to pass, but one turned and gave a stiff and unnatural smile, as if breaking it in. "Excuse me, we looking for lady." The man's voice carried a pronounced Japanese accent. "You seen short lady with blonde hair, okay?"

Brian looked the men up and down. A good three inches shorter than him but from their build and stance, they were fighters.

"No, I can't say I have," he drawled. "If I do, who should I say is looking for her?"

"She is friend of ours. You see her walking on road?"

The truth seemed inconvenient. "Sorry. I got in late last night and didn't see anyone. There are a lot of truckers going through here. She could've caught a ride with one of them."

The smile dropped from the man's face. "Thank you, okay?" He nodded to his partner and they headed for their car. Brian strolled on to the office, but not before he mentally noted the license plate.

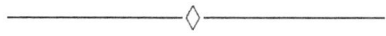

13

When Delta awoke again, it was to the sound of a key turning in the lock. The actor had returned, his arms filled with two large bags of groceries. She pulled herself up against the headboard, tucking the sheet around her as she went, right when a bottle of water and a large ham sandwich landed in her lap.

"Thanks," she said to his back.

"You're welcome," he said and started to unload a pile of food onto the table. "By the way," he said, over his shoulder, "I'm Brian."

She drank down half her water, considering. He'd not left her. He'd gotten her food. He'd…taken care of her. "I know. I read your driver's license when you were asleep."

He halted his unpacking and she tensed, ready for his anger. But after a long, drawn-out moment, he asked, "So what's your name?" He sounded…amused.

She clamped her teeth down on the ham and rye.

"Delta," she mumbled around the sandwich.

Brian plunked down in the armchair and ripped open a bag of chips. "Well, Delta, you mentioned last night some people are after you. Feel like elaborating on that?"

She chewed, swallowed, took another bite. "The less said the better."

"I've got time."

The man talked like an action hero. He was a good-looking guy who'd probably played bit parts in a half-dozen B-list movies and now fancied himself a badass do-gooder in real life. "Look, Mr. Chanse, thanks for everything you've done so far, but if I pay you to give me a lift to Los Angeles, I don't think I should have to tell you my life story."

"Maybe you'd prefer to tell it to those two Japanese guys who were looking for you outside the motel."

14

Shit. "Would it be too much to ask for you to look away for the next couple of minutes?"

The corner of his mouth flicked up. "Already seen you buck-naked."

True. She should get up and get on with it. Her life depended on it. She contemplated wrapping the sheet around herself, but she didn't have time to hold onto that trailing mass.

She was about to fling it back when he said, "I told them I hadn't seen you. They left about a half-hour ago."

She sucked in her breath and tucked the sheet around her again. Chanse was grinning. Jerk. Never mind. How had the bastards found her so soon? She thought she'd given them the slip back in Atlanta, but obviously they were smarter than they looked. She'd be dead if it wasn't for the smirking asshole.

"Thanks." It came out small and grudging to her ears, and she tried again. "Thanks."

"You're welcome. Now the story, please."

She took another long pull on her water. "I have a friend in Los Angeles. He does work that's not entirely legal," she began, choosing her words carefully. "He's gotten himself in trouble with some bad people, and they seem to think I'm involved."

"What did he do?"

"I don't know. I haven't seen him in almost two years."

"So that's why you're headed for Los Angeles, to find him? So why don't you just go to the cops?"

"It's complicated."

The man locked his green eyes on her, his brow creasing into a deep frown. "Delta, let me share something with you. I just finished spending the last six years being jerked around by a smart-ass woman. I didn't like it one bit. If you want my

15

help, then give me the whole story. Or else, I'm paying the bill and leaving you here."

From the bite of his words, he would, too. Her options were telling the truth and chance him calling the cops, or lie and risk him leaving her for the Japanese Mafia. Neither option was particularly pleasant.

"Well?" he prompted.

Delta took a deep breath. "I'm wanted by police on a breaking and entering charge, as well as for escaping police custody. If I go to them I'm facing at least two and a half years in jail, and as cushy as the media says the prisons are, I'd rather not find out for myself."

"Did you do it?"

"Do what?"

"The break and enter?"

"Of course I did. There wouldn't be a warrant out for me if I didn't, now would there?"

Chanse crunched a chip and cracked open a can of coke. "Okay. So what kind of crimes was your friend into?"

"What difference does that make?"

He drank from his can of coke. "The difference between a ride to L.A. or not."

"You wouldn't believe me if I told you."

"Nothing to lose by trying."

"You seem to think you're my only option for getting to L.A."

"I know I'm your best option."

What an arrogant, deluded, interfering…. "We were thieves, okay?" she snapped. "But not like you're thinking. My friend and I are guilty of dozens of b&e jobs, but we never actually stole anything—except for the very last time."

Chanse frowned. "Why would you break into a place and

not take anything?"

"I didn't say we didn't take anything. I said we didn't steal anything. We were reclamation experts. We got back things that had been taken from people."

"You mean like repo men?"

"Sort of, except we'd get back things like art, jewelry, cash...we helped people that had been conned, or were being blackmailed, or who had gotten a raw deal in a divorce. Stuff like that."

"Robin Hood, hmm?" he asked, leaning back in the chair. He was all muscle. He had to be getting tons of audition calls.

"Not really. We charged a percentage. But we never lifted anything that didn't belong to our clients."

"Anything the clients didn't say belonged to them, anyway. So what happened the last time?"

She paused. It had to be said, but even after two full years it still hurt. It hurt to even think about it and now she had to say it. She closed her eyes and sighed. "I got caught is what happened. In the worst possible way."

CHAPTER TWO

BRIAN COCKED HIS head at the power cord dangling from the television. Why the hell had she done that? He sighed, plugging it back in and turning it on.

Snatching up wrappers and plastic bags as he listened to the news, he tossed them in the direction of the garbage bin, then stretched and rubbed the back of his sore neck. Delta had insisted that he take the bed last night while she took the chair. He told her that wasn't happening because she was still sick and that the both of them could take the bed. But she wasn't having any of that, so because he never learned his lesson regarding needy women, he arranged it so that she took the bed and he took the damn chair.

Halfway through the night, he couldn't hack it anymore and had settled himself on the covers. He woke to find her glaring at him as if he were a sex fiend. She stomped into the bathroom and told him they were leaving in twenty minutes. He told her to get her ass out of the shower in ten then, because no way was he driving her anywhere unless he got a shower. She didn't answer, just closed the door.

He snagged her empty bottle of water. What was he doing

picking up after her? Better question: why on earth was he taking her anywhere? The woman might as well have the word "trouble" tattooed on her forehead. What kind of moron would agree to take an admitted fugitive on a road trip, especially when she had Japanese gangsters hunting her? He should've pushed her to expand on that "I got caught" statement but she'd gone into such a lockdown that there was no way he'd have pried another word out of her.

The shower stopped and he paused, imagining how a naked Delta, all warm and pink, would look like, feel like. Nope. Not going there. He fired clothes into his tote bag.

The door opened and out she came, hair all wet and spiky, in her white tee and a motel towel wrapped around her waist.

"Is that a white trash tennis skirt?"

"Jeans are still wet. Denim doesn't dry fast."

"Put on something else then."

Striding over to the bedside table, she grabbed the remote and snapped the T.V. off. "I did."

Brian took in the blank screen, then focused back on her. "You can't wear that in the car."

"Why not?"

"Okay, let me get this straight. You're enough of a prude—an ungrateful prude—to make me sleep on the chair–"

"I told you I'd sleep on the chair!"

"—but it's okay for you to wear a towel that you know when you sit in my car will come up to your crotch."

Delta jerked, and the color drained from her face. And then she went bright red and stomped back into the bathroom. She reappeared seconds later wearing a longer towel. She lifted her chin. "Better?"

Brian pressed his fingers to his forehead. "How about when we get to a place bigger than a block you pick up a pair of pants?"

"I told you. I don't have—"

"And you'll pay me back just like you're going to pay me back for the gas."

Blue eyes narrowed. "I told you I will, and I will."

"That's nice. You finished in the bathroom?"

She gave a mock sweeping gesture. When he emerged, the kink mostly out of his neck, she was waiting by the door, sipping coffee from a Styrofoam cup. She gestured to a second one on the table.

"Where did you get that?"

"From the motel office. Complimentary. I dropped off the key so we could leave straight from here."

"You could've been seen."

"I wasn't. Let's go."

His bag in one hand, he took a sip of coffee. Cream, no sugar, just how he liked it. "How did you know how I take my coffee?"

"I figured you for that kind of guy."

"What kind of guy is that?"

But she was already out the door and making for his vehicle. And the TV was, once again, unplugged.

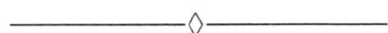

Fifty miles west of Brian and Delta, Kannon Takahama sat in his car by the side of the highway, staring down the long straight strip of asphalt, his eyes as dark and hard as onyx behind his mirrored sunglasses. Though the two men in the back were sweltering, his coffee-colored skin was as dry as a rattlesnake's, and he made a point of not opening the windows.

To control such men as them he had to have their respect.

His mixed black/Japanese heritage meant that he'd never have their friendship, nor ever truly escape their scorn, but respect was something primal and universal. It was the realization that he was tougher than them, meaner than them, and that he would kill them if they crossed him. That was a concept everyone understood, so he strove to establish simple dominance with all he met.

His smartphone chirped, and he took his time answering it.

"Sir. This is Makoto. We check all hotel and gas station. We don't find her."

The news didn't surprise him. Tracking Ms. Fox all the way from South Carolina had challenged even him. He focused on his GPS, scanning the maze of lines intersecting highway 40.

A major traffic accident outside of Edgewood last evening had allowed him to catch up with the piggish trucker who had given her a ride out of Glenrio. The man hadn't been cooperative till Kannon had broken his teeth, at which point the man blubbered that he'd dropped the woman off somewhere past Cuervo. That meant she was likely still east of Clines Corners, the town outside of which he was presently at.

"Park west of highway 84 and watch the traffic. Call me if you spot her." He slipped his phone back into his jacket, even though he heard squawks of protest from Makoto.

Kentaro, one of the two men sweating in the cramped backseat, cleared his throat.

"Yes?" Kannon asked, his voice as deliberately cold as the car was hot.

"Mr. Takahama, we look all night, perhaps she passed us. Maybe we send Makoto to see if she go to Arizona."

Kannon didn't answer. He knew it rankled Kentaro to

have to kowtow to a half-blood, and for his suggestion to be received with silence would piss him off even more. Kannon didn't care. After killing nineteen people, including his own half-brother, the list of people he gave a rat's ass about was pretty short, and Kentaro wasn't on it.

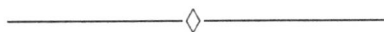

Brian took advantage of Delta's sudden interest in a bunch of cactuses to slant a look at the ridiculous motel towel. Sure enough, it was edging up despite her re-knotting the thing a billion times in the hour they'd been driving. They couldn't get to Albuquerque fast enough.

"So, how did you get into your line of work?" he asked to distract himself.

"Bad parenting," she replied vaguely.

"Your folks were…reclamation experts?"

"No, just assholes."

He glanced at her. She looked ready to spit. "I see."

There was another awkward pause, but this time it was Delta who broke it. "You from L.A.?"

"Not originally. I grew up in Wyoming."

Her eyes rounded. "You don't seem like the Wyoming type."

"What are you talking about?" He grinned. "I'm just like Wyoming—square but fun."

Delta almost smiled. "Cute. I meant you don't sound like you're from there."

"I came out to California when I was eighteen. Guess I've pretty much lost my good ol' boy twang over the years. What about you? Where did you grow up?"

"Hollywood." She uttered the word as if it were a curse.

Brian flexed his shoulders to work out the stiffness. "I lived there till pretty recently."

She turned to him, cocked her head. "You moved?"

"More like moved out. I haven't got myself a new home yet."

"Divorce?"

"Kind of." He shrugged, a little embarrassed. "We weren't married. It's a long story."

"I guess that would be the woman that jerked you around for six years, hmm?"

"Yep, that would be the one."

"You know, you don't seem like the kind of guy that would let himself get strung along like that. At least, not for that long."

Brian eyed her, unsure of whether he'd just been complimented or scorned. The expression in her blue eyes seemed genuine enough. "I guess when we first met we had a lot in common. Neither of us wanted to be tied down. We both liked to party and have fun. She and I were free spirits, I guess."

"So what happened?"

"I grew up."

"And she didn't?"

"No, and I don't think she ever will, either. Marcia is one of those women who equates being young with being immature, and she's scared to death of getting old. That's my take on it, anyway."

"So why did you stay with her so long?"

Brian ran his hands over the steering wheel. It was good to be out in his Mustang. It'd been too long. "I guess because I knew she needed me. She was always getting herself into one mess or another. Every few months she'd lose her job, or have a big blow up with her family, or overdo it at some party. She went in and out of rehab more often than Amy Winehouse, but I stuck with her because between all the crap she was great to be with. Mostly though, it was because I thought she loved me."

"Found out different, huh?"

"Yeah. She started sleeping with this scumbag she work- ed with—one of those secrets everyone knew except me. I had been getting pretty sick of all her drama and I think she did it to get my attention more than anything. She said she was sorry, wanted to work things out, but it was the last straw. All she cares about is herself. I was just too stupid to realize that until the very end."

Delta was silent. Probably mentally agreeing with him but too polite to say so. No, she'd tell him. Bored, more like. What the hell was he doing pouring out his guts to her, anyway? His tongue was as loose as her damn towel. Time to turn things around.

"You in a relationship, Delta?"

She looked as if he'd suggested intimacy with a miniature pony. "What, me? No."

"I guess it's hard to meet guys when you've running from the law."

"Not if they're cops."

Brian laughed and Delta's face softened into a small smile. Made her look cute. Very, very cute. He cleared his throat. "So this guy you mentioned, your old partner, were your dealings with him just business then?"

Delta looked out the window. "No, we're old friends. I've known him since I was twelve."

"Boy next door?"

"We've always liked each other a lot, but not in that way. He's the kind of man who's always changing friends, and I think I'm the only permanent relationship he's ever had. I guess you could say I was sort of a sister to him."

"Must have been rough for him when you left town. How come you two haven't talked for so long?"

She sighed. "We fell out over a job."

"The job you got caught on?"

"Yeah. He was against me taking it."

"Why?" asked Brian.

"Because it was for this loser who couldn't pay us, plus it was high risk. It just didn't make one iota of sense to do it."

"So why did you?"

"Because I was an idiot."

Delta closed down then, and Brian didn't push it. Not worth it. Not. Worth. It. Traffic on the highway was light, and the miles sped away beneath them as they drove through the bone-dry desert. It was more by chance than alertness that Brian noticed the black Acura parked by the roadside. They passed it, and looking into his rearview mirror, he saw it pull out. He squinted, trying to make out the license plate, and frowned as he recognized it.

He looked over at his passenger. She was dozing in her seat, arms still crossed, her eyes shut. And the towel had…hell. "Hey, Delta."

"Mmm?"

"Your Japanese friends just pulled in behind us."

She snapped open her eyes and checked her passenger side mirror. Their pursuers moved into the passing lane, slowly gaining on them.

"This is bad. Really, really bad." She bit her lip. "Why the hell are there never any cops around when you need them?"

Brian maintained his speed. "These guys are really hardcore, huh?"

25

"Yeah." She was scanning the surrounding desert. "Pull over."

"What?"

"Just drop me off and then boot it for the next town. If we split up they won't be able to go after both of us."

Her hand was actually on the door handle, as if ready to bail.

"Delta. No. I don't have time to slow down and anyway they will take us both. There are two of them."

"Then speed up, you idiot! They're almost on us."

He chose not to reply to that. He could already feel the old concentration, the mix of adrenaline and control, taking over. And behind the wheel of his Mustang…yeah, this was going to be good. "Just do me a favor and hang onto that damn towel," he said.

As the Acura moved to come alongside him, Brian hit the brakes and cranked the wheel to the left, the back corner of his car smashing into the Acura's passenger door. Holding the wheel firm, Brian forced both cars across the oncoming lane and off the edge of the highway, only slamming on his accelerator and spinning his wheel back to the right at the last instant.

Tires squealing, the Acura plowed into a guardrail with an explosion of glass and metal, its driver's side wheels lifted off the pavement by the vehicle's momentum. The car continued to slide along the rail in a shower of sparks, then its tires exploded and it flipped, tumbling sideways down the highway for another hundred feet.

Smiling at his work in the rearview mirror, Brian admired the remains of the Yakuza's car upside-down, in the middle of the highway behind them. But sweeter than all that was the look on Delta's face. Shock and pleasure. She shook her head.

"Where the hell did you learn to drive like that?"

"Stunt school."

"You're a stuntman? I thought you were an actor."

"Well, I guess you can't find out everything about a man from his wallet."

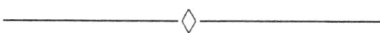

Kannon's eyes stayed fixed on the empty road ahead as he answered his phone.

"Sir. This is Makoto. We find her. She traveling west in red Mustang car with man."

"Follow them," he said, starting his car. "I'll meet you when you reach Clines Corners."

"We cannot follow, sir."

"What? Why not?"

"We crash."

There was a lengthy pause, the only sounds being that of Kannon's teeth grinding together and the acceleration of his car onto the highway.

"Are either of you hurt?" he asked at last.

"We okay, but our car not work anymore."

You not work anymore when I get my hands on you, Kannon decided.

"The man, he surprise us. Make us crash. Very good driver."

Looked as if Fox had managed to get a professional to come and meet her. Despite all the stereotypes about Asian drivers, he knew Makoto was more than a match for the typical *gaijin* behind the wheel. His target had more lives than a cat, but she wasn't going to get away from him again.

Driving into the town, he pulled into a parking lot he'd scouted out the night before. From here he could watch both highway 40 and the turnoff onto highway 285. Several minutes passed before he spotted his quarry: a red Mustang GT, its rear driver's side freshly damaged. The driver was doing the speed limit, and didn't deviate from his westerly course. Perhaps they didn't realize that there were more people hunting them, or maybe they were just very confident. No doubt Fox was armed, and with a skilled driver behind the wheel, she wouldn't be easy to take down, but Kannon didn't hesitate to leave the parking lot and head after them.

"We're going to wait till we're on an empty stretch of road," he explained to Kentaro. "I'll pass them, and I want you to kill the driver. Once the car goes off the road we take her, and don't spare the bullets. Understand?"

The man pulled his silenced pistol from his holster and laid it on his lap. "Yes, Mr. Takahama."

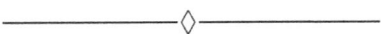

No sooner were they through Clines Corners than Brian pulled into the fast lane and hit the gas pedal. The speedometer needle arced through the numbers and they hurtled down the highway at a velocity that began to rattle Delta's nerves.

"We're going to get pulled over if you keep going like this," she said, trying to keep her voice level.

"Good. I'll get a speeding ticket and then we'll have a police escort to the next town."

"How do you figure that?"

"Simple. I'll tell the police that we were speeding because some suspicious characters were following us, say that we got spooked they were going to rob us or something. I'll take the ticket, if they write one, and ask them to escort us to the next town. Simple."

"Awesome. Except there's a warrant out on me."

"I know, but it's a couple of years old. What are the chances a highway patrolman would recognize you?"

He had a point. "I suppose."

"Anyway," Brian continued, "speeding serves some other purposes as well. If there're more of them, they'll have to move pretty fast to catch up with us. That should make it easy to spot them. If they try to keep a low profile they'll get left behind and I doubt they'll find us again."

Delta nodded and shut up. For the first time in a very long time, someone else was in charge. Someone expert and competent and...willing. By the looks of things she'd sorely misjudged Brian. The man had guts, and brains enough to plan under stress. A man born to his profession. More and more he made her think of Akeno, though she doubted even her old partner would be managing things quite so well.

If she believed in fate, she would have thought Brian and her were destined to meet. But experience had taught her fate was a blind, mindless thing, giving and taking away regardless of one's worth. The world was a hard and uncaring place, and only work, will and blood allowed a person to prevail. Dreamers and romantics fell beneath the heels of the cynics and the manipulators, the real people in charge.

The desert scenery flew by as Delta lost herself in her thoughts, and soon they had covered the better half of the distance to Albuquerque. They shot past a police car that, as luck would have it, was busy giving another motorist a ticket. Although normally she preferred her own company, the drawn-out quiet began to gnaw at her. A little conversation wouldn't hurt, she decided. Just some words to pass the time, and maybe to extend a little gratitude for the risks he'd chosen to take on.

"Sorry about your car," she ventured.

Brian seemed surprised to hear her speak. "It's insured."

"I'll pay for the damages when we reach L.A. I have some money there, and it'll be more than enough to cover your expenses. I'm just cash-strapped at the moment due to my... situation."

He checked his mirrors, answering absently. "That's okay. Not a big deal."

The guy was going to self-destruct with that attitude. "You know what your problem is, Brian?"

"Well, right now I'd say it's your Japanese pals."

She ignored his deadpan witticism. "You're stupidly nice. I mean, why would you turn down someone who's offering to fix your car?"

"Because it's probably going to be damaged a whole lot more in a minute. Take a look behind us."

Delta whipped around to look out the back window. Sure enough, there was another sports car, a low-slung black Nissan, roaring towards them. The vehicle was still a ways back, but even at a distance, she could see the sun glint off the driver's mirrored sunglasses.

CHAPTER 3 THREE

KANNON PRESSED THE accelerator to the floor, the speedometer needle passing the hundred mile-an-hour mark. The broken yellow line of the two-lane highway became a solid blur, yet his advance on the Mustang was slow. Behind him Kentaro opened the window, hot air blasting through the vehicle, and braced his pistol against the vibrating frame. It would be a waste of bullets to shoot now, Kannon knew. The gunman would need a clear shot, which meant he had to get alongside the muscle car. He gripped the trembling wheel and forced the needle to climb. Japanese determination versus American muscle. A battle he'd waged all his life.

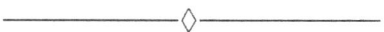

Brian did mental calculations as the Nissan closed the distance. The road ahead was empty save for a lone rig approaching them. Just as well. The last thing he wanted was for some innocent motorist to get hurt, though the oncoming truck presented an opportunity.

"Delta, I need you to climb into the back seat, lie down on

the floor, and brace yourself as best you can."

Unbelievably, she didn't argue. She zipped off her her seatbelt, grabbed a handful of towel-skirt and all but nosedived into the rear, landing with a crackle and crunch into his pile of takeout wrappers.

The Nissan was now a half-dozen car lengths behind them. It was coming up fast, one of its three occupants leaning slightly out of the rear driver's-side window, gun in hand. Right now he was pretty much an impossible target—his pursuer would need the left shoulder of the road to pull alongside him, or risk a head-on collision with the oncoming truck. At least that's what he was counting on.

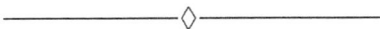

Kannon came up within ten feet of his quarry's rear bumper, steeling himself as he switched left onto the shoulder. As the tires met the rumble strips there was an ear-piercing shriek and bone-rattling vibrations. His right front fender was less than a foot from the back of the Mustang, when the red car veered right and braked hard.

In a fraction of a second the Nissan flashed past, side-swiping the muscle car in a blaze of sparks. Kannon slanted a look at the driver. Goddammit, he was smiling! His own window exploded, showering Kannon with hot glass, and behind him he heard the sickening crack of splintering bone as Kentaro's arm was crushed between the vehicles.

A scream of agony filling his ears, Kannon wrestled the fishtailing Nissan back onto the asphalt as the rig blew past and Kentaro dragged his pulped left arm back inside the car. Small wonder it hadn't been ripped off entirely.

"Sachio!" he growled at the man beside him. "Kill that

bastard!"

His second henchman drew his gun and looked out the rear window. He turned to Kannon in alarm. "Sir! He's stopped!"

The *gaijin* had come to a complete halt in the middle of the highway. What the—? Kannon jammed on the brakes, cranked the Nissan around in a sharp 180°, eliciting another yowl of pain from Kentaro as he tumbled about in the back seat, and faced the grinning maniac.

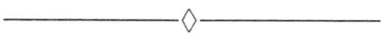

"Brian?" Delta's voice rose uncertainly from the back.

"Yeah?"

"You okay?"

"Uh-huh."

"Why have we stopped?"

Brian watched the Nissan turn. The passenger side window rolled down and another gunman trained his pistol on him, eyes squinted in hate as he took aim.

"Well?" Delta persisted.

Brian adjusted his seat back so that his line of sight barely cleared the dashboard. His smiled broadened, adrenaline crackled along every nerve. He couldn't remember ever being this pumped. And he knew why. This was real.

"We're going to play chicken."

He heard her swallow hard and reply, "Since you're stopped, could I get out now?"

His smile widened. "What, and miss all the fun?"

Then he revved his engine.

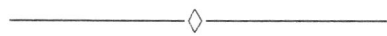

A low growl escaped Kannon's throat as he heard the roar of his opponent's challenge on the desert wind. Sachio was leaning out the passenger window with his pistol, ready to continue the fight.

"We're going to head right for him," Kannon said. "Kill fast." He hit the accelerator, pitching his car forward in a black cloud of burnt rubber. The Mustang responded in kind, wheels screeching against the hot asphalt.

The two cars howled towards one another. Sachio fired his pistol as they went, even though Kannon could see that the lashing wind and recoil almost pulled the gun from his hand with every shot. One of the bullets splintered the windshield, and Kannon hoped for a hit, but the Mustang charged on.

Damn. The man wasn't just a maniac, but a suicidal maniac. No outplaying that. At the last instant, Kannon yanked the wheel to the side, missing the Mustang by a hairsbreadth. The back wheels of the Nissan slid out, and he began to spin down the highway. The desert twirled around him once, twice, three times, and then the front end slammed into the guardrail, exploding an airbag into Kannon's face and hurtling Sachio out the passenger window.

For a few moments the car lay still, steam pouring out from beneath its crumpled hood, its torn tires deflating in a long gusty hiss. Then the driver's door was kicked open so hard it almost came off its hinges, and a snarling Kannon pulled himself out of the wreckage. Teeth clenched, he stripped his busted sunglasses from his bleeding nose and glared down the dusty highway.

Sachio was lying in the middle of the highway like a piece of roadkill, beyond him a receding red dot that represented Kannon's third consecutive failure.

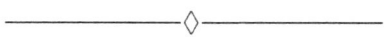

Delta watched the dismay on the mechanic's face, as the once magnificent Mustang sputtered and chugged up to the bay door of the Albuquerque garage, and died.

"Out," Brian ordered. "My door is too crushed to open."

She cinched the towel tight and got out. There was an immediate tug. "Delta, you gotta smooth out the back, your butt is hanging out."

She slapped away his hand and adjusted the terry cloth, while the man in blue observed with interest.

Brian's hand lifted from her backside in a casual wave. "Hey, there. You happen to know where the nearest car rental place is?"

"The other side of town there's a Budget. You want me to take a look at this?"

Delta spun to Brian. "No!" she hissed. "There are bullet holes. The police will be called."

Brian didn't even look at her. "Nah, she's probably totaled. If you could park it out back for me, I'll get the insurance company out. My own fault for racing her." He kneeled to examine a hole in the front grill. "One of the bullets went right into the engine," he said quietly. "Should be interesting explaining that to the adjustor."

Delta stared at him. Brian's relaxed demeanor seemed so surreal she didn't feel entirely sure this wasn't all a dream. "I'll pay for it," she offered weakly.

He stood and dusted off his jeans. "Have you noticed you say that every third sentence? Don't worry about it. It's just a scratch."

She laughed, shaking her head in disbelief, then caught herself. They'd almost been killed, and his prize car wrecked.

What the hell was there to laugh about?

"Why do you do that?" he asked.

"Do what?"

"Act so serious. You know, I'm not going to think you're less of a person if you lighten up a bit."

Delta's back stiffened. "Seems to me that too much 'lightness' was the problem with the last woman you were with."

She watched him turn away, and immediately regretted her words. She had no right to be sharp with him after what he'd been through for her "Look…Brian…"

"It's okay."

"No, look, I—"

"Really, it's okay."

She stamped her foot. "Would you just shut the hell up and let me apologize!"

"Quite the temper you got there," he commented, still not looking at her, his attention all caught up with the mechanic's trek to a tow truck.

Delta's eyes narrowed. "Fine, be a jerk. I'm just trying to say thank you, that's all." She marched around to the back of the car, pulled her now dry jeans from the trunk, and then stalked to the garage's washroom.

He glanced surreptitiously over his shoulder at her backside. He was going to miss that towel. "You're welcome," he mumbled.

After what seemed to Delta like an eternity of sullen silence, the cab arrived and took them to a car rental outlet. Brian chose a nondescript sedan, and in less than an hour they were on their way out of town, still headed west on highway 40. Neither spoke to the other. For Delta, it was because she didn't know what to say to make it better. She had no idea what he was thinking. Half-past noon, they crossed the state line into Arizona, and were fast approaching the town of Lupton.

"You hungry?" Brian asked.

Delta experienced a jolt of relief. Brian was talking to her again. "Starving."

He gestured at the small forest of fast-food signs lining the main drag. "Looks like they have just about everything."

You mean nothing, thought Delta, but she kept quiet. She wasn't a big fan of such restaurants, but was damned if she was going to object. She already owed him plenty. And not just money. She had no idea how she was going to ever repay him for putting his life on the line.

"What do you think? Does a burger sound good?"

"Yeah," she lied. "Sounds great."

They pulled in at one of the eateries, and soon were sitting in the air-conditioned interior, before them meals of chicken burgers, fries and strawberry milkshakes. Delta hadn't had a milkshake since she was a little kid. She took an experimental sip and waited, but all she felt was how thick and sweet and cold and *good* it tasted.

Across from her, Brian swallowed a mouthful of burger. "I don't think we'll be making it to L.A. tonight. If we keep going till nine or ten we should make it to the California border. We can get some sleep there and then finish the drive tomorrow."

"Sounds fine."

"So, how many of those guys we met this morning are there?"

"There's only five, so I think that was all of them."

"They seemed pretty determined," Brian observed.

"They're Japanese."

"How do you think they found you?"

Delta looked around at the other restaurant patrons, lowering her voice to little more than a hoarse whisper. "I've been hitch-hiking since I reached Arkansas. I didn't have a lot of money on me when they kicked in my door, and it's kind of hard to get a bank card when the cops are looking for you. It's been pretty slow going. I suppose they've just been asking around."

"But why didn't you take a car? Couldn't you just…"

"Steal one? No. I'm not that kind of thief. Besides, the cops keep a pretty sharp eye out for hot vehicles."

Brian popped down the last of his burger, wiped his mouth and started wolfing fries. "So this is the second time you've given them the slip."

"The third, actually," she corrected him. "They caught up with me in Atlanta when I took the bus in from Charleston."

Brian stopped chewing. "How did you get away?"

"I climbed into the luggage compartment of my connector bus. That's how I got to Little Rock."

"You rode all the way from Atlanta to Little Rock in the belly of a bus? That's almost five hundred miles."

And thirsty the whole way. It was torture every time the wheels had rushed through a puddle. And then the irony of getting caught in a rainstorm. "I managed to get out when we reached a stop in Alabama. They weren't too happy about me being in with the bags, but since I had a ticket they had to take me the rest of the way."

"Quite the trip. Why don't you just call your old partner and find out what's going on? I mean, why hike all the way across the country?"

"I tried, but his line's disconnected. We haven't talked in well over a year, so he probably got a new number."

"You two didn't have any common friends you could get it from?"

"Akeno has lots of friends, but I never really bothered to get to know any of them except for one. He's the one I need to see."

"Why not just call him then?"

"Because he doesn't have a phone."

Brian frowned. "What kind of person doesn't have a phone?"

"He's kind of old school. I have to talk to him face to face."

"So what about you?" Brian asked, as Delta picked half-heartedly at her fries, "You have many friends back in L.A.?"

"Socializing was never really my strong suit."

"So where are you going to stay?"

She looked at him, unable to suppress a flash of suspicion. "Why do you ask?"

Brian pointed at her fries. "You going to eat those?"

Delta sighed and pushed them over to his side of the table. "Knock yourself out."

"I was just wondering," he continued as he helped her with her meal.

"Don't worry. I'll find a place."

Delta noticed his expression droop ever so slightly. Was that regret on his face? Probably sad that he was losing his chance to crash cars and escape burning buildings.

"How did you get into the stunt business being from Wyoming?" she asked.

"It's all I ever wanted to be." He smiled. "So when I was

eighteen I came to L.A. and enrolled in school. I worked hard. Took some risks. The rest is history. I started up my own company a few years back."

Delta knew all too well about the masses of young men and women who came to L.A. chasing a dream. Only a tiny minority ever got a taste of the fame and fortune they sought, so to make it was no small feat. "You look like you've done pretty well for yourself."

"It pays the bills, but I didn't really get into it for the money."

"Let me guess. For the thrill of it."

His grin turned a little sheepish. She'd called it right. "Okay, I'm an adrenaline junkie. I like testing myself. Is that why you wound up doing reclamation jobs?"

"No, I'm not the kind of person who goes looking for trouble. Especially when there's so much of it lying around everywhere anyway."

"So why did you choose to get into that kind of work?" he asked.

"I didn't. That's just the way it turned out."

Brian gave her a dubious look. "You're telling me you became a thief by accident?"

"Don't make it sound so strange," she replied. "Most people wind up doing what they're doing for the same reason."

"How do you figure that?"

Delta leaned back in her chair, folding her hands together on the tabletop. "Tell me, how many of your friends had a realistic plan for what they wanted to become when they got out of school?"

Brian considered the question. "Not many. Just me and one other guy I knew. He went into the air force."

"Exactly. Everybody else applied for a few jobs, and

eventually got picked by an employer more or less randomly. From that point on, their resume began to dictate what kind of industry they could work in, and that's the field they'll probably stay in till they die. Generally speaking, people's lives are run more by luck than planning."

Brian tilted his head. "Interesting idea, but I don't really buy it."

"Why not?"

"The way I see it, people are responsible for their own actions. You can't go blaming fate for what you choose to do with your life. I mean, everybody starts out with different advantages and disadvantages, but what you ultimately turn out to be is up to you."

Delta felt like arguing, but let it drop. The lucky were always quick to take credit for their successes, and the unlucky to blame others for their failures, but sometimes things were just were and there was nothing for it but to carry on.

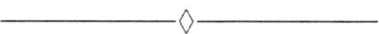

There was a fair bit of construction work on the Arizona stretch of highway 40, so Brian and Delta made slow progress. It was past nine in the evening and they'd only made it to Ash Fork, still a good hundred miles from the California state line.

Delta sighed as they passed yet another hotel with its 'No Vacancy' sign illuminated. "We should have stopped sooner. This is the seventh one."

Brian shifted in his seat. "There's bound to be more up ahead. I'm sure we'll find something."

Always the optimist. Delta gazed out over the darkening landscape. Normally she didn't like road trips, finding them confining and boring, but their trek across Arizona that day

41

had been good. Brian hooked up his iPod and they'd discovered they shared the same taste for cool jazz and blues. They'd chatted about L.A. and how it had changed over the years, then stopped at a small strip-mall and picked up some toiletries and inexpensive clothes for her to change into. Brian had even taught her a stupid car game called "Who am I?", in which one of them would pick a famous man or woman, and the other tried to determine the unknown person's identity by asking questions. She'd discovered she was really good at it, and that Brian was a cheerful loser.

"There's another one." She pointed to a surprisingly large hotel coming into view. The parking lot was pretty full, but there might still be a room. As it turned out, they were in luck. The vacancy sign was still lit, and Brian pulled in and parked without delay.

"Two rooms, please," he said, as they reached the front desk.

The brunette behind the counter smiled at them as if they'd just won the lotto. "Perfect. We only have two left."

Well, I'll be damned, Delta thought. Must be some of that Brian-luck floating their way. He was filling out the registry card when a young family came in behind them, toting a crying baby and a sleepy toddler.

The brunette winced a little, directing her attention to the man carrying the unhappy infant. "I'm sorry, sir, we're full."

"But the sign says vacancy."

"Yes, we just booked the last of our rooms. Sorry about that."

Delta leaned against the counter, eager to be away from the screaming child, then noticed that Brian had stopped writing.

"You know if there are any other places open down the

road?" the father asked, jiggling his baby. "We've been looking for an hour now."

"I'm afraid it's a hectic night. You might find something if you head south to Paulden. It's only about twenty-five miles."

Brian turned, with a weary smile. "It's okay," he said to the man. "You can take one of our rooms."

Delta resisted the urge to slap him upside the head.

"You sure?" Even the father was questioning Brian's sanity.

"Yeah. It's okay."

Saint Brian finished filling out the registry and got the room card, waving off the couple's profuse thanks. As soon as he was done, Delta took him by the arm, ushering him outside where they could speak without having to compete with the baby's bawling.

"You're a softie, you know that?" She poked him in the chest. "No wonder people take advantage of you."

Brian handed over the room card.

"What's this?"

"Go and get some shut eye. I'll meet you out here tomorrow and we'll keep going."

"But where are you going to sleep?" she protested.

"I'll camp out in the car."

Soft in the head, too. "You save my life, drive me across two states and you expect me to allow you to go sleep in the car? What kind of woman do you think I am?"

The corner of his mouth did a little upturn. "Even though you could have it all to yourself? Sounds to me like you're just too much of a softie."

"Yeah? Well, maybe I don't want the bed all to myself," she retorted, then realizing what she'd just implied, felt her face go hot.

"You know what, Delta?" His voice had dropped a notch and warmed.

She looked away. "What?"

He raised his hands to her shoulders and gave them a gentle squeeze. "I really like you, too."

Part of her wanted to lean against his broad chest, to let him hold her like nobody ever had. Part of her longed to go further, and let the night begin with a sweet, loving kiss—to believe for just a moment that this could be real, and be lost in that moment forever. But that wasn't something she could do, either to him or herself.

"You're a smart guy, Brian, but you don't seem to get that this is just business for me. I'm sorry if I led you to believe anything else, but all I want is a ride to L.A., okay? You can save your niceness for the next woman who wants to play you."

His hands dropped from her in a shot. "You know, you're right, I can be a pushover. And yeah, I lived way too long with a woman who could only function when she was taking advantage of me. But you know what? After meeting you, after everything that's happened today, I've decided I'd rather be too soft than just another coldhearted snob."

Her whole body tightened. "I'm not a snob. I've got my reasons."

"We've all got reasons, honey," he said. "Only yours seem all about cutting yourself off from anything with a whiff of happiness to it. I don't think I've heard you say one cheerful thing since I met you. Why live?"

She curled her arms around her middle, half-glaring at him, but not quite able to match his gaze. Moments ticked by. Brian blew out his breath and slung his arm around her shoulder, pulling her to his side. "Come on, I'm wiped. Enough car crashes and bullets for one day. We'll hit the showers, go to bed and finish this tomorrow."

God, he made it sound so simple. It wasn't. It never was. But then again, she saw no point to fighting him because, yeah, she was wiped, too. So she stayed tucked to his side and let him take her up to their room.

CHAPTER
4
FOUR

TURNED OUT THAT the couple in the next room were active. Very active. No sooner had Brian and Delta arranged themselves on the queen-sized bed than Mr. and Mrs. Noisy had started in. Murmuring and giggling, thumping and bumping, then moaning and creaking, and finally joint crying and howling. Then merciful silence.

Brian read the bedside clock. "That was a 75-minute workout." About when the headboard had started tapping the wall, he'd raised a knee because his cock had caught up with his imagination. If Delta hadn't been there, he'd probably have taken matters into his right hand.

Delta didn't answer. She'd spent the time with an arm over her face, no doubt annoyed as hell someone was having fun. He wiggled further down under the sheet and concentrated on becoming unconscious.

He'd almost succeeded when he heard talk and a giggle, a creak and a moan, a bump, a thump...

"Oh, for fuck's sake!" Delta hissed.

Yep, annoyed.

"Someone must've told them to get a room," Brian

decided to comment.

"Why next to us?"

"A conspiracy, no doubt. C'mon, whaddiya think most adults in this hotel are doing right now?"

He could hear her head twist on the pillow towards him. "Bet the parents of those kids are sleeping."

"Didn't get two kids by sleeping."

"And you don't get sleep by having two kids."

Since they weren't going to have sweet dreams themselves for probably another 75 minutes, and since they were on the subject, Brian went for it. "You don't seem to like sex much."

He swore he could hear her teeth grind together. "We're not talking about sex."

"Yes," he agreed. "Let's lie here and listen to it, instead."

"How about we listen in silence?"

He couldn't. If he had to listen to another round of sex, he was sure his balls would explode, and talking to Delta did wonders for keeping his cock down to erratic twitching.

"I wonder," he said conversationally, "what they're doing now."

Silence.

"By the sounds of it, my guess is he's got her on her hands and knees and he's behind her, probably one hand in her hair and the other—"

"Shut. Up."

Brian registered a different sound. "No, have to amend that. Sounds as if her face is in the pillow—"

Suddenly Delta was straddling him, her hand clamped tight over his mouth. "I swear, Brian, shut up or I'll steal the car and leave you to walk home. And don't think I won't do it, either. Got it?"

A dare. She was daring him to lie there and take it. With her sweet round ass just above his cock, her knees pinned to his side, the light pressure of her hand on his bare chest, her palm against his mouth. Didn't matter she might not intend it that way, that's the way it was coming out.

In all his thirty-five years, he'd never refused a dare.

He licked her palm.

She snatched it away and he took advantage. He gripped her hips and flipped her onto her back, following along so his weight came down on top of her. He trapped her upper arms under his, settled his hands on either side of her head.

"Brian!" She strained up against him as he grinned. She fell back and scowled up at him, her brilliant blue eyes flashing.

There was no way he was backing off. Not on their last night together, not after what they'd gone through, not when he knew she'd nothing to fear from him.

"I'm thinking," he whispered, "they've changed position. They're like you and me, right now. Him on her, her all soft and curved and smelling like hotel soap. And him, happy as hell he's made her come and knowing it's his turn now—but he's holding back because she's wrapped tight around him, and he wants that connection to last a little longer, 'cause they'll probably go to sleep after this and in the morning they gotta be up early, lot of driving to do—"

"Brian." His name came out different this time, softer, almost a whimper. Her arms relaxed under his. Progress.

"They're pressed tight, lifting and rolling against each other—" he lowered his mouth until his breath was on her lips "—their lips brush against each other and he gives her a hard kiss, he'd give her more but it's moving to the final build-up—"

"Brian." Almost there.

"She feels it, too. Braces herself, rises with his pounding. He hears her breathing change, gets more like his, ragged and hard, and he smiles because damn, she's going to come again with him—"

Delta gave it to him. She slanted her head and tapped her lips against his. That was all he needed.

He pressed his mouth to hers, slid his tongue against the slit of her mouth and her lips parted and he was inside for a long, hungry time. She didn't kiss back much, didn't wiggle or rub, but she gave in, surrendered, didn't fight him one little bit. She'd let his hand underneath her tee, he figured. Cup those squeezable tits or slide down to curve around her ass. Only his hands were busy on her face, his thumbs were getting the measure of her cheeks, his fingers forked into her spiky hair….

There was a howl and a cry from the other side, louder and longer than the first time, one of the bumps clapped like thunder. Delta stiffened underneath Brian, and he knew it was over for them, too. But he didn't pull away yet. He eased his mouth from hers, whispered, "You should know better than to dare a stuntman."

"It wasn't a dare," she whispered back. "It was a threat."

He thought he'd gotten through to her. He thumb-stroked the side of her throat and explained, "Delta. Dare, threat, promise, whatever you think to give me, I don't back away from any of it."

Under his thumb, he could feel her swallow. Enough. Their time together was all but over, no need to spook her. He rolled off her, settled himself down on his side of the bed.

"You still planning to drive off without me?"

"Guess you'll find out when you wake up." Her voice had got back its edge but he liked to think it wasn't as sharp as before.

"Goodnight, Delta."

"Goodnight, Brian."

Brian grinned into the dark. Yep, definitely softer.

Kannon lit a cigarette as he walked across the hospital parking lot with his two remaining men. Although both Makoto and Renji had come out of their crash with no more than bruises and scrapes, the same could not be said for their colleagues. The surgeons had barely managed to save Kentaro's mangled arm, and Sachio had broken several bones, not to mention his face, when he had been thrown from the car.

To make matters worse there had been a hundred questions from the police, who were reluctant to believe his story about falling asleep at the wheel. If he hadn't hidden the guns, he'd still be stuck in their interrogation room, and as it was he'd been slapped with a hefty fine for speeding and reckless driving.

And it wasn't yet eight in the morning.

He had his phone to his ear as he slid into the driver's seat of their rental SUV. Jeanelle, his employer's wife, answered it.

"I have a message for Mr. Matsuda."

"Good news?" she asked, her sugary voice untroubled.

"No."

"Not having much luck, are you?"

Kannon shut his eyes, forcing himself to remain calm. He despised having to deal with the arrogant whore his boss had chosen to wed. "We'll be returning to Los Angeles today. I'll need to meet with Mr. Matsuda tonight."

"That *may* be possible. I'll have to ask him about his

schedule."

"I'll call this afternoon to confirm."

"Actually," she replied, "I'll call you."

Kannon's eyes flicked open as he heard the line disconnect. "Bitch." He cursed under his breath. He thought for a moment, taking a long drag of his cigarette, then blowing twin streams of smoke through his nose, he dialed another number.

This time the phone rang once before a female voice croaked, "Yes?"

"Iolana, this is Kannon."

He heard the old woman hiss. The harridan owed him for the work he'd done back in Hawaii, but that didn't mean she had to be happy about him calling to collect the debt.

"What do you want?"

"I have a license plate number. I need to know who owns the car and everything about them."

"That all?"

"No. I also need to find someone. Delta Fox."

"Fox?" the crone spat. "She's not in L.A. anymore. Everyone and their dog knows that."

"She's coming back. She's probably there already."

Kannon let her absorb the news. She made her livelihood by dealing information, and word of the thief's return was probably worth something to someone. "Why are you looking for her?" she asked.

"Guess."

She chuckled. "Best be on your toes, killer. That woman still has powerful friends even after two years under a rock. I don't know if you heard what happened to Judge Hall, but you'd best watch your back."

Kannon had never heard of any Judge Hall, nor had he

any idea who the thief's allies might be, but he wasn't in the mood to reveal his ignorance. He'd learn what he needed to soon enough, and he wouldn't be in Iolana's debt to do it. "Just get me the information and keep your mouth shut about my job. Then we'll be even."

"Hmmph," the woman snorted. "You in town?"

"I will be soon."

"Call me this afternoon. It won't take long to find what you're looking for."

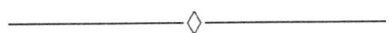

Delta had Brian park by a nondescript alley, its grimy walls tagged with Chinese characters. She had business here on the edge of L. A.'s Chinatown, and it was time for them to say their goodbyes. Going any further together was out of the question. Not that she didn't trust Brian, she did. But the man she had to see trusted her, too, and part of that trust was that she respect his privacy.

And the cold heart of the matter was that she needed the trust of that man more than she needed Brian's. She couldn't ever repay the stuntman, especially not the hottest kiss of her life, a miraculous event that neither of them mentioned since waking that morning. Their drive into L.A. had descended into virtual silence. Delta became weighed down by what she had to do and Brian, too, seemed to grow preoccupied. But now that they were here, there was one last piece of business.

"The man I need to see, he's holding some cash for me. I'll be done in an hour or so. We could meet somewhere...."

"Don't want your money."

"Why not?" She realized what he was probably thinking. "Mine's as good as anyone's."

He sliced her a look. His eyes were hidden behind his shades, but from the tense line of his jaw, she knew he wasn't impressed. "Look, Delta, I guess I'm coming off my adrenaline high. You're in a line of work which I'd probably be better off not getting involved in. At least, not any deeper. I don't know I want your money in my account. I mean, if the police investigate it might not look good. As it is, I'll have to come up with a good story about the bullet holes in the car."

Guilt, worry, helplessness. The last time she'd felt these emotions was for Akeno. "I'm sorry, Brian." She drew a deep breath and on the exhale, pushed out the words, "I owe you, big time, I know that. The only thing I can give you is money. Not enough probably but it's all I got. And if you don't want that, then I guess…then I guess…."

"Then I guess you need to say goodbye and get out of the car," Brian finished. The words came out low, firm and very, very final. And they got her right in the gut. She nodded, got a good hold on her bag and went for the door handle.

"Bye," she mumbled.

He growled in annoyance, clamped his hand on her arm. "Listen, against my better judgment, I'm saying this. You need my help, you can get me at Cause & FX. Okay?"

She wasn't going to need his help ever again. Even if she did, she wasn't going to him. That was what she could give him. Her absolute absence from his decent life.

"Yeah, okay," she lied.

The corner of his mouth did that quick upturn that in their few short days together, she'd come to identify as classic Brian Chanse. "Quick, then, out of the rental car before it gets shot up."

She got out, they exchanged waves, and she turned away and cut down the old familiar alley a few steps away.

Brian Chanse was officially a memory. One of the few good ones. Though in a way, it hurt as much as all the bad ones.

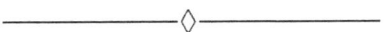

Halfway down the garbage-strewn alley, Delta came to a battered steel door with faded letters reading *Han's Grocery*. Beside it was a small intercom with two unmarked buttons. Delta pressed both three times in rapid succession. After several seconds, she heard a loud buzz and the door unlocked. With a squeal of rusty hinges, she pulled it open to reveal an immaculate polished hardwood stairwell, its olive green walls illuminated by soft lamps of frosted glass.

It felt strange to climb these stairs again after so long. There was a time when a wave of relief washed over her as she entered this place, knowing it to be a safe haven from all the horrors and dangers of the world. Now it felt different, as if she were stepping back into a bad habit that had been hard to break. She reached the second floor landing but passed by the door there, continuing on to the very top where she stopped before an ornate oak door, a lion's head knocker at its center. She rapped it three times, then let herself inside.

The apartment within was straight out of the 1920s, decorated in the Art Deco style of the period and filled with fine antiques. Its walls were lined with shelves of hardcover books, its hardwood floor adorned with a huge Persian carpet, and its large bay window inset with an intricate pattern of colored glass. Delta took off her shoes and headed inside, settling herself in a leather armchair to wait.

She eventually heard footsteps climbing the stairwell to the door, and an elderly gentlemen appeared, immaculately groomed and dressed in a fine, if dated, suit. Despite his years, he looked remarkably handsome and debonair, so much so that one might not have even noticed the metal claw where his left hand should have been.

Delta felt the excited rush of seeing him again, but she merely stood and nodded to him, as if it had been only yesterday and not two years since they'd last spoke. "Mr. Hadrian."

He returned the gesture, his face remaining neutral. "I was wondering when you might turn up, Delta. I'm glad to see you made it back in one piece." He didn't sound glad. Then again, he didn't sound much of anything. That was Mr. Hadrian.

"Then you know about the men hunting me."

"I know what Akeno told me, which I'm afraid wasn't very much."

"Is he all right? Where is he?"

Her host sat on the nearby couch, motioning for her to resume her seat as well. She perched on the edge, waiting for an answer.

"Delta," he said quietly, "Akeno is dead."

Dead. Akeno. Her arms, her legs, her brain, her insides felt heavy and wooden.

"He died a week ago in Florida," Mr. Hadrian continued in his usual passionless voice. "He'd gone to Miami to try and hide, but the Yakuza found him. He was gunned down in Little Haiti."

Taken out like a stray dog. Her old friend. His wit and courage had made him seem invincible but in the end, bullets didn't play favorites. Bile and tears rose in her throat, and she choked them back down. Emotional displays made her mentor uncomfortable, so she would do her grieving elsewhere. Alone. There was the memory of a strong arm across her shoulder. No. No. She couldn't think of Brian now, or she'd fall apart.

"I see," she managed at length. "But why are they after me?"

"Akeno teamed up with a new partner. A woman named Susan. She worked as a maid in the home of a Yakuza boss named Hiro Matsuda. Perhaps you've heard of him."

Delta had. In his day, Matsuda was one of the most feared men in the Orient, well-known for his ruthlessness and savagery. He'd become one of the Japanese mafia's key people in California about twenty years ago, starting up a host of legitimate businesses through which to launder their prostitution, drug, and extortion money. The man was as rich as he was dangerous, and held the respect of the top mob leaders in Japan.

"Akeno tried to rip off the Yakuza?" she said in disbelief.

"I told him to drop the idea, Delta, but he went ahead with it anyway. His partner gave him everything he needed to do the job. A layout of the house, imprints of the keys, the codes to the security system, the combination of the safe…everything."

"He really thought he could make a clean getaway?"

"Yes. The plan was to leave Los Angeles as soon as the job was done and fly to Miami. They knew Matsuda would pin the job on Susan, but Akeno felt confident that the two of them could just disappear. It was going to be his last job, Delta. He had a good amount saved up from his previous work, and with this haul he was planning to retire with her."

"What went wrong?" she asked.

The old man stood up slowly, and wandered over to the window. Delta knew the view there was of brick, clay and graffiti. But always the harder the conversation, the farther Mr.

Hadrian withdrew. Facing away from her, he folded his hand and claw behind his back. "The woman, Susan, came with him on the job."

"What? Why?"

"I don't know. From what Akeno told me, I can't see any reason why he would have taken her in with him, but apparently he did."

"That's impossible. Akeno would never have taken a risk like that, especially if he gave a damn about her."

"I can only tell you what he told me, Delta, and he never chose to explain why he'd made that decision. The long and the short of it was that Matsuda's teenage son, his only son, discovered them."

"Was he able to identify Susan?"

Mr. Hadrian's hand convulsed around his claw. "I imagine he would have if she hadn't shot him in the face."

The bottom fell out of Delta's stomach.

"Oh God you mean…"

He turned to her, giving her his profile. "She killed the boy, Delta. She and Akeno had the money, however, so they wisely decided to run. Akeno stopped by here to tell me what had happened, then left immediately. It was the last time I ever saw him. A couple of weeks later they caught up with him in Miami, and you know the rest."

"But how did they find him?"

"I don't know, Delta. Perhaps Akeno made the mistake of telling someone other than myself where he was headed. Who can say?"

Delta mulled over the story. "So that bastard Matsuda got his pound of flesh. I still don't get what brought his thugs to my doorstep."

"I can only assume that they thought you were involved.

57

Vengeance is not a matter to be left half-finished with these people. If they suspected you were part of the job, they may have simply decided to kill you for good measure."

Delta's fingers dug into the soft leather of the armchair. Repressing the sadness, anger and fear flaring inside her was like holding her hand in a fire, and she felt a desperate urge to scream. "But anyone with two brain cells to rub together would know I wasn't part of it. All they'd have to do is talk to my neighbors in Myrtle Beach to know I haven't been any-where. How the hell did they learn I was there anyway? Only Akeno and you knew where to find me."

"I suppose Akeno must have told his new partner about you."

"Akeno would never have betrayed me like that! Never!"

Mr. Hadrian turned his head back towards her, and she saw that his face was suddenly old and very weary. "He loved her, Delta."

She swallowed hard, trying to still her trembling nerves. "Then where is she? Did they get her too?"

"I don't know. Maybe. I only heard about Akeno."

Delta had to do something, anything. "Well, you know what, Mr. Hadrian? I think this whole thing stinks of a set-up. She's on the job with him when we both know he'd never have allowed it. She brings a gun and shoots Matsuda's kid. The Yakuza find Akeno in just two weeks, and no sooner is he dead than they show up at my door? I don't know who this Susan is or was, but I'm damn well going to find out."

He faced her. "How?"

Delta hesitated. "I'll...I'll go to Morgan. He can get the details on what happened in Florida."

Mr. Hadrian frowned. "Once upon a time I warned you about a job too, Delta, and while you didn't lose your life over it, it was a fiasco, nonetheless. You're going to go ask for help from the same self-serving cop that used you on the Hall case?"

Delta shook her head. "Morgan couldn't help what happened, but he owes me a favor. A big one."

Mr. Hadrian walked back and resumed his seat. He crossed his legs and templed his fingers. "I heard word about the fate of Judge Hall about a year ago, Delta."

"Yeah?"

"Apparently some guards 'accidentally' put your old friend in the wrong cell and he wound up in the company of some gentlemen he'd sentenced. I heard they took the opportunity to cut off his genitalia and choke him to death with it. Seems there might be a little justice in this world after all, wouldn't you say?"

"A little," Delta replied, not sure where Mr. Hadrian was heading with this. "Too bad that's not the way to bet."

"That's my point, Delta. Justice might show her face on occasion but more often she's nowhere to be found. That detective will as likely turn you in as look at you."

"Then, what would you suggest, Mr. Hadrian?" It was a struggle to keep sarcasm out of her voice, but the man had both saved and trained her. If nothing else, she owed him respect.

"I would suggest you take the ten thousand you left with me and start fresh somewhere. Akeno knew the risks, and he wouldn't have wanted you to die, too."

Delta crossed her arms over her chest, her blue eyes fierce as she set her jaw. "That's not happening, Mr. Hadrian. I'm going to find out what really went down that night, and if Akeno was framed, then God help the person who did it."

CHAPTER
5
FIVE

BRIAN PULLED INTO the parking lot of Cause & FX, his feelings about returning to work definitely mixed. His crazy time with Delta had cured him. After three days with the woman, he'd felt truly alive again, and as maddening as she was, he already found himself hoping for her call.

He headed into the office. Gina, the tattooed, pierced and pink-haired woman who ran the front end, looked up from her computer and greeted him with one of her face-splitting grins. She rounded the counter and he braced himself just as she caught him in a full body hug.

"Hey! Look what the cat dragged in! How you doing, Bri?"

"Not too bad. Everybody been relaxing since I left?"

"Yeah, right." They released each other and she leaned against the counter. "We might have if you hadn't left Attila in charge. She was cracking the whip the second you walked out the door."

Ursula, his operations manager, had once been a Catholic nun back in her native Austria. She was a model of honesty and efficiency, but had so much of both, that Gina had gifted her with the nickname, "Attila the Nun" . Not that anyone dared call her that to her face.

Gina craned her neck to look out the large window that fronted the building. "What happened to your chick magnet?"

"Got totaled."

She threw him a disgusted look. "I thought you were a highly trained stunt driver."

"You should see the other guy's."

Gina gave a bark of laughter. She was the kind of super high-energy employee bosses dreamed of. She loved the challenge of running the company's phones, accounting, permit and legal affairs almost single-handedly, and was about as friendly and chipper as a person could possibly be. She was also pretty offbeat and liked to poke fun at the company's more serious-minded staff, Ursula being her prime target.

"Soooo…how was your trip aside from the car crash?" Gina's brown eyes sparkled with the anticipation of gossip. "Have any fascinating adventures?"

"A few," he said, deliberately enigmatic.

"Hmm… let me guess…." She tapped her long pink nails on the countertop. "Did you go rock climbing again?"

"Nope."

"Hang gliding?"

He shook his head.

"Deep sea fishing?"

"I hate fishing."

"Orgy? Come on, tell me you went to at least one orgy."

He rolled his eyes.

"Well, I'm out of guesses. I wouldn't mention the car wreck to Ursula. She'll flip when she finds out you raised our insurance premiums."

"She here?"

"In her office, probably alphabetizing the paperclips or something. She's been such a tyrant I've had to cut my lunch breaks back to two hours. Be sure to tell her that too, okay?"

The phone rang. Gina flashed him a parting grin as she reached over the counter to put the receiver to her ear.

Brian made his way to Ursula's office, knocking before entering. She was standing behind her desk, an old conference table, scowling as she checked off items from a thick schedule book, her printer busy spitting out columns of figures. Her office was a reflection of her: spartan, efficient and organized. And the command centre.

"Ah, Brian." Her expression shifted to a near-smile and she inspected him from head-to-toe. "How was your trip?"

"Very good. How have things been going here? Everyone been behaving themselves?"

"Aside from the antics of a particular pink-haired employee, everything's been good. We just completed that huge fight sequence with Mr. Stratham yesterday, and last week we finally signed off on the contracts with Syfy. Right now, most of the crew is out prepping a shoot at Long Beach. You remember that gun battle we choreographed for the big ship there?"

"Yeah, the Queen Mary. Sounds like you've been busy."

She nodded at the printer. "And wait until you see the financials. And then we need to talk about what's coming up. Thanks to our safety record and our relationship with the unions, we're no longer having to bid on the Sony contracts. By the looks of things we're going to be swamped with work this fall. I was just about to drive out to the site in a few minutes. Come and I'll get you up to speed."

"Is that an order?"

"Yes."

"Can I go to my office first?"

"Ten minutes, then. Meet me at the front."

"Yes, boss."

Brian closed the door behind him and crossed the hall to his own office. Ursula had tidied and organized it since he'd left, and he sat down behind the clear desk with a sigh. Three weeks away and from the sound of things, everything had run smoothly. With Marcia gone and his head free of all the crap he'd had to deal with over the past few years, his life was finally back on track.

He should be happy but he wasn't, and he knew why. Years back, when he'd come to Los Angeles full of dreams and determination, life had been a grand adventure. He'd thrown himself into his training and excelled beyond anyone's wildest expectations, even his own. Working the most daring and dangerous jobs, he'd earned a formidable reputation for himself, and gone on to start his own business. It had been a challenge finding the right team to pull off the kind of amazing stunts he'd wanted to do, but he'd done it, and made his company successful.

Now he rarely did any of the stunts himself. He could go away for weeks and the business ran without a hiccup. All the excitement and enthusiasm he'd had as a youth had been slowly ebbed away by routine, disappearing so subtly that it had taken his wild ride with Delta to make him realize how tame his life had become. After years of toil and risk, he'd achieved all the goals he'd ever set for himself. The question now was what did he want to do next?

"I want to help Delta." He said it aloud. It sounded simple and foolish. Almost as foolish as 'I want to be a stuntman.' or 'I want to own a successful FX company.' Both had happened, so why should this be any different?

Because, he knew, just like he knew how soft her lips were, that Delta Fox would walk on hot coals before she asked him for help.

There was a short clipped walk down the hall, followed up by two knocks on his door. Ursula had summoned him. She handed him a stack of paper when he reached the front desk, simultaneously rattling off instructions to Gina who was bobbing her head, either in agreement or to the music coming up through the iPod bud stuck in one ear.

Ursula pointed at her. "See? This is exactly what I'm talking about. Unprofessionalism in action."

Gina's jack-o-lantern grin widened. "Why is it unprofessional to enjoy myself while I'm working?"

"How about you seek pleasure elsewhere?"

"But *you* are what gives my life pleasure, Ursula."

God, they'd bicker all day if they could. It was who they were. But they were also as loyal as dogs. Ursula had been with him since the beginning and Gina had come to him after she'd blown the whistle on a stunt company that had been cutting corners on safety. He loved them like family, but like family, they drove him nuts.

"Girls, I haven't been back an hour. How about you lavish your attentions on me?"

Gina looked ready to accommodate his wishes. Ursula poked the stack in his hands. "You want attention, I'll give it to you. Here are the financials. I have an appointment with the accountant in less than an hour and you should be there, so let's go."

"Sounds good," Brian fibbed, trailing after her. He paused at the exit, and turned back. "If a woman by the name of Delta Fox calls, tell her I want to talk."

If possible, Gina got even more perky. "You got it, boss

o'mine." She'd never disguised her dislike for Marcia and had actively promoted him to other available women. "This Fox lady, she business or pleasure?"

Brian considered. "Is there a third option?"

"A wife," Gina said, at the same time Ursula said, "An education."

Brian called upon his years of experience with his two trusted employees and said nothing more.

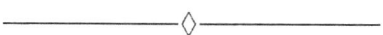

Delta leaned against a battered payphone in the downtown, listening to the baritone rumble of Detective Morgan's voice. *"You've reached the desk of Detective Lawrence Morgan. Leave your name, number and the time of your call and I'll get back to you."*

There was a sharp beep. "Hey, Morgan. I'm back in town, and I need to speak to you. Be when and where we first talked about the job. Don't be late."

She hung up but didn't move, the small enclosure giving her privacy to think. Perhaps dealing with Morgan wasn't the smartest thing. Mr. Hadrian hadn't lived to become the most successful thief in the history of the West Coast without having a keen sense of survival. Sure, Morgan had been the one to let her go, but then if anyone knew she had stolen evidence for him, the case he was working on would have collapsed. Maybe her mentor was being too cynical, but there was no guarantee that Morgan wouldn't just slap the cuffs on her the second they met again.

If the detective was to arrest her, it would be game over. She'd be packed off to a state prison, and in the unlikely event she wasn't murdered there, she'd have assassins waiting for her when she got out. Akeno would go unavenged, and that would be that. Mr. Hadrian was right. It was too much of a risk.

But how else to learn about Akeno's last weeks? There were one or two fixers in the city that could obtain such information, but with the Yakuza's price on her head she wasn't about to risk dealing with them. She could hire a private eye in Miami to dig around for her, but since PIs couldn't fully access police files, the results would be sketchy.

Morgan was her best bet, though it would be better if she had someone backing her up. Mr. Hadrian's hatred of the police ran long and deep, and he'd have been insulted if she'd requested his help. Technically she could deal with Morgan over the phone and have him fax or email the files to her, but she knew the detective would never go for it. Like Mr. Hadrian, the man was strictly old school, and as such, only did things face to face. For all he knew, it could be a sting by internal affairs to catch him handing out classified documents, and she knew he'd been on their hit list since he'd gone after Judge Hall.

Brian. If Brian helped her, things would be different. With a second person she knew just how to set things up so that the risk would be next to nil. No. She'd promised herself she wouldn't involve him and to take advantage of his stupid need to help would be the height of hypocrisy.

The old thief and Akeno had been her only friends, people as scarred as she was but tough enough to carve something out of the horror life had handed them. Together they had lent each other the strength to shut out the nightmares of the past and build themselves cocoons of solitude and anonymity. Someone like Brian, who'd grown up amongst sane people in a sane world could never understand what that was like, no matter how well-meaning he might be.

She banged open the payphone door and stepped into the flow of pedestrians. She'd go it alone.

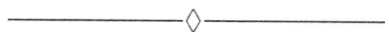

Kannon had flown into LAX late that morning, rented a car and checked himself into a downtown hotel. By the time he'd reached his room, it was almost two in the afternoon, time to call Iolana back and see what she had found. As always it rang only once before her croaking voice answered.

"This is Kannon. Do you have my information?"

"You're early," she rasped. "I said to call me this afternoon."

"It's one minute to two. It *is* afternoon."

She muttered something incomprehensible, and no doubt blasphemous, in Hawaiian.

"Did you get what I wanted or not?"

He could hear her flipping through papers. "Yes, yes. Keep your gun holstered. Here it is. The car belongs to Cause & FX. It's a company that does stunts and special effects for Hollywood. The place is owned by some guy named Brian Chanse, and from what I could dig up, the car is insured only for his use."

Fox hired a stuntman? Different. "Where does he live?"

She gave him an address in West Hollywood. Not the fanciest neighborhood, but certainly not a bad one by any means. "The guy's not filthy rich," she added, "but he sure is doing better than most in this economy."

"Have you heard of this man before?"

"Never. As far as I know he's just another *haole*."

He must be an old contact of Fox. "You'll tell me when

you get word of the thief?"

"Sure. If she's back in town to work it shouldn't take long to find her. The girl's got quite the reputation."

"So you mentioned," Kannon replied, his voice hard and dismissive. "You have my number. Don't disappoint me."

Iolana cackled unpleasantly. "If she's in the city, I'll know soon enough, killer. You just better hope it's before she finds you."

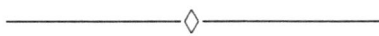

Kannon walked into Cause & FX and made straight for the pink-haired receptionist. "I'm here to see Mr. Chanse," he clipped.

One finger with a long glittery nail came up. "I'll be with you in a moment, sir. Texting lunch orders for the guys in the back. Not something you want to screw up."

He reached over, stripped her of her smartphone and leaned in. "I said, I'm here to see Chanse."

Before he could register the fact, the smartphone was back in her hand. "No one touches my phone except me. That's a law." She went right back to her tapping. For a surreal moment Kannon didn't know what to do. He'd never met a woman who hadn't been knocked back on her heels by his brand of raw intimidation.

She finished with her e-waitressing and glanced up. Her eyes, light brown and jewel-bright, widened, and the small smile that had played about her lips during her time with the smartphone deepened and curled into something he'd not received in years. An invitation. "Well, handsome. How can I help you?"

She was flirting with him. "For the third time," he ground

out, "I'm here to see Chanse."

"Not in." She leaned forward on her elbows, the pose giving a boost to her already plentiful chest. "Perhaps, I can help you."

"You take messages?"

She didn't break eye contact, didn't reach for paper and pen. "Sure do."

"Tell him he gives me what I want and his receptionist won't have an unfortunate accident."

She didn't so much as flinch. He had to give it to the man, Chanse had hired himself one ballsy staffer. "And how may he contact you?"

Kannon picked up a business card from the counter. "I'll be in touch with him. Soon."

"And what name should I give?"

He tried giving her another look, and she responded with an extra bright smile. "You tell him I still owe him for New Mexico, he'll know who I am."

"Okay. Kinda weird and creepy, but okay."

He turned and walked away, as if he couldn't be bothered to talk to her anymore. But she hadn't finished with him.

"Have a nice day!"

"He told you that? He told you he'd hurt you?" It was all Brian could to do speak through his rage. Gina had filled him in the second he came back. That Yakuza bastard had walked into his place of business and threatened his staff.

"Yeah, but listen, Brian, don't worry. He was just trying to motivate me to pass you the message. I'm not worried. After all, how dangerous could he be?"

"Plenty dangerous, believe me."

"How did you get involved with the likes of him?" Ursula said, as if Brian had gotten into the wrong crowd at school.

He didn't want to get into it. "I picked up a hitch-hiker."

"You should know better than that."

"It was pissing rain. She was wearing practically nothing. What was I supposed to do?"

"Drive on!" the ex-nun explained.

"Delta Fox," Gina chirped. "That's who you picked up. That's who the badass wants. Am I right or am I right?"

Brian didn't answer. Gina slapped her hands above her head, giving herself a high five. "I'm so cool."

He knew Ursula was worried, because she studiously ignored Gina. "You need to go to the police."

"You think that's going to stop him?" Brian said. "No, I know what I need to do."

Gina's hand shot up. "Get in touch with Delta, right?"

He pointed at her. "You, go home. Call me when you get there and stay put."

Gina grinned. "You're so bossy. I love that in a boss."

Brian gave her a stern look.

She dove under her desk and reappeared immediately with her purse, a fat, shiny gold bag. "This is a real bummer, you know. I didn't bring my bike today because I was psyched for an evening of power-shopping and now—" Her eyes caught Brian's, and she was out the front door in a flash.

Now it was Ursula's turn to look stern. "You can't get involved, Brian."

He strode down the hallway, bound for his car keys. He'd have to turn the rental in first thing tomorrow. The Yakuza man would've spotted it. He'd see what wrecker the guys in the back had going. He'd only need it for a few days.

"Brian, did you hear me?" Ursula called after him.

"It's too late for that, Ursula. Go home, be safe."

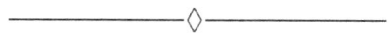

Through her binoculars, Delta watched as the unmarked police cruiser came to a stop on the shoulder of the highway overpass, a few hundred feet from where she stood on the roof of a nearby apartment building. She waited the time it took for Morgan to cautiously get out, look around, and walk over to the bright orange bag she'd left for him. Unzipping it, he pulled out a matching pair of binoculars and a walkie-talkie dialed in to her frequency.

So far, so good. From there, he could see it was really her even in the darkening evening, but there was no way he'd be able to make an arrest. It would take him at least five minutes to make it from the highway to her, by which point she could easily disappear. She adjusted the small headset she was wearing, impatient for Morgan to hail her.

"Where are you?" his deep voice crackled at length.

"Seven o'clock. On the roof."

Morgan pivoted till his binoculars were trained on her. "How've you been doing?"

"Been better," she answered.

"I thought you quit L.A. Why you back?"

"Akeno's dead."

"I heard about that. They said he got hit in Miami."

"That's right. So now I need a favor."

"You're wasting your time, Fox. Your partner got what he deserved."

Delta stiffened, her silence forcing the detective to reconsider his words. "Fine, I take it back, but a kid got killed there, Fox. I can't say I'm surprised his dad put a hit out on your partner. Hell, you of all people should get that."

"I understand what happened, but Akeno didn't do it. You didn't know him the way I did. There's no way in hell he would have taken a gun on a job, let alone used it."

Delta heard the soft gust of Morgan's sigh. "It's not my department. Perhaps if he'd come to me I could have done something for him, but he took off to Florida. What was everyone supposed to think?"

"I don't give a rat's ass what anyone thinks. What I need are all the details on what went down, both here and in Miami."

"You expect me to just hand over case files?" His voice was crackly and full of static. "Judge Hall might be gone, but a lot of his pals are still around. If I get caught giving you anything, they'll crucify me."

Delta gripped the radio. "I lost my work because of you, friend. I lost my home. I lost Akeno. Don't tell me you don't owe me, because you know damn well you do."

"You're appealing to my conscience?" Morgan asked, his tone edged with sarcasm.

"Just like you appealed to mine," Delta snapped. "Akeno was a thief, but he was no killer. It's my bet that whoever shot that boy is the same person that set Akeno up to take the blame for it. The killer's still walking around out there, so how about you take a break from the donuts and help me out?"

Morgan's radio went silent and Delta heard only the rush and rattle of night-time traffic, but their binoculars stayed trained on each other.

"Okay," he said at last, his voice grudging. "I'll see what I can put together."

"I'll be checking your voice mail every day at noon. As

soon as you have something for me, change your message. I'll get back to you with a time and place for our next meet."

Morgan lowered his binoculars. "Fine."

Delta clicked off her radio. Once again she was doing the cops' job for them. Then again, how could she expect them to care about people like Akeno or herself? It was exactly as Mr. Hadrian had taught her, she thought, as she slipped away into the shadows. If she wanted something done, she'd better be ready to do it herself.

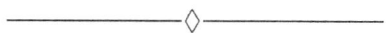

Jeanelle posed on her husband's favorite armchair in the library, checking her long black hair yet one more time as she awaited the arrival of her old adversary, Kannon Takahama.

The appointment was for eleven at night, and she'd instructed the doorman to show Mr. Takahama to the room. At 10:59 there was a knock, and in came the man she loathed more than any other.

Despite the hour, his eyes were hidden behind mirrored sunglasses, but she knew what they were doing: scanning the room suspiciously, then moving over her body, finally rising to meet her eyes. She'd noticed the same pattern in every visitor her husband had, though his teenaged son's gaze had always skipped checking the room.

"Hello, Mr. Takahama." She smiled, her practiced voice cool and silky.

His face was expressionless. "Where's Mr. Matsuda?"

Why couldn't he pretend to be polite? "There's been a change of plans. He's instructed that you give your report to me. Please have a seat and tell me all about your progress...or lack thereof."

Kannon's hands balled into fists. Good, Jeanelle thought smugly. You want to hit me. You want to wipe the smile off my pretty face, but you won't dare. I can say anything I want and as tough and dangerous as you are, you have to take it. Oh, how the tides have turned.

There had been a time when the two of them had been the most hated of rivals, her trying to win the affections and trust of Matsuda and Kannon thwarting her at every turn. Of course, he had been right to think her a gold-digger—exploiting the lust and loneliness of an old monster, to say nothing of his son. But Kannon was a half-blood, and despite his Japanese father and impeccable reputation, she had fought for months to turn the racism of the Yakuza against him. It hadn't worked, so she'd had to take more extreme measures. Every man had his weakness, after all.

The assassin removed his glasses with exaggerated slowness, sliding them into an inside pocket. He took a seat across from her and adjusted his clothing. Only then did he speak. "Fox has acquired aid from an associate of hers. He picked her up in New Mexico and, to make a long story short, he managed to…disable us."

"Meaning?"

"He ran our cars off the road. A couple of my men are in hospital."

"How terribly sad. What are you going to do now?" she enquired. Not that she cared but she so loved to make Kannon account for his mistakes.

"Continue." He made it sound as if she'd asked a stupid question. He could cut her down with one word.

She pretended not to notice, appraised him from polished shoe to closely cropped head, her disparaging smile in place. "I'm sure you'll understand, Mr. Takahama, that my husband is becoming somewhat upset by your lack of progress. The news you're bringing today is only going to deepen his concerns about your abilities."

Kannon sat still as a statue. She waited, but apparently there wasn't going to be a response. "How long will it take to finish the job, Mr. Takahama?" she was forced to ask.

"It's impossible to say. These things take time."

"Oh, silly me," she said in mock apology. "Should I just pass that estimate along to my husband, then?"

"I have a lead on her associate, and contacts searching the city for her. It will be easier to find her here in Los Angeles than when she was traveling across the country."

"So your estimate would be...?"

"A week."

"Really? That sounds rather optimistic."

"Tell your husband a week," he repeated.

Who was he to order her what to do? With a supreme effort, she shrugged her shoulders and nodded. "All right, then. I'll let him know."

She meant to dismiss him like a servant but he was on his feet and going. *One day*, she vowed. *One day, you'll bow to me.* But first....

She glided upstairs, her path bringing her to the very spot her stepson had died. She tapped on the office door, waited a few seconds, and then entered.

Hiro Matsuda sat behind his desk, his head in his calloused hands, his hair gray at the roots since he no longer bothered to dye it. Even now, in the depths of despair, his robust build and angry countenance made him a fearsome figure to behold, and one could still see how he had once been one of the most notorious criminals in the world.

"News?" His quiet voice was edged with menace.

"Kannon has tracked her back here to L.A., but he doesn't have her yet."

"She should already be dead," Matsuda fumed, with the growl of an irate dragon. "I gave him four men. How many does it take to kill a thief?"

Jeanelle made appropriate noises of agreement. Right from the start, Fox had been unexpectedly well-prepared, forcing Mr. Takahama and his men to deal with two guard dogs and reinforced doors before they could enter her home. The delay had allowed her time to escape out a second-story window, and by the time they realized she was no longer in the house she was long gone.

It had been a pleasure to hear of Mr. Takahama's humiliating failure, but that he would ultimately succeed she had no doubt. His record to date had been flawless.

"Anything else?" Hiro asked, obviously not in the mood for her unnecessary presence.

"Just one more thing. The police finally found Maria's body out by Griffith Park this morning. I saw it on the news."

Her husband hadn't much liked the chubby Filipino maid, and when he had learned that the thieves had used her pass code and that her bank book recorded a recent hefty deposit, he hadn't been very forgiving. Of course, the woman had protested her innocence to the end, but what else could one expect?

Mr. Matsuda nodded. Now that his fury on Maria had been spent, word of her remains was of only minor interest. All of his power and influence was now focused on completing his vengeance, and nothing else much mattered to the old man anymore, including his wife.

Jeanelle understood. After all, the two of them hadn't married for love. He had wanted a warm young body in his bed, a white woman to please him in ways the demure ladies of his homeland would not. She had wanted to enjoy the riches and power he possessed, luxuriating in a life of opulence. She'd fought hard for his affections—even killed for them, and for the past two years they had been able to suit each other's needs quite well, but recent events had done much to shift his focus.

"I'll leave you now, if you wish," she said softly.

He looked up at her, his eyes bloodshot from sleeplessness and secret tears. "Let me know when that bitch is dead. Kannon had better catch her soon."

She was turning to leave when he spoke again. "And make sure nobody touches Kei's urn but me. If anyone does, I'll cut their hands off. Understand?"

"Yes, Hiro. I'll make certain of it."

CHAPTER SIX

DELTA NEEDED MORE money. She'd already blown through the three hundred she'd taken from her stash at Mr. Hadrian's to get the equipment for the meet with Morgan, and that meant she had no cash for a room for the night. She should've taken more but she hated carrying too much—more than once in her life she'd handed over her money roll to punks with knives. So here she was back at her old mentor's, about to bring down his wrath for intruding on his sleep time.

She reached out to press the unmarked buttons beside the doorway. Then she was off her feet, a hand clamped over her mouth, being hauled deeper into the alley. Delta reacted immediately. She shoved her legs between his, balling up his backward walking and bit his hand. Hard.

"Fuck, Delta!"

Brian.

She froze and that allowed him time to drag her behind a dumpster where he let her go so fast she stumbled. He shook his hand. "You drew blood." He sounded pissed off, as if it were her fault for defending herself. "You got your shots or do I need to go for mine?"

God. High on adrenaline from his jump on her, she whirled on him. "You ever think of saying 'Hey, Delta, it's me, Brian.'? A few simple words but nah, that would be too easy."

"Except you would've scampered down your little hidey-hole. I've been waiting five hours for you." He hissed out the last words. He was angry. Really angry. She paused. This wasn't about the bite or the wait. He'd put up with a whole lot more from her and shrugged it off. But right now, there was rage in every line of his body.

"How'd you know about this place?" She tried to make it sound like a topic of conversation.

"I followed you this morning instead of driving off."

"What? How did you do that?"

She saw the glint of his eye, and his voice dropped to an edgy softness. "If you'd bothered to look over your shoulder, you'd have seen me. But you were so set on not looking back."

He had her. She'd been too afraid she'd run after him. But damned if she was going to tell him that. "Congrats, you're a regular Colombo. Now, what do you want?"

There was a weird kind of silence. "Colombo?"

"Yeah, Colombo. The detective. In the trench coat. The television show."

There was more silence. What was the matter?

When he spoke it was slowly, calmly, as if counseling a psych patient. "I've heard of Colombo. I haven't watched the show. It was before my time and definitely before yours, Delta."

Here she was, standing in the dark with a man she'd met three days ago, who'd stalked her, dragged her off, and now it seemed she was obliged to talk television with him—the subject she despised more than any other.

"Whatever. Last time I watched T.V. I was twelve, so

why are we going on about it?"

Suddenly the dumpster erupted. Out shot two full plastic bags of garbage and then up popped a head. It began shouting rapid-fire Mandarin and arms waved at them.

"Seems we're disrupting the quiet of the neighborhood," Brian commented. "Let's go."

He took her elbow to lead her farther down the alley, away from the irate homeless man. She pulled back, he tugged, she pulled back. He rounded on her and his mouth to her ear, he said, "Listen, Delta. I put myself out there for you. I dodged bullets, I got my car totaled, I took you to where you wanted to go, I took it without getting anything in return except for one real sweet kiss. And I was okay with that. Only today, a big black Yakuza man shows up at my place of work and threatens to take out my receptionist unless I tell him where you are."

Delta jerked, because blowback on Brian was the one thing she'd not wanted to have happen. He must've thought she'd wanted to get away, because his grip tightened and he kept talking. "I'm not okay with that. Gina's like a sister to me, and considering I've already got three biological ones, that's saying something. I'm not going to let anything happen to her or to anyone where my name appears on their paycheck. So, you're coming with me, you're going to tell me what the fuck's going on and then we're making a plan that does not involve you messing up yet another person's life. Got it?"

He didn't wait for her to agree but pulled on her again. This time, she let him take her wherever he had in mind.

Brian swung into the back lot of Cause & FX, stopping to watch the security gate close behind them. "We were broken into a couple of times when we moved into this building." Brian explained. It was the first he'd spoken on the forty-minute trip there, other than telling her they'd talk when they got where they were going. She hated his silences because it wasn't who he was, and she regretted her part in making him who he wasn't. "The insurance companies made us set this place up like Fort Knox, plus we have security that comes by on patrol. But I suppose you could get inside no problem, hmm?"

Delta didn't let on she was counting cameras. Old habits and all. "I wouldn't say no problem, but it certainly wouldn't be the hardest place I've ever hit."

Brian grunted and parked behind one of the company trucks, then led the way to a reinforced back door. Once inside, he flipped on the lights to reveal a large loading bay filled with floor-to-ceiling special effects equipment and supplies. She followed him through a maze of neatly organized shelves and worktables, and past a long line of heavy steel lockers marked with hazard symbols and padlocks that'd require heavy-duty bolt-cutters to crack.

"What's in these?"

"Explosives."

Good to know. He palmed open a swinging door and headed into the wide hallway that she assumed led to the front office. He stopped at the first door on the left and pushed it open.

"Here we are. Home sweet home."

Inside was a huge and well-appointed lunchroom, complete with a pool table. Delta looked around at the stainless steel appliances and granite countertops. Most people didn't have as nice a kitchen in their homes.

"Your employees must love you."

He opened the fridge. "What do you want?"

She didn't know how to answer that. "Nothing. You came to me."

Still turned to the fridge interior, he cut her a look over his shoulder. "Delta. Beer? Coke? Water? What?"

"Oh. Uh...water."

He took out a bottle and set it on the table. Her cue, she supposed, to park her ass on the seat in front of it, which she did.

He had his beer and settled his butt against the counter. "Give me an update."

She took a deep breath. "My former partner...my friend is dead."

Brian made a low sound of sympathy. One piece of bad news and out came the old softie. She hurried on, "The thing is...the thing about it is I think he was set up. In fact I know he was."

Out came the story Mr. Hadrian had told her, about how Akeno had partnered with some mysterious woman and how his last job had ended in disaster. She told him why the Yakuza were after her, and the reasons she thought the whole thing had been a set-up, and though it was a struggle not to let her emotions get the best of her, she was proud and relieved when she pulled it off well enough.

"So, what are you going to do now?" Brian asked.

"I have a contact with the police, a detective here in Los Angeles. I'm not 100% certain I can trust him, but he's in the position to get me all the details on what happened in Miami. With those, I might be able to piece together what's going on and clear my name with the Yakuza."

"Isn't it his job to bust you?"

"Well, actually he's the one who let me go."

"He let you go? You mean he let you escape? But why?"

Delta was instantly sucked back to the night that had changed her life. The first in the chain of events that had led to her leaving Akeno, and, ultimately, to his death. "Because that detective was my last client, Brian. Remember me telling you about the repo business?"

"Yeah, Delta. Every word." The way he said it, low and with a kind of disbelief, made her think of his sexy talk before they'd kissed. It had the same intimate, got-you-on-my-mind softness. And thinking of that kiss completely messed with her mind.

"You were saying?" he prompted.

She felt herself go hot with embarrassment, and rolled the bottle across her cheek. "Anyway, so like I said, Akeno and I had a partnership with Mr. Hadrian, the man who taught us how to steal and found us our clients. Things went well for a few years. We got back millions of dollars in stuff, and there was nothing the people we stole from could do. Being criminals themselves they couldn't call the police, and though a few of the cops knew what we were doing, they turned a blind eye to us. We even went semi-legal and started paying taxes on some of our fees. Akeno and I were the best on the coast, and we developed a real reputation."

"So what happened with this detective?" Brian asked.

"The guy's name is Morgan. A few years back when he was in vice he discovered that a certain judge was dealing in child pornography. Not just looking at it, I mean making and distributing it. Morgan tried everything to get enough evidence on the guy, but every time he seemed to get close, internal affairs gave him a hard time and interfered with his case. He needed an unedited video that had the judge in it, something that tied the bastard directly to the crime."

Brian nodded. "And that's what he hired you to steal for him, huh?"

Delta snorted. "Yeah, like cops ever pay for anything. Morgan approached Mr. Hadrian, but the old man hates police and told the detective to get lost. So then he came to Akeno and me directly. He didn't have the money to pay our fees, so he just appealed to… I don't know… to our duty as citizens, I suppose. Anyway, Akeno didn't care for police any more than the old man, so he told Morgan to get lost, too."

The corner of Brian's mouth twitched. "But you didn't."

No, she hadn't. It had been personal. An old hurt she'd thought to heal. Instead, it had torn her life apart. "I told him I would do it. Just that once. Akeno and Mr. Hadrian were furious, but I went ahead, alone. I got into the judge's house and found what Morgan needed, but I slipped up on the exit and set off an alarm. I cleared the place but then a police dog took me down. I got busted, and while I was in the cop car, Morgan showed up.

"You gave him the videos?"

"Yeah, Hall kept them on flash drives. Almost a dozen of them. I shoved them under a bush just off the Judge's property, and I told Morgan where to find them. In return, he let me escape. I made it back to Mr. Hadrian's, but by that time, there was a warrant out for my arrest. I was charged with breaking and entering and evading police custody, and I knew the judge had powerful friends who would make sure I got serious time. So I retired."

"Why didn't Morgan just admit he'd hired you? I mean, no jury would have convicted you if they'd known you'd been put up to it by a cop."

"Because then the evidence I got for him would have been inadmissible, plus he'd have been kicked off the force.

Really, he didn't have much of an option if he wanted to nail the judge."

"Uh-huh. Right." Brian chucked his beer can into a tall bin and opened the fridge again, this time for a Dr. Pepper. "I take it the judge went to jail."

Delta felt a flash of that same triumph as when she'd first heard the news. "Oh yeah. Big time, and all of the people that worked with him, too. He turned state's evidence against them, but even that got him three years in the pen. Apparently some of his cellmates found out what he'd done and, well, I guess you could say he wound up serving a life sentence." She couldn't keep the gloat out of her voice.

Brian regarded her. "So now that Morgan has put the judge away he doesn't have to worry about you. He's free to arrest you now if wanted to, huh?"

"Bingo."

"Do you really think he would, though? I mean, you put everything on the line to help him bust the creep."

"Tonight, I met with him. That is, across buildings and with binoculars."

Brian froze, soda halfway to his mouth. "Across buildings and with binoculars?"

"Yeah."

"Alone?"

"Yeah."

His mouth thinned. "Did it occur to you to call me?"

"It occurred."

He made a disgusted sound. Sucked back the rest of his soda and sent it the way of the earlier beer. The cans crackled against each other, and Delta reacted by scurrying out more info. "He said he'd do some digging. I don't know, Brian. Maybe he's honorable and maybe he's not. No telling with cops."

Silence. He was angry, and she understood why. She'd lost one person. Brian had at risk every single employee.

"What's the story with this Gina?" she asked.

"A Yakuza man matching the description of our guy in the Nissan came in while I was out on site, tried to intimidate her into telling him where I was. Failing that, he told her I'd better tell him where you're at, or he'd hurt her."

"Did you tell him?"

His eyes flashed. "Of course not. I'm not giving up, and I'm not giving in. We're going to settle your trouble because your trouble is now officially my trouble. You got yourself a new partner."

One look at him and she knew she couldn't talk him out of it. At least, not tonight.

"Okay," she replied.

He eyed her suspiciously. "Okay? Just like that?" He walked over and stuck out his hand. "Shake on it?"

"Yeah, yeah." She took his hand, and he didn't let it go.

"In my world, a handshake means a lot. It's a promise. Understand?"

"From your wild west days in Wyoming."

His expression stayed solemn. "Something like that."

She didn't know what to do with that look. He smiled during a car chase and went serious on a handshake. "Okay. Partners. I'm shaking on it."

He slowly released her hand.

"Mind if I go now?"

"Go where?"

"Back to where you found me. I need money."

"Why?"

"For a room, for starters."

"Stay here."

"Here?"

"Why not? It's where I spend my nights."

"Here?" She repeated.

"Haven't got a new place since, well, I gave my home to Marcia." He winced. "I'm kind of in transition."

He pulled out a folding cot from a tall cupboard, and began to wrest it flat. "Anyway, a hotel isn't going to be half as secure as this place. The washrooms are across the hall, and they have showers and towels if you want to clean up." He pulled out a second cot and started working on it.

She shoved her hands in her pockets. "Once again we're roommates, huh?"

Brian gave her a look that felt like a small heat pack had cracked open on her belly. "Yeah, once again." And the way he said it, the heat radiated everywhere through her body. "Especially when it's" —he glanced at the microwave clock— "1:12 in the morning. Seems to me the best thing we can do for now is sleep."

The heat stopped its progress. By 1:18 the lunchroom was dark, and they were both stretched out fully clothed on the cots set up side by side. They didn't need to be so close together, but she didn't mind at all.

"Delta. I'm sorry about Akeno."

She got a lump in her throat and tears flooded her eyes. She was going to lose it. A reaction to all the drama, the sleep deprivation, the fear. If she was alone, she'd let it all out. Have a good cry. She swallowed to get the lump down so she could answer him, tell him thanks and that it was all right. Only it wasn't working. Her gut clenched, her legs curled, she squeezed her eyes shut and hot tears leaked out, and then to her utter shame, she sobbed.

She was lifted straight off the cot and resettled with Brian as her bed. Her head was on his chest, her legs between his. He arranged the blanket over them, and then his arms were around her.

"Hey," he whispered. "Let it all out."

And she did. Because she couldn't hold back any longer and because with Brian, she didn't have to.

CHAPTER 7
SEVEN

DELTA WOKE IN the dawn of the lunchroom, still bundled with Brian, his arms heavy and warm around her. She'd cried like there was no stopping last night, and he'd held her, only letting go once to tear off paper towel for her nose. She still had it wadded in her hand.

Ever so slowly, she peeked up. His head was turned to the side, his face calm and strong, like it always was when he slept. God, she knew how he looked when he slept. She'd never actually slept with a man before, and here she'd done it every single night with him. The smell of coffee wafted across from the maker on the counter, and her eyelids closed to its burping and wheezing.

Then, from the hallway, the clipped march of heels. The staff, already. Delta squinted at the microwave clock. 7:38. The two feet about-faced in front of the door, and there was the muted beeping of a code being punched in. Delta burst from Brian and was on her feet when the door swung open and the lights were clicked on.

"Oh!" A tall, very solid woman stopped short. Her hair was steel gray, her pantsuit was steel gray, her chest seemed reinforced and her gaze was like that of a bird of prey.

Delta blinked. "Um… hi. You must be Gina."

If possible, the woman grew taller and more solid. "Does my hair look pink to you?" From the cot came a suppressed roll of laughter. "Delta. Meet Ursula. Operations manager."

Ursula's gaze swept over Delta, and she knew what the imposing woman saw: messed hair, red eyes, wrinkled clothes. A waste of space. "You're the hitch-hiker?"

Brian swung himself up to sit on the cot. "Ursula..." he warned. "Delta is my guest."

"You brought her here? To your workplace?

Brian scratched his head, yawned. "Have some pity for the homeless. What time is it anyway?"

"Time to get up. Please, before someone else sees this."

"Oh, for Christ's sake, we were just sleeping. That's all."

"Ahem." Ursula glowered.

"For goodness' sake," Brian said automatically. He stretched and pushed off the cot. "Okay, okay, we're up already. Is that coffee I see?" And stumbled towards it like a blind man.

Ursula's eyes narrowed on the pot. "Yes. Yesterday it failed to turn on, and so today, I came early to see that it didn't happen again."

Delta felt for the poor appliance that had barely escaped disciplinary action. She saw Brian take two cups from the cupboard and anticipating his next move, she made for the fridge. "And it is a blessing I did," Ursula informed them. "You now have twenty minutes to clear away this"—she waved at the cots—"evidence before the others arrive. Especially that rumor-monger." Ursula pointed in the direction of the front office. "Remember at ten, the producers for the Globus account are coming. Your suit is in your office. Socks and underwear are on your desk."

"Thanks, mom," Brian said, as he poured.

"Speaking of which, she's flying in a week tomorrow to help you find a new place." Brian groaned and turned to Delta as she came up alongside him with a carton of cream. "Look at me, Delta," he mock whispered. "A grown man and not one woman in my life believes I can take care of myself."

"I heard that!" Ursula said and opened the door. "Fine. You can show up in your pajamas for the next meeting for all I care." She clipped out. Delta could hear her continue further down the hallway into the bay area, probably off to chastise the machinery for just sitting there.

Brian passed a full cup to Delta which she took in exchange for the carton of cream she had at the ready. He took it, as if he expected it, as if having a morning coffee was something they always did. "Don't mind her. She's more concerned about people coming to the wrong conclusions."

Delta thought of what he believed about her, about them. That they were partners, and maybe even a little more. Talk about wrong conclusions.

His arm came around her shoulders. "How you doing?" His voice was low and tender against her ear.

"Much better. Thanks." She sipped her coffee and tried to ignore how good it felt to be tucked against his side again. It wasn't going to last. It couldn't.

"Ursula's probably right," Brian said. "We should figure out another place to stay. The cots are spine killers."

We? *We*? She wiggled against his hold on her shoulders. "Here, let me put the cots away."

Brian held her to him. "Hey, I don't care who knows, okay? And if I don't care then neither should you." His grip tightened and he angled her so her front was against his side, his mouth against her hair. "I'm thinking that after we sort out this craziness, you and I should spend some time figuring out the two of us. Yeah?"

The two of us. As if they were already a couple, and there remained only a few technicalities to sort. And in some ways they were. Only one cot with mussed blankets, two cups of coffee, a road trip together, shared meals, shared beds. God, they'd done everything a couple could do, except have sex. And she knew how that would end.

"Yeah. Okay."

He gave her hair—her hair!—a loud smacking kiss, followed up with a push away and a smack to her butt. "That's my girl. Now, why don't you go scrub yourself up? Maybe find a toothbrush, too."

It was the world's most unsexy kiss and comment, yet Delta felt a stupid, giddy-girly rush of happiness. This wouldn't do. She folded her arms. "I'm not a girl. I'm twenty-nine, you know," she said, quickly putting distance between them by heading for the door.

Brian grinned. "Big deal. I'm thirty-five and I still haven't grown up. How about when you finish you meet me in the back and we'll go for a quick breakfast?"

"Yeah," she said. "Okay."

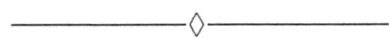

The shower room had heated floors. And an armoire with fluffy white towels. And another unit with soaps and different kinds of shampoos and conditioners. On the counter above the double sinks were lotions and creams. And toothbrushes individually wrapped, in individual real glasses. It was a spa. All the female employees must adore their boss. It was a good reminder. Generosity was a habit for Brian.

Delta stripped and stepped into the shower area with its three shower heads. Three? How many female employees were there who required showers simultaneously? Delta lathered up her hair from something that smelled like coconut, and pushed thoughts of Brian out. Focus on staying alive and getting even.

Morgan probably wouldn't take long to get hold of the files on the Matsuda murder, seeing as that crime was local, and it would give her a place to start while she waited for data from the cops in Florida. She also had to find a safer place to hole up. His workplace was a Yakuza target now and her anywhere near it was not good for him or his people. Made her gut queasy to think about it.

The bathroom door opened, and wiping the soap from her eyes, she peeked out of the shower. It was a woman, dressed in a tight fitting cycling outfit, her shock of pink hair fanning out as she pulled off her helmet. Gina.

"Mornin'," she said with a grin.

"Morning," Delta said, acutely aware she was naked in front of a woman who was in the process of stripping herself down to that condition, too. Okay, time to rinse and go.

"Have a nice night in the lunchroom?"

Delta winced, provoking a giggle from Gina. She stepped in beside Delta, twisted on the other two shower heads, angling them and herself so water blasted her front and her back.

"Soooo, how was he?" Gina asked, as if they were BFFs from way back.

Delta suddenly felt at one with Ursula. Gina really was a gossip. She turned to face the woman, tipping her head back to rinse out the shampoo. "Isn't that kind of a personal question?"

Gina gave Delta's front a once-over, squinted and handed Delta a razor. "Need to smooth out the pits there, m'dear.

Anyway, just curious. Bri hasn't had many girlfriends, so I've never really had anyone else to ask."

Delta took the razor and, after a moment's hesitation, commenced 'smoothing'. "What about his last one?"

"Marcia." Gina lathered up her hair, the effect of white suds and pink hair making it look like a ball of cotton candy. "There was a head case if there ever was one."

Delta skimmed the razor over her legs, her face conveniently hidden. "Oh?"

"Yeah. I don't know what Brian ever saw in her," Gina breezed on. "He's a good guy, but man is he a sucker for a sob story."

Delta concentrated on getting the troublesome hairs around her knees. "What was her story?"

"Oh, the usual one in this town. She'd had an unhappy childhood. Mommy and Daddy didn't pay enough attention to her. She never got that pony they promised. Yadda-yadda."

Delta handed the razor back. "Thanks. Doesn't sound as if you liked her very much."

"Hated her," Gina said. "She was one of those needy types that lean on a guy till he breaks. She couldn't get over whatever bad things happened in her life, and always expected everyone to feel sorry for her."

Delta stepped out of the shower and dried herself off. She had to get out. Out of the shower, out of the building, out of Brian's life. She wasn't Marcia. She was way more dangerous.

"Oh well," Gina shrugged. "Live and learn. I'm probably being hard on her because of Bri. He's done a lot for me, and I don't like seeing my friends jerked around, even if they go asking for it."

Delta wiggled on her underwear over her damp skin as fast as possible.

Gina paused in the midst of soaping up the section between her legs. Delta had never met anyone so uninhibited. "I guess I can't blame her for going after a good thing," Gina mused, her fingers resuming a slow, rhythmic pattern. "If I was alone when I met Brian, I probably would have tried to get with him as well."

"You have a boyfriend?" Delta asked, eager to have the subject shift away from Brian's poor choice in lovers.

Gina laughed, her hands traveling up to her breasts. "Girlfriend at the moment, but it's casual."

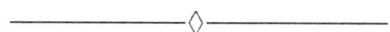

Delta slung her bag—the one containing the sum of her worldly possessions—over her shoulder as she left the ladies room. She walked determinedly into the large back bay, making her way past the stacks of equipment and ignoring the curious looks of the men at the worktables.

One of Cause & FX's vans was backed up to the open bay door, and a pair of young men were unloading high-performance motorcycles from it with Brian's aid. Spying her, he smiled, and she waited as he finished helping his employees get the bikes parked on the shop floor.

"All set to go?"

"Actually, Brian, can we have a word for a second?"

He raised an eyebrow. "Sure." He led her behind a large tool rack that more or less separated them from the workers.

"I don't think this is going to work," she said, as fast as she could.

"What?"

"Look, you've been very kind to me, Brian. I owe you, and I know it. When everything gets cleared up maybe we can get together sometime, but for now I just don't think this a good idea."

"Come again?"

"Listen, there's people in this city who want to *kill* me. Get it? This isn't some goddamn TV show. It's real, and people have already died. Real people. Real death."

He backed her into the corner. "We shook on it."

"Sorry, I'm not into your code of honor thing."

Everything about Brian changed. Not yet anger but the kind of stillness before a storm broke. She checked her exits. "Delta. I risked my life for you."

"I know. That's why I'm breaking the promise. You do stupid things. Like believing in handshakes."

He stepped back, stared at her. "Un-be-lieve-able."

Delta stood firm. "I get it, Brian. I get that I'm going back on a handshake. But I don't care, get that, too. I came here last night because there was no way you were going to let me be. And yeah, okay, you deserved an explanation. I would cheat and lie to keep you and yours safe. Which means that I'd cheat and lie to you. And so yes, I'm okay with going back on a handshake."

His face changed, softened, and she didn't need that, right now. "Don't, Brian. Don't go all stupid and soft on me when you ought to be thinking straight."

His jaw hardened. "This better, Delta?"

She hated how he looked. "Yes."

"How about if I say, 'Get the hell out of here?'"

"Even better." She spun around and headed back the way she'd come. She stalked back into the hall, making for the front doors of Cause & FX.

She didn't notice the danger till it was too late. Striding out into the front office, her eyes locked on to the man at the counter, her shocked expression reflected in his mirrored sunglasses as he looked up from Gina at her. Time seemed to stop as predator and prey locked eyes, then with the force of dynamite, the situation exploded.

Leaping over the counter like some jungle cat, Kannon sent Gina sprawling as he drew his handgun. In the same instant, Delta grabbed a handful of paper from a desk and, hurling it over her shoulder, bolted down the hall.

Once, twice, three times the pistol fired, but the space between the counter and the hall was filled with whirling papers, drawing even the assassin's trained eye off his target. He sprinted through the storm of paper just in time to see Fox disappear through a door at the end of the hall. He fired again, blowing a hole through it, then burst into the crowded back bay. Stripping off his glasses, he scanned the room, and spying her tearing past a set of lockers, he steadied his hand and pulled the trigger.

There was a bright flash as a locker, full of explosives, detonated.

Delta felt herself lifted into the air, then slammed onto one of the work benches, a shower of hot metal ricocheting in every direction. The impact ripped the breath from her, but instinctively she rolled off the table, hitting the ground running. Smoke and flame filled the room behind her, but she didn't risk a look back to see if she was still being pursued. Startled men stood in her way but she weaved between them, into the back of the van and up to the front where the keys were in the ignition. Leaping into the driver's seat, she started the van, threw it into gear and pressed the accelerator to the floor.

Brian was still picking himself off the floor as he heard the squeal of tires, barely audible over the ringing in his ears. A sprinkler went off, filling the room with a haze of water and smoke as he looked about. Out of the swirl of chaos came a tall, dark-skinned man, suit torn and scorched, a massive gun in his outstretched hand. Narrowing his eyes, the stranger aimed the weapon at the back of the retreating van, till Brian hurled himself against the hitman's legs, slamming him to the concrete floor.

Brian lunged to get on top of the killer, but a square kick to his chest sent him flailing backwards into the tool rack. A weighty socket wrench cracked him across the head, and by the time he stumbled to his feet again, the gunman was no longer there. Leaping over wreckage with incredible athleticism, the assassin reached the bay door just as Delta crashed the van through the security gate, sparks showering the area as she accelerated down the alley.

Brian made to pursue but his head swam, and he barely caught himself before he lost his footing entirely. Staggering to the rear entrance, he shook his head, trying to clear it, and looking up, he could see the killer was still in pursuit at a full sprint, aiming his gun even as he ran, too fast for Brian to even hope to catch,.

The side of the van scraped against the alley wall as another shot rang out, and swinging back barely managed to clear the corner where the lane intersected another. The hitman only ran faster, and at near Olympian pace, rounded the corner after Delta, disappearing from Brian's view.

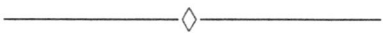

Kannon wasn't about to lose the thief now that he'd

finally caught up with her. He redoubled his efforts, muscles straining, rounding the alley with every ounce of his speed— just in time to see her reversing straight towards him.

He dived to the side, but one of the rear doors clipped him, throwing him against the alley wall with bone-crushing force. Bouncing off the wall, he was thrown hard against the vehicle, which in turn sent him reeling face first to the dusty pavement.

For several seconds he lay there, head spinning, then rolled himself over, trying to find the gun that had been torn from his hands. Through the spider web of cracks in his sunglasses he located it in the worst possible place.

Standing over him, Delta trained the massive gun on the Yakuza, and for a long moment the two simply looked at each other, both fighting for breath, their eyes locked over the barrel of the weapon.

What was she waiting for? What would one more death matter to her at this point? Then, to his utter surprise, she lowered the handgun.

"I…didn't…do it," she gasped out, then flung the weapon down the alleyway, sending it clattering beneath a dumpster. Turning on her heel, she ran to a nearby drainpipe, and fast as a monkey, clambered up it to the rooftop and disappeared.

Kannon blinked against the hard sun, then with a pained grunt pulled himself to his feet. His side ached. Definitely a few cracked ribs, but considering his brains could be on the ground right now, he was lucky. The police would be here in a matter of minutes, and unless he wanted to be healing up in a prison hospital, he'd best make himself scarce. Clutching his side, he jogged off down the alley, pulling out his cell phone with his free hand.

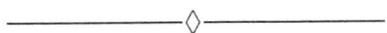

The blow from the wrench had been more severe than Brian had first realized, and he didn't made it halfway to the crushed security fence before tripping over his own feet. His crew picked him up and helped him back to his office. By some miracle, he had been the only one injured.

Gina appeared with the medical kit as soon as he sat down, and Ursula shooed everyone out of the room.

"A couple of nasty gashes you got there, Bri, but I don't think you're concussed," Gina said, poking away at him. "Guess that thick skull of yours comes in handy sometimes."

"Gina, Ursula…I need a favor."

Both women looked at him in surprise. "Sure, Bri." Gina said. "What's that?"

"Don't tell the cops about Delta. Just say that she came in to use the bathroom, and that some guy came asking for her a few minutes later. Okay?"

Gina flashed him a conspiratorial grin. "Okay."

Ursula's reaction was predictably the opposite. "You want us to give false testimony to the police?" She said, obviously shocked and offended by the very notion of his request. "Have you lost your mind, Brian? That's a serious crime!" Her voice grew higher pitched with every question.

Outside a cacophony of police and fire sirens shrilled towards them. "I can't explain now, but I swear to God—and Ursula, I'm not saying His name in vain this time—there's a very good reason. You know I'd never ask you to lie unless it was a matter of life and death, and in this case it is. I need you to trust me."

Ursula looked at him with a pained expression, but reluctantly nodded.

"Tell the crew they saw me arguing with what looked like some homeless woman. Tell them I told her to get the hell out." That part, at least, was true.

Police, paramedics and the fire department soon descended, and Brian had to argue with a couple of medics to keep from being hauled off in an ambulance. No sooner did they relent than the police began questioning him. He described the assassin as accurately as he could, but when they turned their attention to Delta he told them as little as possible, vaguely relating how some woman wandered into the back of the shop, trying to hit him up for a few bucks and he'd shown her the door. The next thing he knew she was running back through it a moment before the explosion. They took his state-ment and left him alone.

He got to his feet, unable to suppress a low grunt as he touched the back of his head, and walked out the bay door and over to the alley to see what he could see. He had no idea what had become of Delta, and was sick with worry. The police had already cordoned off the area and had forensics people on the scene. From his vantage he could see them carefully going over the battered van, but not much else.

There wasn't anyone from the morgue, so Delta had out-run her pursuer at least this far. It was impossible to tell if she had ultimately eluded him. He was about to head back inside when Ursula confronted him." Are you sure you're all right, Brian? I know Gina has her medical ticket but you really should go to the hospital."

"I'm okay," he assured her. "Really, I'm fine."

She gave him a long, piercing look. "All right, then." She lowered her voice. "Now, what are you and that hitch-hiker up to?"

Hell if he knew. "It's a very long and complex story,

Ursula. I promise I'll tell you all about it as soon as I can, but right now I have to deal with more than just this situation."

"Did you know she had a crazed lunatic after her? Gina told me that man had been here before! Why didn't you call the police about him?"

He sighed. "Like I said, it's a long story."

"It will be longer when the cops lock you up for questioning. Do you know how much damage she caused?"

"I get the feeling you're going to tell me."

"Tens of thousands of dollars worth! Our pyrotechnical supplies went up in smoke, our security gate is ruined and the van she took is probably a write-off. That's to mention nothing of all the smashed equipment and the bullet holes in the walls."

"It's all insured, Ursula," he said. "And anyway, she's gone now. I've talked to the police, and we'll all get through this mess. Let's just be thankful that nobody was hurt, okay? It could have been much worse."

Ursula set her hands on her hips, her expression unhappy. "Fine," she said in resignation. "I'll go phone our adjusters and start reorganizing our schedule."

Good, he'd survived Ursula. And then he realized what she'd said. "Don't claim my car. I'll pay for the repairs myself."

The scowl on Ursula's face deepened. "Why?"

He'd had enough. "Do as I say, Ursula."

"Fine, then." The woman stalked off, clearly annoyed, though Brian could tell she felt a little hurt, too. She wasn't used to him keeping things from her.

"Damn woman." He wasn't sure to which woman he was referring. Delta said she didn't need him, but how was she going to get by without help? The women had no identification, no credit cards…she couldn't even rent a car or get a decent hotel room by herself. Where was she going to stay?

He did know of one place she might go. He might catch up with her there before the Yakuza did. Because, dammit, whether she liked it or not, they were partners. He had shook on it.

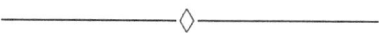

Delta knelt on the leather chair, slumped over the back of it as Mr. Hadrian worked on her. She let out a hiss of pain as he wiggled a small shard of metal from her upper back, then again as he dabbed the wound with a peroxide-soaked cloth.

"Don't be a baby," her mentor said quietly, dropping the quarter-sized chip of metal into a bowl. "I'm almost finished."

Delta gritted her teeth as she felt him slide a needle into her skin and begin sewing up the wound, holding the thread taut with his mechanical claw. "It hurts, okay?"

"Try getting your hand crushed by a sledgehammer," he replied coolly.

He had her there. The sewing needle wove in and out of her back a few more times, but at last she felt him snap the thread. He wiped the wound again with the cloth, applied a bandage to it, then straightened and turned his back to her.

"I'm done. You can get dressed now."

Delta put on the linen shirt he had given her to replace her bloodied tee. She'd dropped her bag during the chase, and in so doing, lost what pitiful few belongings she'd possessed. His shirt was naturally much too big for her, and she had to roll up the sleeves until they hung like bagels around her wrists. "I'm dressed."

Mr. Hadrian turned, wiping the blood from his hands with the last remaining clean cloth. Delta picked up the tray of medical supplies and carried it to the kitchen. He followed her, and wordlessly they tidied up together. When they were done, she put on the kettle to boil, then sat down with him at the small kitchen table. They'd often shared tea, back when, and today she needed the ritual, needed something ordinary to do to keep her mind off Brian. Her point had been proven. She prayed it wasn't at the cost of a bullet to his body.

"So…how have you been?" she asked.

He shrugged. "I'm enjoying my retirement. How was your time in South Carolina?"

"Quiet. I rented a house a little ways out of town."

"Find employment?"

"Not in our line of work, no. I got a job as a climbing instructor, though. I managed to talk them into paying me cash, so it was all good."

"Meet anyone?"

The question took Delta aback. Her mentor had never talked about personal relationships in all the time she'd known him. It had been as if he didn't know there were such things. "No, I didn't."

"Why not?"

She frowned. "I don't understand your question."

"I'm asking why you didn't start a relationship with anyone in Myrtle Beach. You're an attractive enough woman. You're young. Why didn't you find someone?"

"Because…" She trailed off.

"The truth now," he instructed, his tone polished and precise as a scalpel.

"Because I was afraid," she admitted.

"Afraid of being hurt? Afraid of being used? Afraid of being turned in to the police?"

"All of the above."

He nodded, his expression one of satisfaction." That's good."

Delta cast a dubious look. "It is?"

"Yes. It means you have a clear understanding of both yourself and your situation. You know your limits and weaknesses, and as such you can live within those boundaries. That is, you did."

God, a lecture. "Please come to the point, Mr. Hadrian."

"The point is you've forgotten who you are, Delta. Instead of going to ground you're trying to fight back against an enemy you can't possibly defeat. Your desire for vengeance might be very noble, but we don't live in a storybook world. There are no happy endings, least of all for those who ignore reality."

Exactly what she'd been telling Brian. Was she guilty of the same romanticizing? The kettle began to whistle, and she got up to make the tea. She could feel Mr. Hadrian's eyes on her as she poured boiling water into the teapot.

"You used to do that years ago, you know."

"Do what?" he asked.

"Watch me like that. When I wasn't looking. Only when I wasn't looking."

His reply sounded careful. "I suppose I didn't want to make you uncomfortable, given your experiences."

"Why were you looking at all?"

There was a slight pause. "What are you implying, Ms. Fox?"

Her back still to him, she smiled slightly. He always called her that when he was uncomfortable. "I'm not implying anything, Mr. Hadrian. I should think the question's as straightforward as the one you put to me."

"I suppose it was because I was...fond of you. You were

like a…" He searched for the right word.

"Daughter?" she suggested.

"More like a pet."

She placed her hands on her hips and turned around, catching the last trace of a smirk on his lined face. "I see. Well, I daresay if anyone had harmed your 'pet' you would have had to do something about it, being still in your prime at the time."

"Perhaps," he conceded.

"And that's why I have to do something about Akeno, Mr. Hadrian. Just as I'd have to do something if someone harmed you."

The expression on his face shifted, to something almost like tenderness. Or was it disappointment? He folded his hand around his claw as she poured his tea, dropped in two teaspoons of sugar and set it before him. She prepared her own, and they silently drank together.

CHAPTER 8
EIGHT

WHEN DELTA EMERGED from Mr. Hadrian's at noon, she headed straight for the nearest phone booth. She punched in the number to Cause & FX and waited a couple of rings before Gina answered the phone.

"Gina? This is Delta."

"Mom!" Gina replied. "You wouldn't believe what happened today."

"Oh?"

"Yeah. Some woman shows up asking to use the bathroom, and no sooner does she go in when this big black dude comes by looking for her. As soon as he saw her, he went postal and started shooting up the place."

Delta swallowed. "Is—is everyone okay?"

"Oh, yeah. The guy couldn't hit the broad side of a barn. The boss got banged up, but he's walking and talking. The place is a bit of a mess, though."

Delta took a deep breath. "I'm sorry, Gina. Please tell Brian I'm sorry, too."

"Well, what can you do?" Gina carried on as if she hadn't heard a thing. "Crazy things happen in this city. Anyway, the boss is cool with it all. He's more worked up about his new girlfriend."

"What?" Delta breathed out the word.

"You remember the short blonde he found on his road trip? Apparently she ran off without telling him where she was going. I hope she calls." Gina's voice dropped. "I don't think she knows it, but she means a hell of a lot to him."

Delta's throat tightened. "I don't think that would be in Brian's best interests."

"I know what you're saying, but I think a man like him can decide that for himself. Don't you?"

Delta closed her eyes.

"Oh, got to go, mom. Ursula just brought donuts and I want to get one before the cops eat 'em all. Talk to you later."

The line disconnected, and Delta leaned her head against the door of the phone booth. Why was it so hard to walk away from Brian Chanse? At least he was safe and more or less sound, and thanks to Gina she now knew the cops weren't aware of his connection to her.

She opened her eyes again and pushed another couple of quarters into the phone." *You've reached the desk of Detective Lawrence Morgan. Please leave your name, your number and the time you called, and I'll get back to you as soon as I can.*"

The message was altered already, which was both good news and bad. Morgan had rounded up the Matsuda files, but he'd done it too fast for her suspicious mind. Was this just bait for a trap? She needed to think this through before leaving her message. Hanging up, she noticed a street kid eyeing her from across the way. Perhaps it was her blonde hair in the middle of Chinatown, but something about the girl's fixed stare gave her bad juju. There was always the possibility the girl was eyes for her hunters. Delta was certain they didn't give a damn about her innocence. Or the fact that she'd spared the killer's life. Their pursuit would continue until she was dead, which meant that she'd best make herself harder to find.

A little game of hide-and-seek was in order. She exited the booth and merged with the flow of pedestrians. She ducked into a drug store, beelining for the hair care aisle. With hair her color, any dye ought to radically change her appearance. Her eyes scanned the shelves. It shouldn't have mattered which one she took, but Delta picked through box after box before realizing she was imagining which one Brian would like the most.

She snatched up one with a pouty brunette on it, made the purchase and went into the store bathrooms. She was about to become some neutral brown color called 'Country Dawn'. It was the first time Delta had ever dyed her hair, and she was interrupted by a stream of moms, toddlers, Goths and school girls using the two stalls and filing up at the one open sink Delta hadn't commandeered. Every single one of them looked at her wide-eyed, probably wondering what insane woman dyed her natural blonde hair dark. One frustrating hour and a heap of paper towels later, she was looking at herself sourly in the mirror, her natural blonde hair now a light ginger color. She looked at the model on the package and then back at her reflection. "What the hell is this?"

Her next stop was at a store to buy a couple of changes of clothes, along with a backpack for her stuff. As she left the store, she spotted another street kid eyeing her, this one in a ratty leather jacket, skateboard tucked under his arm. The boy couldn't have been much older than fourteen, but already had a hardened, feral look about him.

She openly returned his look, her expression fierce. "Want something?"

"That really your hair color?"

"Yeah, I'm from Mars. Fuck off."

The boy gave her the finger and sauntered off. She didn't like the looks of the kid, nor the fact that he posed that particular question. She needed off the streets. Now.

She cut across one intersection, then another, down an alley, switching and zigzagging til she slipped inside a butcher shop. Five minutes of hard bargaining in Cantonese with a shriveled Chinese woman got her a room on the second floor. She switched out of her denims into a cami with a handy built-in bra and cargo pants, also with useful pockets. The hiking boots were ditched for sneakers.

She folded what remained of her cash into one of the pockets and shoved the backpack under the bed.

There was a knock on the door.

Shit. Likely the old woman wanted another twenty. She and Akeno had rented from her when they'd needed a second safe place, and she had the annoying habit of hitting her tenants up for cash more or less at random. Still, better safe than dead.

"Mh'hóu gáau ngóh," she called through the door, making it clear she wanted to be left alone even as she pushed open the small window that led to the fire escape.

"It's me."

Brian! Delta's eyes widened, and she rushed to the door, flinging it open. "How the hell did you find me?" He had a bruised cheek and blood on his shirt collar. Her hand halfway to him before she checked it. His eyes followed the retreat of her hand back to her pocket.

"There're a few street kids I hire as extras. Put out the word I was looking for you." He swept her a hard look, then as if he could see right through her body, he eased her around, and she felt his thumb skim the bandage on her shoulder blade.

110

"That Mr. Hadrian fix you up?"

"Yeah. Fifteen stitches, that's all."

His hand dropped from her. "So, why aren't you with him now?"

Mr. Hadrian wouldn't have allowed her to bring trouble to his door. Not that she would've stayed but it hurt that he hadn't offered. She faced him. "I was out getting my hair done."

He gave her do a critical squint. "A box job, huh? You should've got Gina to give you the name of her hairdresser."

She crossed her arms. "Are you finished? Because I've got to go and find a new place now that you've advertised where I'm staying. Did it occur to you there are others looking for me?"

He pushed past her into the room. "My nephew's got a hamster cage bigger than this dump. C'mon, get your bag and let's go someplace with a real bed."

"Brian..."

"You walking or am I packing you down the stairs?"

Why wouldn't he listen? "Brian. You nearly got killed this morning. I told you that might happen and I was right. So, listen to me this time. Stay. Away. From. Me."

"I would, except I shook on it and unlike you, I keep my promises."

Oh God, back to this honor crap. "It's not a promise if you don't intend on keeping it in the first place."

"Then, you're a liar."

"Yeah, okay," she replied, rolling her eyes.

His mouth twisted, thinned. He stepped right up to her, so close she had to arch her neck way back to see him. "You have this real annoying habit, Delta, of saying 'Yeah, okay' to things that you're not actually feeling 'Yeah, okay' about."

111

She bit her lip because she was about to offer up 'Yeah, okay'.

"Which is really, really annoying because in between that you come out with things like how you'd lie and cheat to keep me safe, and that's a really, really nice thing to say."

His voice went low on the last bit and continued on that level as he added, "And so, I get confused. What's the lie, Delta? You and the 'Yeah, okay' thing or you talking so nice I hunt you down all over Chinatown because I'm scared that you've taken a bullet and are in an alley somewhere bleeding out and there's no one to take care of you because you refuse to accept help from the one person who has lied and lied to save your lying ass."

He said all this in a low growl, his body still close. From a distance it looked as if they might kiss. One look at his face, and it was clear that wasn't going to happen. "Well, Delta?"

She couldn't deal with his anger. Not thinking, she touched his hurt cheek. He flinched. "I'm sorry you got hurt."

"Not an answer."

She shifted. God, he was close. His shirt had sweat stains. He really had been all over Chinatown. She had to give him a straight answer. No, she wanted to give a straight answer. It hit her that she'd held out on Brian not to protect him—or at least, not entirely—but to protect herself. She'd lost Akeno. Mr. Hadrian was the only person she had left, and he—well, he wasn't exactly someone whose shoulder you could cry on.

"The truth is"—she could barely hear her own words past the pounding of her heart—"the truth is—I could really use your help."

Nothing about Brian changed. His body stayed close and tight, his mouth still a thin, hard line. "Tell me something I don't know."

She bent her head. "The truth is—I'm sorry you had to go all over Chinatown for me but a part of me is stupid happy that you did because I wanted to see for myself that you were okay, and because—because it means that you care enough to look for me."

And still nothing changed about Brian. His body stayed close, his face hard. "Why should I believe you?"

She felt her eyes bug out, felt them actually go dry. "Because," she said, "because it doesn't hurt like this when I say, 'Yeah, okay.'"

He changed. He wrapped himself gently around her. After a very long time, he whispered into her hair, "You coming with me or am I packing you down the stairs?"

"I'm coming," she whispered into his neck.

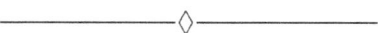

Delta sat at the little table in the hotel suite, watching the digital display on the bedside clock click to eleven. Gina had personally booked the suite, so there was little chance the Yakuza would be able to trace either Brian or her to the place. Her new partner had left close to two hours ago to pick up the files from Morgan, and she was beginning to worry about how long it was taking him when the phone rang.

"I'm back," Brian's voice greeted her when she answered it. As an added security precaution, he was to call before coming up.

"You okay?"

"I'm okay."

"Did you get the files?"

"That I did. See you in a moment."

When she let him in, she couldn't help it. Her eyes shot to

the folder in his hand, and she followed him like a puppy after a treat to where he dropped it on the table.

Brian opened the bar fridge. "Morgan said everything of relevance to the Matsuda case is in here. He's going to need more time to get the files from Miami, but seems pretty confident that he'll have them in a few days."

She itched to open the file but she had to know. "Are you sure—?"

"Yes, I'm sure I wasn't followed."

"Good." She sat at the table and moved to the file, but suddenly Brian's hand was on top of it, holding it firmly closed. "You know, I think you're right. I give way too much to others and get nothing in return."

Delta paused. He sprang open his Cola with his free hand, the hiss of the vented can electric to her nerves. "That's not really fair, is it?'

"Uh...no."

"And I know you don't want to take advantage of me."

"No."

"And I have saved you a lot of time by picking up those files."

"What would you like?"

His reply was instant. "My hands on you until I'm done."

A tingle shot through her entire body and settled between her legs. God, he hadn't even touched her and she was hot for him. This had never happened to her.

She attempted to answer him, but her throat had gone dry. She tried again. "I'd like that."

Brian's mouth upturned and he set aside his can. "Then get your cute ass over here."

When she got within arm's length, he spun her so that cute ass was up against his thighs. One hand crawled under her cami, flattened against her belly, the other hand released the catch on her built-in bra, and then both hands were on her tits.

Oh God, his touch. She ground against him hard and they stumbled back against the wall.

"Whoa, Delta. Easy." Except he wasn't taking it easy, either. He squeezed and rolled her breasts, plucked and palmed her nipples, until she was rubbing her backside, right from her ass to her shoulders against his front.

"Take off the top." And she did, tossing it away like it was on fire.

"You know how we slept together this afternoon, Delta?" Her eyes drifted to the bed. They'd slept, spooned tight together. Slept the entire afternoon away and she hadn't woken until past seven, still tucked close against him.

"I woke three times. My cock hard for you."

Any other man, and she would've felt weirded out. But this was Brian, and his statement of arousal felt the same as if he'd drawn his hard cock along her folds. She moistened. She gave a reflexive grind against him and his head dipped to her bare neck. "Each time I thought about sliding away, going into the bathroom and doing something about it. But then, that might mean you'd wake up and I really, really wanted you to be able to sleep. To feel safe with me." His lips brushed up her neck, and then his tongue traced the curve of her ear. "So I laid there but I tell ya, Delta, it was hard, really hard."

Her heart stopped, and restarted with a thud. "I'm—I'm awake now."

"Yeah, I see that. Feel that." He gave her tits an extra tight squeeze and her pussy muscles squeezed back. He sucked in his breath. "Smell that." Then he said what she'd been waiting for. "Unzip your pants."

She did, had her thumbs hooked over the waistband to

strip them off when he whispered, "Hold it. Like that." With one hand still working her tits, his other hand glided slow as a honey trickle down her middle onto her lower belly and his fingers played the skin inside her right hip bone. She gave a gasp-giggle and wiggled her ass against him.

"Lying there all hard this afternoon, I wondered if you'd like that. That question's answered. Now I wonder about the other side." And they discovered the answer was once again affirmative.

"I'm ready for you to lose the pants, Delta."

And they went the way of the cami. Panties, too. She was hot and wet for what was going to happen next, not that she knew what it was going to be. It didn't matter, it was going to be with Brian.

His cock bumped against her ass cheek and she rubbed against it, and he replied in kind, and for a while, his bulge encased in the roughness of his jeans sweetly chafed her. One hand cupped a breast and the other hovered low on her belly. She moaned, aching for his fingers to inch farther down.

"Brian?"

"Yeah?"

How to say this? How to say she was totally sexually pumped for him? How to say she wanted him to stroke her pussy and rub her clit, or to give her his cock, to give her something hard and fast? Anything, so long as it was him, so long as he didn't stop. "I'm ready."

And his hand was there, cupping her. "Christ, Delta. You're soaked." His finger stroked through her wetness. Arm banded around her belly, he hauled her up against him until she was on tiptoe. "Hold on, Delta, hold on."

He started on her swollen clit, a slow tickle that had her bearing down on him, hunting for the orgasm. But he kept with the feather touches. She climbed him, wrapping her legs around him, opening herself to him. He adjusted, braced himself, still rolling her clit. Two fingers stroked through her swollen folds. She squirmed, wanting. God, she'd never wanted so much. Never even thought she could.

"Please. Oh, God. Please." She was whimpering and didn't care.

Still, he stroked and rolled. Her abdomen clenched and warmed. She ground against his fingers. "That's it, Delta." His grip around her midsection tightened, his legs braced again, preparing, then he slipped his fingers inside her.

She yelped, her body going flat and tight against him. For a second, she couldn't move and then his fingers ever so gently flicked inside her. She gave a mighty buck. And then she lost it. She fucked his hand hard, thrusting and arching and twisting, her ass pounding against the hardness in his pants. He held on, she didn't know how and she was beyond caring. All she cared about was getting off with him.

She looked down. At his arm tight under her tits, past that to his hand on her, in her, and then she felt his lips on her ugly ginger hair. And he kissed her, a soft gentle kiss that went against everything they were doing. Or maybe, just maybe, it didn't.

And that's when she came again. Came so hard, her ass lifted off him and her feet jumped up to his knees and she stretched out nearly perpendicular from him.

Then she collapsed against him and she heard him give a soft 'woof'.

"You done?" he whispered.

"Yeah," she panted.

"Then me too."

She twisted in his arms, stared up at him. "But don't

you...want to...."

"Yeah," he said, squeezing her up against him. "I do. But no condom. And I'm not losing my first load with you unless I'm deep inside."

She felt incredible relief. It would've hurt so bad, if he didn't want her. "That a code thing with you? Like a hand-shake?"

"Handshakes apply to everyone. This applies only to you."

Only to you. "How do you do that?"

His hand ran over the curve of her ass. "Do what?"

"Say things like 'we need a new place' and 'only to you' and other stuff, too. Like we're a couple, even though we can't be after just three days together but you say it in a way that has me believing it."

He gave a slow grin and his finger stroked her cheek. "Delta, get your clothes on. *We* got work to do."

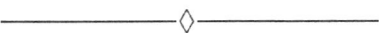

Not ten minutes later, they were at the table, drinking soda, sifting through the file, their minds a million miles away from where they had just been. Or at least, Brian's seemed to be. Delta was still wrapping her head around getting the first orgasm of her life. In this room. Against that wall. With that man. Now, if Gina were to ask again how it was with 'Bri', she'd have a story. It felt unbelievably good to know what sex was supposed to be like.

"Hey, Delta. You're smiling. Police writing jokes down?"

Oh, God. "I'm not smiling. It's my focused look."

"Uh-huh."

He didn't believe her and she refused to respond. She

concentrated again on the spread before her. There were photos of the crime scene, ballistics and autopsy reports, a plan of the room and adjoining hall where the murder had taken place and translated statements taken from two 'security guards'. Lastly there was a brief statement from Mr. Matsuda himself.

"Looks like whoever killed him was a pretty good shot," Brian observed. "The bullet was fired from a small caliber pistol from about twenty feet, and hit the kid square in the forehead. That's not easy to do, especially if you don't have time to aim."

"And in the dark. Too good of a shot for Akeno," Delta murmured. She ran a finger down one page. "The guards say they spotted two intruders escaping the grounds, dressed in black bodysuits. One male, the other female, both small in stature."

"That explains why the Yakuza would have thought you were involved," said Brian. "But how did they figure out it was your friend who pulled the job?"

Delta had asked herself that a thousand times. She flipped through papers. "Here's something. Seems the codes he used to access the house were assigned to a maid named Maria Bustoses, but according to security she didn't show up for work the next morning. The police found her remains yesterday in Griffith Park, no autopsy report here but yeah, it wouldn't have been pretty."

Brian tossed down his pages and sat back. "So what do you think?"

"Okay, let's see if we can put it all together. Akeno goes into the house armed with all the codes, combinations, layout, everything he could possibly need. That means his partner must have either been an insider at the house, like she claimed, or been cooperating with someone who was. Supposedly her name was Susan. I can't see Akeno going in with his partner unless she was a trained infiltrator. Let's assume she was."

"How so?"

"If he went in with her, it meant she was experienced. If he didn't then she must have gotten past the guards on her own. Either way, she knew how to evade security."

"But if she had all that information, couldn't she figure out a way in without having to be a professional?"

"Maybe, but you have to remember that they also got out. That meant moving fast and silent, getting over the property's fence quickly and dodging the police to make a getaway. Even with Akeno leading her, that would have been a trick for a regular citizen."

Brian drained his can, rolled it between his hands, the aluminum crinkling away. "Okay, we know she was a good shot, and we can safely assume that she was a skilled burglar. The next question is, how did she get all the information about the house? I mean, I can see her getting the layout and door code, but the combination to Matsuda's safe?"

"You're right. Maria Bustoses wouldn't have known that, so it's safe to conclude she wasn't involved. Someone used her codes to frame her, probably to divert suspicion from themselves."

"So Akeno's partner couldn't have been Maria's co-worker. More likely one of Mr. Matsuda's staff." Brian stood, tossing his empty into the garbage, then walked the room, picking up wrappers and hanging up jackets.

To Delta, his present activity showed his ignorance of Japanese culture. "The Yakuza aren't exactly equal oppor-tunity employers. I doubt Matsuda would have any women working for him. More likely his wife, or maybe a mistress."

Brian paused, empty sandwich wrapper in hand. "Didn't it say in the file that his wife was next to him in bed when all this went down? Obviously she didn't pull the trigger, whatever else her involvement. Which brings us to the victim. Was the kid's death an accident, or was this all some elaborate plan to kill him? I mean, what was the boy doing at the office door in the middle of the night, anyway?"

Delta gnawed her lip. "Yeah, that's the thing. To the Yakuza it might seem like the kid heard the thieves and walked in on them, but if they were professionals they would've been silent. He would never have heard them, especially through a closed door. Someone must have arranged for the kid to be there. You know, Brian, you don't have to pick up after me."

"Been doing it since the day we met."

She was about to call him on that when he carried on. "So, we're getting a bit of a clearer picture, but we still don't have a clue why everything happened the way it did."

Which brought them to her next point, one that had darted around her mind since they started going through the reports. She cleared her throat. "I don't think we have enough information to figure it out at the moment. Right now, we should just concentrate on finding a short female burglar, good with guns and with connections to either Matsuda's staff or family. And to Akeno, of course."

"How are you going to do that? Yellow pages?"

"Ha-ha. The report from Miami might give us some leads when we get it, but I know a place we can start."

She tried to sound casual but it didn't work. Brian turfed the garbage bag and went to alert-mode. "Where's that?" The man really was an adrenaline junkie.

"One of Akeno's old haunts. I've never been there

myself, but I know he used to be a regular. He made a lot of his acquaintances there. Could be where he met Susan."

"So what's the place? A nightclub?"

Given their activities of the previous hour, talking about this should be way easier. But she was pretty sure that right now she'd rather run naked down the street.

Brian flexed his fingers. "Delta...."

"Okay, okay. It's a swinger's club called *The Sweet Pepper*."

Brian suddenly went super-casual himself. "Uh...that one out near Malibu?"

Something in the way he said it... "You...know it?"

"Yeah, well, uh..." He blew out his breath. "I've never been to *that* club in particular, but Marcia introduced me to the lifestyle. It was...uh, stimulating, met some great people but..."

Delta went still. "But what?"

"Didn't save our relationship." His voice was flat, sad.

"Oh."

"Yeah. 'Oh.' Akeno was a gold member, huh?"

"I...guess," Delta started fussing with the pages, tucking them back into the folder. "Akeno was kind of short, but he was good-looking, and very athletic. He used to go there to meet...couples. So, you know which street it's on?"

He was watching her carefully. "No, but it shouldn't be too hard to find their phone number. They have a website."

Delta drummed her fingers on the folder, "You wanna come?"

"Our first date is at a swinger's club?"

"This isn't a date. It's business."

"Then, it's a pleasure doing business with you, Delta."

She wasn't entirely sure whether to thank him or

apologize. "Anyway," she said, "it would probably be a bit more discreet if we looked like a couple. We might even find this Susan there."

He was already scrolling on his smartphone. "Let's see…here they are. You want to call them, or should I?"

"I'll do it."

Brian handed her the phone, and she entered the number while he sat on the edge of the bed.

"*The Sweet Pepper*, Julie speaking," a cheery voice answered, the sound of dance music and laughter in the background.

"Hi there. My partner and I heard about your place from a friend, and wanted to come and check it out. Tonight. If that's possible."

"Wonderful. And is your partner male or female?"

"Uh, male."

"Great. We like to keep a good mix. Have you been in the lifestyle long?"

"No, actually. We're kind of new to the whole thing." Brian grinned, laid back on the bed, crossed his hands behind his head.

"Well, that's no problem at all, everybody's welcome. We're open tonight till three if you'd like to come by for a tour."

"Okay. Can I get your address?"

Delta scribbled it down, and was about to disconnect when another question popped into her head. "Oh, by the way, is there a dress code?"

"Normally we're pretty casual but tonight we're having a toga party."

"Togas?" She repeated in a squeak. Brian burst out laughing and Delta winged a bottle cap at him. He caught it. Jerk.

"But we don't have any togas." She tried Brian with an empty water bottle. He caught it with his other hand. Jerk.

"Not a problem. We have some here."

"Okay," Delta muttered. "Sounds...good."

She got off the phone and Brian got off the bed. He snagged the key card and pulled open the hotel door, waiting for her to grab her card.

"You know," she said, walking up to him, "you should seek help for your adrenaline addiction."

"If I wasn't always having to save your ass, there wouldn't be a problem," he said, cuffing her body part in question as she went by him out the door.

She'd told him. She'd told him a hundred thousand million times that her problems were not his, hadn't she just this afternoon told him that very same thing, that he should leave her al—

He was grinning, his back turned to her while he checked to make sure the door was locked, but she could see enough of his face to know it was there.

He was teasing her. No one had ever teased her. Not even Akeno. And she freaking loved it. She reached down and goosed him. Then she ran like hell, fully expecting him, fully wanting him, to catch her.

CHAPTER NINE

THE CLUB TURNED out to be a large house, with only a small tasteful sign on the front gate designating it as *The Sweet Pepper*. If Delta hadn't known what kind of establishment it was, she never would have guessed. The lights in the place were on, and the sounds of what seemed like a quiet party drifted through the cool night air.

"Looks like a bed & breakfast," said Delta as she climbed out of the car. "I was expecting something more...X-rated."

Brian came around the car to join her. "Don't worry. I'm sure there'll be some of that inside. You're not nervous, are you?"

That morning was the first time she'd seen a naked female body other than hers. Two hours ago, she'd discovered what an orgasm felt like. She had no idea how to give head and she'd never had sex that wasn't kinda painful. "Yes. I am." She could hear the hiss of fear in her voice. Sure as shit, all the memories would rise up, like vomit in the throat. It'd feel the same way, too.

Then, there it was. Brian's arm curled around her waist, cinching her tight to his side. "Hey, Foxy."

She snorted out a half-laugh. "Brian, that's dumb."

"Don't care, made you laugh."

That was sweet. He said, "Listen, I've seen you naked and trust me, you're hot. But this is business, not pleasure, right? We're here to chat and look around, and see what we can learn. Okay?"

"Yeah, okay."

Brian gave a low growl, and she knew why. "I mean it."

But then, as soon as she rang the doorbell, she felt nauseous and turned to Brian. "One ground rule. We stay together, right?"

He shrugged. "Of course."

Her deep blue eyes narrowed on him. "Together and *alone*."

His mouth thinned. "'Yeah, okay' wasn't 'yeah, okay', was it?"

"Not really."

He gave her a look of pure exasperation. "Then, think about this. We haven't had sex yet. Not full-blown, me-in-you sex. Until we do, why would I let someone else get in on it? I've got first dibs." He squeezed her right ass cheek.

And so it was that when the hostess of *The Sweet Pepper* answered the door, it was to Delta squeaking not entirely with displeasure, and Brian slipping his hand back to where it belonged. The polite smile on the woman, dressed in a short silk toga and high-heeled slip-ons, deepened into a genuine one.

"Helloooo. Can I help you?"

Delta did her best to look like a sex sophisticate. "Hi. Yeah. I phoned earlier this evening and talked to Julie…"

"Oh yes! I'm Julie. Please come on in."

Their hostess, who Delta judged to be in her forties, led

them into a foyer, offering seats on a large leather couch. She sat on a matching armchair, her robe riding up, up, up. Delta wondered if the backs of her thighs were sticking to the leather. "Just wanted to go over a few quick ground rules," Julie said. "To begin with our club is purely a social one. Just couples and select singles interested in the lifestyle. Nothing too naughty ever happens here. If people want to play they meet off-premises. Okay?"

Relief flooded through Delta. "Got it."

"Once inside you're free to talk and dance, just like you would at a regular party. There are complimentary beverages, and you're allowed to bring your own alcohol, but we don't allow any drugs. As this is your first visit there's only the door coverage, which is fifty dollars for the two of you. If you wish to come again you have to provide us with a copy of your I.D. and buy a membership, but we can discuss that later if you're interested. The rules inside are simple. No means no. And if you have any STDs be upfront about it. That's about it. Any questions?"

Delta glanced at Brian. He was staring across the foyer at a large framed picture of a woman's torso arched in passion, and hands—dark, white, female, male, large, small, ringed, plain—all over her. What the—? Wasn't he the one who'd gone on about how this was all business? She drove her shoulder into his.

Brian turned to Julie. "Uh, yes. One, actually. I was wondering if you might know our friend. His name's Akeno."

When would she learn that the man was more than he let on? Julie's eyes lit up. "You're friends of Akeno? Oh, oh," she said to Delta in rising excitement, "you're not Delta, are you?"

"Um… yes, actually."

"You should have said so earlier! Akeno told me so much

about you! It's great to finally meet you."

Delta made a point of not looking at Brian, even though she could feel his eyes on her. "What…what exactly did Akeno say about me?"

"Oh, not that much I suppose. Only that you're his step-sister, but he always used to talk about what you two got up to as kids. They were great stories. We used to kill ourselves laughing."

"Really?" Brian piped up. "What stories are these?"

Julie gave a giggle, that finished on a 'mmmm…', the kind of little sexy noise that seemed to come natural to all women, except Delta. "She hasn't told you? From what Akeno said the two of them were a real pair of rebels back when they were teens."

"When they were teens," Brian echoed. "Good thing she's tamer now." His arm circled her waist, his hand coming around to rest on her upper thigh. "At least, out of bed."

Delta felt her face go hot. On-fire hot. She whipped to Brian. The teasing look on his face suddenly wiped clear, replaced by something way more intense, the loose hold on her thigh tightened. *Play along*, his expression said. And then another message. *Play with me*.

A throat was cleared. "Delta, everyone at the club has been wondering what Akeno's been up to. Where's he disappeared, hmmm?"

Delta tore her eyes from Brian. Business. She swallowed. She and Brian had decided not to divulge Akeno's death, hoping that information might drop more easily. People might clam up if it came out that a member was victim of a gang-related killing. "He's gone to Miami."

"Oh. You know when he's coming back?"

"It's kind of permanent. He went there with his girlfriend,

Susan. You ever met her?"

"Yes, she was a member." Julie's voice had gone strange, forced. Delta wanted to look at Brian, to see if he'd noticed the same thing. Fingers tapped against her thigh, same as when he was reading the files and thinking. He *had* noticed. "I was wondering what happened to her," Julie said. "So they're together now, hmm?"

Brian cut in. "Tight as jeans. I guess they met here, huh?"

Julie's voice became vague. "Yes. She's been a member here for a few years, but didn't stop by all that often." She waved her fingers, as if Susan was just another name. Except—.

Delta went with her gut. "I never met her but from what Akeno had—has—said, I'm not sure I like her."

Julie transformed into a picture of vehemence and anger. Her face went hard and she leaned forward, her perfect nails digging into her knees. "The woman's a real piece of work. A bitch to end all bitches."

Julie closed her eyes, sucked in her breath and when she opened them again, the gracious hostess mask was back in place. "We should get you inside. The party's only going for another couple of hours and you'll need time to mingle. Oh! And seeing as you're Akeno's little sister…" She clipped across to an armoire, and produced two togas similar to her own. "On the house!" She handed them the silky strips of cloth. "The bathrooms are just through those doors. Have fun!"

And then she was gone, leaving Brian and Delta to stare at each other.

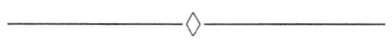

Delta cringed at herself in the bathroom mirror. Although

the robe had enough material across the back to cover up her stitches, the neckline plunged to her belly button. She leaned forward experimentally and gasped as the robe completely failed to contain her breasts. She wrapped and rewrapped, tied and retied, but there was nothing for it. The garment was designed for exposure.

To hell with it. She was here to talk to people, not obsess about her appearance. Still, it would've been nice to have proper shoes, but bare feet it was. She followed the music down a short hallway into a large room filled with people.

The place consisted mostly of a dance floor featuring a pole, with a few couples dancing, if rubbing against each other could be called dancing. A dozen more were either perched on stools by the bar or reclining on the couches that lined the room. And judging from how indiscreetly the robes were donned and the intimate angling of the bodies, the event was in full…swing.

A body came close behind her, and for the third time since arriving, a familiar hand slid around her waist, kept on sliding through the slit in her toga. "These things feel a lot better on you than me."

She twisted around to take a look. His hand stayed caught in her toga and out popped her right breast.

"Brian!" She jerked the cloth and her breast back into place, and she darted a worried look around. A couple at the bar smiled and waved. Brian waved back with his free hand. Delta tugged on the other hand. "This is supposed to be business."

"Right. Business in a toga. Next time I've got a meeting, I'll ask Ursula if she's picked up my toga from the dry-cleaners."

Delta pulled back to give him the once-over. He was

wearing a dark purple toga. And flip-flops. She sucked in a cheek not to laugh. She sucked in both.

"You look fine," she said through puckered lips.

"I look gay, which I dunno, might be the effect they're going for tonight." His gaze shifted and his head came up. "Waving couple inbound." Brian extracted his hand, but upward first so his fingertips grazed her nipple which immediately hardened. God.

His hand slipped to hers, twined his fingers with her own, and when they turned to face the couple, it was as if they were on an old-fashioned date. The pair looked to be in their late forties, Delta guessed, both fit and tanned, and when they smiled it was with polished white teeth.

"Hi there," the man said. "New to *The Pepper*?"

"First time," Brian replied. "I'm Brian, and this is my partner, Delta."

"Delta?" said the woman, "You're not Akeno's sister, are you?"

If her old partner wasn't dead, Delta decided she'd be ready to kill him about now. "Um, yeah."

The woman's face lit up, just like Julie's. Delta wondered what it would do if she mentioned Susan. "Oh, he told us so much about you. My name's Mandy, and this is my husband, David. Why don't you come over and have a drink with us?"

A minute later the two women were sitting on a pair of love seats across from each other, waiting for their men to bring the drinks.

"First time?" Mandy said sympathetically.

Delta winced. "That obvious, huh?"

"It takes a little getting used to, darling, so no need to feel shy." The woman reached forward and patted her knee, her hand staying. Where the hell was Brian?

Delta crossed her legs, neatly slipping out from under Mandy's hand but now slitting open the toga skirt. Mandy's gaze lingered appreciatively.

Delta scrambled to think of a topic of conversation. "So, I guess you know Akeno pretty well?"

"Oh yes. We played together several times." Mandy stroked her inner thigh. "It's awesome being with a bi-male, especially since my husband is one, too."

Where the hell was Brian? "Oh. Yes." Delta fiddled with the hem of her robe. She really need to hurry this interview along. "Did you ever meet his girlfriend, Susan? I heard he met her here."

Sure enough, Mandy's face got the same buttoned-down expression as Julie's. "We played. Once. She had boundary issues."

Delta wondered if it was out-of-bounds to ask what those boundary issues were. God, she wished Brian was here. He'd know how to work his good ol' boy charm. "I've never met her actually," Delta confessed, "but Julie—indicated that Susan was, er, difficult."

"Not surprised. Julie and Akeno were play partners for a time, maybe even more. She doesn't let single men join the club but she made an exception for Akeno. Some nights we'd arrive to see him coming down from her place upstairs. She might be jealous. More likely, she's right about Susan. The woman's incredibly exotic and beautiful but there's some-thing...off with her."

"Oh?"

Mandy gave her a straight look. "I don't know how much you and Brian know about alternative lifestyles. But Susan wasn't just in the lifestyle, she was a Domme. And Akeno was known to be a submissive. The thing is, Susan liked to Domme

132

24/7. And Akeno, the word is, could take a lot of punishment."

Delta felt as if she'd been stabbed. Yes, anyone who knew anything about how Akeno was raised would know he could take a lot of punishment. Delta hated this unknown Susan, and she was damn happy the woman was likely dead. She gave Mandy a straight look back. "I think I need to have a word with this Susan. You know how I can reach her? Where she works?"

Mandy shook her head. "No idea. Our meet-up was arranged through Akeno. I suppose Julie has all the particulars but she keeps the identities of our membership very secure. You can imagine the kind of scandals there could be if people knew who belonged to the club. Oh, here come the men."

For the next hour, they talked about the club and its membership. It turned out the clientele at the *The Sweet Pepper* was fairly exclusive, consisting primarily of high-paid professionals. Mandy flirted with Delta and Brian, David with Brian. If she wasn't so occupied with the news about Akeno and Susan, Delta might've felt amused at Brian's clever duckings of David's very overt come-ons. They eventually managed to extricate themselves, Brian offering his business's number and typing Mandy's into his smartphone.

Back in the car and back in street clothes, Brian turned to Delta. "Was that as good for you as it was for me?" He aimed for casual to cover up the fact he was as horny as hell. Delta looked so damn sexy in that toga, forever tugging at it, her fingers slipping in where he wanted his to go.

Delta rolled her eyes. "I swear if Mandy touched my knee one more time I would have screamed."

Brian rubbed her knee and assumed Mandy's husky tone. "You mean like that?"

"Argh!" Delta pushed him away. "Then again, I saw the way David was sizing *you* up."

Brian's cock softened. "I guess we learned one thing tonight. We're both straight."

Delta started to laugh, then stopped. "Turns out Akeno wasn't. He was also Susan's punching bag." She paused. He waited, willing to give her to the count of five before he strangled the information out of her. He got to three before she spilled. "Mandy was like Julie, didn't like Susan very much. The way Mandy put it, Susan was a Domme with boundary issues."

Brian drummed his fingers on the wheel. "So you're thinking that maybe Susan and Akeno took the relationship outside the bedroom and into Matsuda's house?"

"Might explain why he acted so strange. Akeno had a pretty messed-up start. Sexually abused, physically abused. Wouldn't take much for him to be persuaded that the only way to get love was by being punished."

Brian watched Delta battle with her emotions. He was about to reach for her when she sucked in her breath and carried on. "Anyway, that's not all. I also learned that our hostess has files on the members. It's probably not a huge amount of information, but maybe enough for us to get an idea of who Susan is and where to start looking for her."

"Yeah, but how are you going to get access to...?" Brian's question trailed off as he saw the gleam in Delta's eyes.

"I checked out the security while we were inside. Should be easy."

It took him a click or two to catch up to her thinking.

"You want to go in tonight?"

"Why not? Mr. Hadrian always says, 'Strike while the iron's hot.'"

Christ. She was right but—Christ. "So, no chance of going back to the hotel and having sex instead?"

She did it again. She blushed. He couldn't remember the last time he'd seen a female blush. Not in this city, that's for sure. She did it all the time with him, and then she'd gone all pink sitting beside him on the couch, it was all he could do not to kiss her. It was so sweet and sexy. His cock started up again, even as she murmured, "We're here for business. Got to finish that first."

Just to see where the pink in her cheeks would go, he said, "How about here in the car?"

The pink stayed and then she squirmed. He could hear her butt wiggling against the leather seat. "We can't," she whispered, flustered and annoyed.

He was about to tell her that he already figured that, when she added, "No condom, remember?"

That was it. He punched off the interior lights, unsnapped his belt, then hers, dropped back his seat and hauled her across. "Gotta get my hands on you" was all he could come up with.

His mouth found hers, like iron to a magnet, and his tongue spread apart her lips. He wasn't in the mood for slow, and neither was she. Their tongues flicked and sucked at each other, and when she made a little mew, he grabbed her ass and pulled her tight against him. Her hip bone ground against his, making it damn uncomfortable. But to move meant giving up on his handful of ass and the wet softness of her mouth. So he held on.

He spoke, his lips moving on hers. "You know, Delta. This has been no ordinary day in the life of Brian Chanse. No

135

sooner do I wake up with a beautiful blonde cat burglar than she walks out on me, only to return being chased by a hitman. The guy blows up my business and cracks me over the head, while she totals one of my vans and runs off."

He stopped talking, Still uncomfortable but for a whole different reason. He started up his chatter, because he needed to say this and because he needed the distraction. "Next, I track her down which, may I add, is no easy feat considering she hasn't told me where she's gone, or that she's changed her hair color. I spend the evening getting police documents, then it's off to a swinger's club. It looks like I'm going to round off the night by helping her with some B&E to steal some information on some mysterious dominatrix."

Delta looked at him blankly.

"Do you have the faintest inkling the point I'm trying to make?"

She shook her head.

"I got into the stunt business because I love doing wild, crazy, dangerous things. For the first time in years, I really feel like I'm living again. So what I'm saying is that I find it totally hot that I'm with a woman who lives a wild life and yet blushes at the word 'sex'."

"Brian—" She was drawing breath, he knew, to give him another damn lecture about him getting himself killed. As if she were one to talk. But he didn't want to go into it. Not with her still on his lap, not with her about to commit a serious crime that could remove any chance of her ass being on his lap again, much less being in bed with him.

He drew her face to his, cut her off with a kiss and with her mouth wet on his, he said, "What's the plan?"

———————◊———————

It was almost four in the morning before the last guests departed, and Brian had allowed Delta to sleep while he kept lookout. The late hour, coupled with his frantic day and lack of sleep the night before, was making him extremely drowsy, and it took all of his willpower not to slip unconscious. When the last car disappeared and the lights of the house went out, he nudged Delta awake. "Time to steal us some clues."

As usual she was instantly alert, and adjusting her seat upright, she looked over at the house. "How long since the last person left?"

"About ten minutes ago. The last light in the place just turned off."

"Means Julie's beat. I'll give her another few minutes to get to sleep and then I'll go in."

"Don't you need lock picks or a mask or something?"

"Not for something this easy. Akeno and I used to break into places like this when we were kids." Delta pointed up to the second story of the house. "See? She's even left a couple of windows open."

Brian looked. Sure they were open, but getting to them would be another matter. There was nothing but open space between them and the ground, and the roof above had a considerable overhang. "How you going to reach them?"

"You'll just have to wait and see." She smiled slyly.

"Won't you need gloves? I mean, not to leave fingerprints?"

"She'll never know I was there. Anyway, gloves are for amateurs. They're hard to work with."

Must be the fact he was sleep-deprived, but he couldn't follow. "So you're saying there's a way to touch things barehanded without leaving fingerprints?"

"Uh-huh."

"How?"

"A little bowl of sulfuric acid, slightly diluted."

"I don't get it."

"From the time I was fifteen till I was nineteen, back when Mr. Hadrian was training me, I used to have weekly acid treatments on my fingerprints. I'd burn them off, then let them heal, then burn them off again, over and over."

Brian grimaced. "Didn't that hurt like hell?"

"Of course it did, but after about two hundred treatments my prints were permanently erased." She wiggled her fingers at him, "No pain, no gain."

He shook his head. "Didn't any of your teachers call social services when your fingers were bandaged all the time?"

"Mr. Hadrian was my teacher. I didn't go to school after I left home."

"What about friends?"

"Akeno was my friend. With the long hours of training I didn't have time for anyone else. I mean, we studied lock-smithing, safecracking, climbing, contortionism—the whole nine yards. He taught us stealth and surveillance, demolitions and escape artistry. We had to learn to overcome our fear of heights and enclosed spaces and guard dogs, and, of course, we had to master working in the dark. By the time we were done, we could operate in pitch blackness."

"Sounds pretty brutal."

"No. It was hard, but it was never brutal. Mr. Hadrian's a good teacher. He taught me a trade. He fed and clothed me for all those years. And he sure as hell was more of a parent to Akeno and me than our real folks ever were."

Brian leaned back, imagining a young Delta making her way through the years of her strange education. Then again, it wasn't so much different than his own, or that of any professional for that matter.

Delta smiled. "You're tired. Get a little shut eye and I'll be right back." Then a small miracle happened. She kissed him. A quick touch on the lips, but it was from her, so it felt pretty damn good.

She slipped out of the car, closing the door quietly, and padded off back to *The Sweet Pepper*. Despite being tired as a dog, there was no way he was going to miss her getting inside. He watched her reach the corner of the house where she pressed her hands and legs against it and—Holy Fuck!—began scaling the brick wall like a bug.

Faster than he thought possible, she'd reached the roof, and in one quick moment, pushed off from the wall and grasped the overhang, dangling by her arms for a second before hauling herself up. In the moonlight, he watched as she crouched, then slipped to where the windows were located. Clutching the edge of the roof, she lowered her head to take a cautious look inside, then let her legs slide down so that again she was hanging in open space.

Gently swinging back and forth she caught the windowsill with the tips of her sneakers, then stretched herself across the underside of the eave till she could reach down and take hold of the window frame. Then she simply swung herself though the window in one graceful movement and was gone.

She was a real-life Spider-Woman.

In less than a minute she was inside. She would make an incredible stunt person.

If she didn't get caught.

Or killed.

He locked his eyes on the window and because there wasn't a goddamn thing he could do to help, he counted.

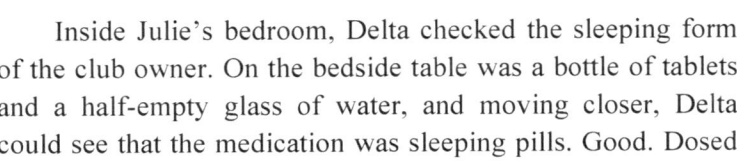

Inside Julie's bedroom, Delta checked the sleeping form of the club owner. On the bedside table was a bottle of tablets and a half-empty glass of water, and moving closer, Delta could see that the medication was sleeping pills. Good. Dosed up like that, it wasn't likely her hostess would be waking anytime soon.

Delta placed her ear to the bedroom door, then carefully opened it a crack. The upstairs hallway was empty and silent, illuminated only by a small nightlight, and stepping forward, she closed the bedroom door behind her. Sinking to one knee she carefully examined the carpet. Apparently Julie hadn't vacuumed in a few days, but Delta saw no trace of animal hair. No dogs. Excellent.

There were three other doorways along the hall, and Delta began a systematic inspection of what was behind them. The first led to a bathroom. The second to a small kitchen. The third to Julie's home office, and in a heartbeat, Delta was inside, the door closing noiselessly behind her. Within the room was a tidy desk, a computer perched on top, and beside that was a filing cabinet. A compact bookcase contained rows of sex manuals and self-improvement titles, and on the walls, hung a couple of erotic abstracts.

Delta tried the filing cabinet. Locked. She took a couple of paperclips off Julie's desk and straightened them, and not half a minute later, had the cabinet open. She examined each and every file. Nothing but tax and business records. Shit.

Muting the computer speakers, Delta switched on the PC, trying the desk drawers as it booted up. The first contained stationery, while the second was locked. Out with the paperclips, and before the computer had warmed up, she had the drawer open.

Within were a pair of leather-bound photo albums. She sat cross-legged on the floor and began to flip though them. They seemed to be shots from various special events at the club. Halloween masquerades, members' birthdays, Pride Day celebrations, Christmas parties. She turned a page and her breath stopped. Akeno, his tanned face smiling at the camera. He had his arms around the shoulders of two women: Mandy and the other being a sly-looking one with luxurious dark hair and cocoa-colored skin, classic Eurasian features and dark pools for eyes.

Delta let out a long breath. This had to be Susan.

Delta didn't like her. That the woman was sexy she couldn't deny, but her perfect face wore an expression of feline arrogance. The look of someone used to getting her own way and damn the cost to others. She eased out the picture, replacing the empty spot with a photograph from the back of the album. Julie would never notice without a careful inspection.

Tucking the photo into her waistband, she returned the albums, then fished out a thumb-drive from her pocket. Turning to the computer, she found the usual publisher programs, some adult clip-art and—bingo—a scan of each club member's driver's license.

Plugging in the thumb drive, Delta copied the entire file to it. She'd sort through it when she got back to the hotel room and find Susan's I.D., which ought to give her an address and birth date to track down the bitch.

Delta powered down the PC and returned the volume control to its normal level, then relocked both the drawer and filing cabinet. Nobody would ever know she'd been there.

She retraced her steps to the bedroom. Lowering herself

out the window, she hung down from it, then dropped the ten feet to the ground. She landed in a crouch, then returned to the car.

"Thank God. You're safe," Brian said, as she took the passenger seat. "I lost count at twelve hundred and something."

She was supposed to know what that meant? But she couldn't mistake the relief in his voice and it did weird things to her system. It was also kind of annoying, the feeling she decided to go with for now. "Well, yeah. I am a professional."

His green eyes narrowed dangerously. She thought fast. Flashing him a smile, she pulled out the picture from her waistband. "Brian, meet Susan."

CHAPTER TEN

BRIAN WOKE FROM a mixed-up dream of Delta in a toga scaling a brick wall into the hotel room where he waited for her, reclining in a cot while watching porn. Turned out the hotel room was cool and dark, the curtains drawn, the air conditioner purring, and thanks to the dream, he had a hard-on.

Rising to his elbow, he looked at the other bed. Empty. "Delta?" he called, but there was no reply. His erection died. He checked his phone. 11:23. Nearly half the day shot and Delta who knew where. He had to get the woman a GPS tag.

Rolling out of bed, he opened the curtains and squinted as the sun flooded the room. The brightness tore away the last shred of sleepiness, and he had his jeans on and was looking for a shirt when he heard the snick of the door, and there was Delta pushing it open with her butt, her arms filled with paper bags. "Ah, good. You're up."

All bright-eyed and bushy-tailed, she wore the same cami and pants she'd shimmied out of last time he'd had his hands on her. What would it take to get her out of them again?

"Yeah. How long have you been up?" he asked, taking the bags from her which required brushing his arm across her breasts. Her nipples were perked. She didn't seem to notice, and she slid past him to the bed, saying as she went, "For a while. There's a deli just down the block so I got us some lunch."

So it wasn't sex but at least she was offering up another necessity of life. He unloaded one bag. Two huge sandwiches, sushi and…a bottle of wine?

"I thought we'd have a little bit of a celebration."

Okay, maybe it wouldn't be so hard to get her out of the clothes. "Oh? Why?"

She grinned. "There's a computer store next door to the deli. It was closed so I went in and checked out the records from *The Sweet Pepper*." She paused, fiddled with the plastic lid on the sushi. "Would have been back sooner but it took forever to get the alarm activated again. Those wireless systems are such junk."

"Delta…"

She looked up, her eyes full of fun. "Her name is Susan Chang, and she lives down by Venice Beach, probably in one of the studios there. Now we can get Morgan to pull her record and find out more about her." She popped a piece of sushi into her mouth. "I'd like to stop by her place tonight and check it out."

"So you're saying we need to figure out how that's going to work." He had his sandwich unwrapped but he was thirsty as hell and the wine wasn't going to cut it. He reached inside the second bag, feeling through stuff. "You buy any soda or—?" His hand closed on a suspiciously familiar box. He blinked, then looked inside to confirm. Yep, condoms.

Brian turned to Delta. She was blushing, a hot delicious pink that even trickled down her neck. "If you want to…I'd like to," she said softly.

If he wanted to—! He snatched out the box, but then he read the packaging. "Um…I would like to. I'd like to very much. But I can't use these."

"Why not?"

"They're too small."

Delta stared. "How could they be too small? Those things blow up like balloons."

How to explain this without sounding like a macho bull on steroids? "Yeah, but their openings are meant to stay tight, so I find them sort of…restrictive."

"Oh." She crossed her legs, then gave a crooked smile, and uncrossed them. "Wow."

"Fortunately, I have a solution. In the drawer by the bed."

Delta opened it, and he watched her take in what was next to the bible. "Large," he explained.

"But I thought you didn't have a condom. Last night you said—"

"That I didn't have one. Yeah. But the newsstand in the lobby is surprisingly well-stocked."

Delta took out the box, slit it open and tore off a condom from the roll, and set it on the bedside table. She tore off a second and lined it up behind the first like ammo for loading. She gave a shy smile. "Just in case."

In a beat, she was flat on the bed and he was on top, his mouth all over that sexy blush of hers—her pink cheeks, the cords in her neck, her earlobes. His hands raked her crazy-colored hair, squeezed her ass, tugged up her cami so their bellies were warm and naked together. Her little moans and pants made him hot and hard, but then she began to withdraw. Her kisses became short and dry, her body stiffened. He pulled back to examine her. The blush was gone, and she was pale.

She reached out, and her hand was shaking. "Brian...

please don't stop. I'm fine. I want to do this. I do."

The way her eyes were pleading, the way she'd been so jumpy when they first met—"Delta, you're not a virgin, are you?"

She flinched. "No. It's just that I've…I've got some sexual hang-ups, I guess."

He waited, and right before his eyes, the woman who thought nothing of walking alone in the cold rain, dodging bullets and scaling walls became small and sad and frightened. Christ. This was not good.

He pulled himself up against the headboard, lifted her onto his lap and hugged her hard. "Delta, you can talk to me."

Her eyes dropped. "I don't think that's a story you need to hear."

"If we're going to get through these condoms, I think it is," he whispered, the joke meant to tease out a smile.

"Yeah, okay."

Not those two words, not now. She must've felt it herself because she breathed and on the exhale, out went her stray-cat tension. "Brian. You came from a good family, didn't you?"

"I like to think so."

"Well, my parents weren't so nice."

"Okay."

"They worked in television. They weren't exactly movers and shakers, but they wanted to be. They went to all the big parties and tried to get to know all the top people, but they could never seem to really get the break they wanted, you know?"

Brian knew. He'd stomached plenty of the brittle, desperate types in his time.

"Anyway, one day they had a party at our house. I had just turned twelve a couple of days before, so I can still remember it. They managed to get some pretty serious V.I.P.s to come. There were actors and producers and directors and network executives, every one of them a back-stabbing narcissist."

Brian tightened his hold on her.

"Anyway, there was this one guy who they all sucked up to," Delta continued. "A major media financier. Really rich. Helped get a lot of major television shows off the ground. Everybody was falling over each other trying to get on his good side, because with the backing of a guy like him, you could get to the top pretty damn quick."

Brian felt a knot of sickness form in his gut as she brought her knees up to her chin like a frightened little girl. He circled one arm around her legs, tightened his other around her back.

"My mother slept with him that night, and for some weeks afterwards, and he did a lot to make my parents' dreams come true. My mom got a major role in a soap opera, and my dad got the funding to produce a show of his own. But then…then he wanted something more from them…" Delta's voice trailed off.

He knew where this was going. He wanted her to stop, stop ripping her heart out, stop ripping out his. But into the room bright with L.A. sunshine, she whispered it. "They sold me, Brian. They sold me to him."

Her head fell against his shoulder. There was more to the story but all the rest was details. She'd told him the worst, trusted him not to hurt her with it. And he wouldn't. Only she needed to understand he had expectations of her.

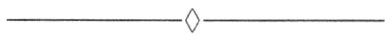

S.M. STELMACK

Delta had only told her story to one person before, and that was Mr. Hadrian when she'd been thirteen. Even Akeno hadn't known any details of her life before meeting her on the street, and she certainly hadn't shared them with any of her very occasional one-night stands.

She'd thought she could make love with Brian and let the sex gloss over her emotions. But this time she was in too deep to ignore them.

God, what must he think of her now? A real mood-killer she was. His arms were still banded tight around her and she couldn't bring herself to pull away. But she should, because knowing Brian, he'd think he needed to take care of her, and that wasn't fair to him.

His hand loosened its grip on her thigh, and his finger crooked beneath her chin and tilted her face to him. He whispered, his lips so close to hers.

"But you beat them, didn't you? They betrayed you in the worst way a person can be betrayed, but you didn't lie down and die. You found your own path in one of the toughest cities on Earth. You found friends and a mentor and became this ninja wall-climbing super-thief. And then, if that wasn't enough, you saved who knows how many kids from that pedophile judge by locking him away. You're a hero, Delta."

She blinked. She'd thought of herself as a lot of things in her life, but a hero had never been one of them. She felt her face go hot again. He grinned, caressing her cheek.

"Truth is, Delta, you're a smart, brave, beautiful woman, and nothing in your past could possibly ruin how I feel about you." His mouth dropped to hers, and the kiss was as wonderful as all the others he'd ever given her. The long one back in Arizona, the tender one on her hair here in the hotel room and the sexy, risky one in the car last night. And yet it was even more. It was loving and knowing and intimate, and somehow made her feel stronger than she'd ever had before.

"I want to make love to you so bad right now," he breathed into her mouth, "but if you're not ready, I'll wait, because a woman like you is worth it."

Delta closed her eyes. No, she wasn't going to make him wait. It was time she decided the path her life was going to take. Mr. Hadrian had made his opinion on love clear from the very start, and had ingrained in her a cynicism bordering on paranoia. She wasn't a hero—just a desperate survivor who'd hit the streets running before she was even a teen, the product of the selfish, vile parents and the monster who'd used her.

But she wasn't garbage either. She'd fought hard to survive. To carve out a small piece of decency in a sick, shallow world. Everything she had, from her printless fingers and scarred body to her lean physique and masterful skills, she'd earned with pain and sweat and raw determination. Sure, she was a thief. And a liar. And a fighter. And to some people's thinking, a whore. But she'd never given up, and she sure wasn't going to now.

Delta opened her eyes and reached for Brian, easing him into a deep kiss, to which he deeply responded. She pulled her lips from his long enough to strip off her cami and then she had her mouth back on him, grazing her nipples across his chest.

"I wondered how I'd get that shirt off you," he said into her mouth.

"Mmm…there's still the pants," she murmured, her fingers curling in his hair.

"Yours or mine?" His strong hands skimmed her sides, slipped around to her taut stomach, no longer gentle as their mutual need fed one another.

Delta straddled him, stroking his chest. She'd fantasized about his naked torso since the motel in New Mexico. Her answer was to unbutton his jeans and make sure she had hooked her fingers around the waistband of his boxers before pulling them down.

His cock—and he'd made a good point about the size— sprang free, and even as she tossed his clothing aside, he was stripping Delta of the last of hers. Their mouths met again in a fierce kiss, and when it broke she lowered her head to taste a part of him she hadn't yet.

Brian leaned back on his elbows, inhaling sharply as her lips wrapped around the tip of his hard cock, his jaw clenching as she took him fully into her mouth. She knew she wasn't particularly skilled, but by his happy moan, she suspected that what she lacked in experience, she was making up for with enthusiasm.

"I need to be inside you," he said, his hands raking her hair, his voice almost pleading.

She nodded and got in a couple more licks on his swollen cock before Brian grabbed a condom, knocking over the bedside lamp and alarm clock in the process. A rip of foil and a snap of latex, and he was on top of her, his cock at her moist entrance. He slipped in, and nothing, nothing had felt more right in her life.

This was her choice. She was giving her lover pleasure and claiming it as her own. It wasn't enough to survive any-more. Not enough to hide and steal and exist. Death could come for her tomorrow, but at least this day, this moment, she was really and truly alive.

"Missed seeing your face when you came yesterday." His voice was husky. "That's not happening today."

God, he filled her up, and still she bumped up against

him, begging for more. He smiled, not a full one because his expression was already intense, his attention clearly on their grinding connection. Her muscles around him tightened and he thrust in response. She moaned. This was more than good. This was what she *needed*.

He gave her long hard strokes, and her orgasm built. This one was going to be different from last night's. Not hard and fast, but slow and hot. She closed her eyes and gave in to the feeling. It spread out from her G-spot, pulsed in her nipples— she touched them and she heard Brian give a sexed-up rumble of pleasure—and she slid her hands to his ass, his muscles flexing with each thrust, caught his rhythm and when he moved to thrust again, she rammed him hard into her. The heat shot through her, she arched, electrified, and then she lost it, her orgasm throwing her against him, her panting heightening into a long, shrill cry.

She started coming down and Brian took over, pounding into her again and again, his pace even, yet his thrusts growing more urgent. Her body writhed, her moans deepened, her hands fisted into the sheets as he gave himself to her. Then, with a savage growl he drove up into her, raising her hips from the sheets, a second cry bursting from her as they climaxed as one.

With a gasp she fell back against the bed, and Brian collapsed onto her, bracing himself so as not to crush her. She reached up and ran her tongue along his sweaty throat.

He moaned out a laugh. "Christ, Delta. You're killing me." He stroked his cock lazily inside her. "Though of the all the ways you've nearly done that, this is my favorite."

Her slim, nimble hands skimmed and raked his chest and sides, and with a playful arch of her body, they rolled so that she was on top, his cock still deep inside her. Then, she stretched out and picked up the second condom.

He let out a whimper. "Woman, what do you think my recovery time is?"

"How about we find out?"

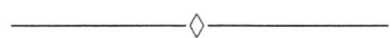

Brian and Delta were necking in the shower, the hot water slicking and slapping over their bodies, his hand working the softness between her legs when his phone on the bathroom counter chirped to life. He broke off their kiss.

"That'll be Ursula. I gotta answer it," he said. "I want to make sure it's not more trouble." His hand wasn't listening, and Delta had to tug it away before turning him out of the shower.

Drying off his hands, he picked up the smartphone. It was Gina.

"Hey, Bri. Long time no see."

"Yeah, sorry I haven't been in. Delta and I have been taking care of some business."

"Would that be the same kind of business my girlfriend and I took care of last night?"

Brian sighed, Gina laughing as she heard his exaspera-tion. "Not that I can blame you. If I were single, I don't know which of you two I'd like to jump into the sack with first. Then again, I heard a rumor you do threesomes."

"Gina..."

"Okay, okay. Can't a girl fantasize? So, when can I tell the Nun you'll be in? I'd say she's PMSing, but how the hell can you tell?"

Brian looked at Delta's silhouette behind the curtain, did some quick calculations. "When do I need to be in?"

"According to God's little angel, three hours ago. There's a whack of stuff you need to sign, and then there's the meeting happening at Universal in oh, ninety-two minutes, and the question of whether you want me to extend your stay at the hotel, and—"

"All right, all right, I get it. I've been a little lax in my role as CEO. Tell Ursula I'll meet her at Universal and to bring those papers and my suit, and get me a couple of more nights here at the hotel. As for everything else, I'll call you when I'm on my way and you can fill me in then."

"Sure thing. When are you going to leave?"

Brian rubbed his forehead. When Gina started nagging him about his responsibilities, he knew it was time to take care of his company. His staff had done an incredible job of keeping things running while he tried to straighten out his personal life, but he couldn't keep leaning on them forever. "Give me fifteen minutes."

The shower clunked off and Delta pulled back the curtain.

And there she was, naked as a jaybird, her body pink and warm. Damn. He disconnected and tried not to think of all the unused condoms on the bedside table.

"Delta, I hate to say this, but I have to head into work for a few hours. There's a whole pile of things I need to look after."

"Good," she replied, reaching for a towel.

"Good?"

"Yeah, because I have work to do, too. Need to go case Susan's place."

"Isn't that—?"

"What I'm trained to do?" Delta's tits and tush disappeared under the towel. "Don't worry about me. I'll be back before you are. Besides, casing a place is best done alone. I might need you later on as a diversion so it's better Susan doesn't catch sight of you."

He followed her out of the bathroom, snapping up his shirt from where it hung on a chair. "Call if you need any help, okay? I'd feel a lot better if you didn't run off on me again."

"I'll come back." She flashed him a grin. "For more."

His fingers paused on the buttons and he had to order them to continue. "Yeah, well be sure you do. Disappear now and you'll break my heart. You seen my socks?"

Delta slipped by him, all wet hair and warm body, and bent over the bed, the too-short towel riding up her backside. She snagged his socks and came back. "Here you—"

He grabbed her, lifted her against him and took her mouth. She opened for him, wrapped her arms around his neck and hung along his body, her toes suctioned to his calves.

"Think fifteen minutes is enough time for a quickie?" she breathed.

It was.

CHAPTER 11
ELEVEN

A ROLLERBLADER DUCKED past Delta on Venice Beach, reminding her exactly why she didn't like the place. Too crowded, chaotic and bizarre. Along the beach were stalls of numerous local artists, their wares in every imaginable medium and, crammed between them, vendors of every description. On the blinding white walkway, tanned locals, wearing little more than their wheels, swerved around gawking tourists, hulking body builders released from nearby Muscle Beach, and all kinds of street performers from African drummers to belly dancers to pianists.

Few buildings facing the beachfront were numbered, and Delta wandered back and forth trying to locate the address. At last, she found it: a small and somewhat weather-beaten brick facade with the sign, *Venice Beach Psychic Connection*.

Delta stepped back and honed in on the second floor. The upper windows suggested an apartment, though it was far too crowded to climb up and take a look. She and Brian would have to return tonight to check out Susan's place, but in the meantime, she could scope out the main floor.

Skirting a errant fire-juggler, she pushed open the door of

the establishment and was immersed in pungent incense. The place was dark, grubby and vaguely sinister, like a circus sideshow. Charts of Chinese and Arabic astrological symbols hung from the walls, interspaced with a hodgepodge of photographs including famous psychics, occultists and madmen. Coming to the silk-draped counter, Delta spotted a little silver bell inlaid with what looked like Egyptian hieroglyphs.

Tinkling it summoned a short, elderly woman of uncertain ethnicity, clad in a kimono-like dress of crimson and violet. Her long gray hair was braided in African style, and about her neck hung a dozen golden talismans, which looked Asian in origin. Delta could see from her grace and symmetry that the woman had once been a beauty. Even now, she was undeniably striking.

"Hello, my child," the woman greeted, "Welcome to my humble establishment." Her voice was friendly yet aloof. Like royalty engaging a commoner in small talk.

Delta struck the attitude of a New Agey free spirit. "Whoa, this place is so cool. I was walking by and noticed the apartment upstairs. I'm looking for a place here in Venice, so I said to myself, 'Why not?'"

The woman looked at Delta as if she'd suggested she'd bring her pet rats, too. "Ah yes, there is a place, but I'm afraid it's not for rent. My daughter and I live there."

Delta was careful not to reveal more than a mild curiosity. "Ah man, my karma's all off today. You and your daughter live and work together? That's cool."

"Oh no, I'm afraid the gifts I was blessed with were not passed on to her. She's gone on to pursue her father's line of work. But tell me, my child, have you ever had your fortune told?"

The woman was trolling for business, and Delta decided

to humor her. The more she could learn the better. "Twice. That's what brought me here to Venice Beach. I'm from Seattle and the woman there said I'd be traveling to a sunny place. And so I was going home and I thought, why not? And so I took the bus, and here I am." She looked about and wondered if she was laying it on a bit thick. Akeno had always been better at the clueless stoner method of casing places. "Now I'm not sure what I should do, so maybe I need to connect with the spirits again. How much does it cost?"

The woman didn't bat an eye. "Just eighty dollars. My readings are very accurate, my child. Well worth the investment."

"Eighty dollars? That works for me. Long as I still have money for the hostel tonight. By the way, my name's Susan." Delta stuck out her hand.

"Oh really?" The woman took it more easily than she'd anticipated. "That is the name I gave my daughter. It means 'full of joy'. I see you suit your destiny name. I'm Xia."

Xia wasn't entirely wrong. Delta would feel joy if destiny brought her Susan." Whoa, cool. You Chinese?"

"Partly. My mother was Egyptian. Now, come and I'll do a reading for you."

Delta followed the lady into a back room, decorated similarly to the one they had just left. There was a small table and a pair of chairs, and sitting, Xia invited Delta to do the same. "Now, Susan-my-child, there are several arts of divination in which I am practiced, including tarot cards, palmistry, tasseomancy and crystal scrying. Looking at you, I would think that the tarot would be the best suited, especially for a general forecast of events."

Tasseo—? Scrying? At least she understood what tarot was all about. "Yeah, okay." The woman produced a deck of dog-eared tarot cards, shuffled them, and then began to lay them out in a pattern upon the table.

"Oh, my. Very intriguing. Very intriguing indeed."

Delta pretended to be very intrigued, too. "What, what?"

"They say that you've been lonely in the past. That you've been misunderstood by others, but that you possess a deep sensitivity to art."

Just like her and every other wannabe along the beach-front, but Delta ooh-ed and aah-ed like a good little hippie.

"I see a period of struggle ahead, both spiritual and financial, but your talents shall not go unnoticed. You shall meet a man, and he shall recognize in you a genius even you do not fully appreciate...."

Xia droned on, painting a picture of an ideal artist's life, filled with angst, struggle, romance and eventual triumph. Plenty of time to assess security while still feigning fascination.

"That was amazing!" Delta said, at the end of the half-hour session, handing over cash.

"Oh, my child. It was a pleasure," the charlatan cooed, recounting the bills. "You have a very bright future ahead."

A bright future. And for a split second, Delta thought of her and Brian and what ifs. But only for a split second. "Hey, I have a friend who'd be totally into getting his future read too, but he's only free in the evenings what with work and stuff."

"Oh, that's fine, my dear-Susan-child. I do private readings, so have him call and schedule an appointment. Here, I'll give you a card."

Delta followed the lady back out to the front room, and pocketed the card. "Whoa, thanks. I need to call my friend first. Can you see him tonight? He's messed up and could do with celestial guidance and stuff."

Xia confirmed with a regal gesture that she would grant an audience that evening. Delta gave a happy nod and skipped out, losing herself in the crowd again.

She cut across a grassy space on her way back to the street and unable to resist, grinned. For under a hundred bucks, she'd confirmed Susan's presence at that address, scoped out the ground floor of the place, and found a way to ensure that she could enter the top floor and poke around for a good half-hour without risk of being disturbed. All that was left to do was check times with Brian, which she'd do once she got back to the hotel room, probably two hours ahead of his ETA.

She pulled out the business card to memorize the number, but one look at it and she ground to a halt. She read it again and again, her stomach knotting tighter and tighter. No. God. No. But the name was too much of a coincidence, and as she thought about what Xia had told her, Delta saw the terrible web that had ensnared Akeno.

The name on the card was Xia Hadrian.

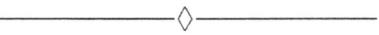

Kannon leaned on the railing of his hotel balcony, and scanned the wedge of L.A the view offered him. Somewhere out there, somewhere in this city of fame, fortune and fuckups was the woman he needed to find. Problem was when he caught her, he didn't know if he wanted to kill her or talk to her.

Mr. Matsuda's order was very clear: kill the people responsible for his son's murder. The crime lord had already identified who they were and knew where to find them, so the job had seemed straightforward enough.

The first target had been right where Mr. Matsuda said he

would be, and confronting the thief on the street, Kannon had put a bullet in the man's heart, then one more in his head for good measure. Within an hour, he'd been out of Miami and angling north to the home of his second target. He'd thought taking Ms. Fox down would be simple. Instead, she had become the most challenging person he'd ever hunted. Nobody had ever eluded him more than once. Nobody had ever sent his men to the hospital. Nobody had ever had him helpless on the ground, his own gun leveled at his head.

Nothing about the woman made sense. Why come back to a city where she was known, both by the underworld and the police? Why hadn't she killed him when she'd the chance? When she said she hadn't done it, was she implying that it was her partner that had killed Matsuda's boy, or that the two of them had been completely innocent of the crime?

This was turning into a clusterfuck. His cracked ribs reduced his physical edge. The police were looking for him, so he had to keep a much lower profile than he wanted. He'd promised Mr. Matsuda that he'd have Fox's head within a week, but he had no idea how that was going to happen. Or even if it should. He didn't hurt innocent people. At least, not knowingly. In this hell of a life he'd created for himself, it was his one code.

Except if he didn't break his own rule, if he didn't kill the wrong woman, if he didn't do what he was told, he endangered the life of someone more important than the woman or himself. His daughter, Zoe.

Like all criminal organizations there was only two states of being in the Yakuza: you were either in the boss' good books or you were dead. Weakness and incompetence were not tolerated, and it was too risky to just let people go. Because of his mother's Nubian heritage, he only had status amongst his xenophobic peers because of his perfect kill record. Failing any job, let alone one so important, bordered on suicide. Since the death of her mother, her father was all Zoe had anymore. She was only sixteen, and without him, she'd be left to the mercies of a vicious world. He had to be there for her till she was old enough to stand on her own, no matter what the cost.

His phone rang.

"It's me." Iolana said, her rasping voice smug. "Calling to clear my debt to you, killer. I've found the hotel she's staying at. Even got you the room number."

A minute later, he was on his way, his mind made up.

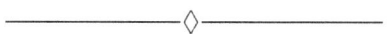

Delta walked up the stairwell to Mr. Hadrian's apartment, dread deep in the pit of her gut. She'd never thought she'd take the steps in doubt, even in fear, but here she was. She'd always known her teacher kept secrets. That was the way of their profession, but just how deep those secrets ran, she had never guessed.

She tapped at his door, then let herself in. Mr. Hadrian was in his armchair, a book in his lap, a cup of tea by his side. "Considering the recent frequency of your visits, I'm surprised you haven't requested residency."

He couldn't have spoken to her more formally. Of course, he didn't want her there. Did he know? Delta held up Xia Hadrian's business card. Mr. Hadrian leaned forward to inspect it, then settled back into his armchair, his face blank. He did know.

Delta locked down her anger. "Who is Susan?"

"That, Ms. Fox, is none of your business."

"I see. Was it any of Akeno's business by chance?"

161

Mr. Hadrian shrugged, and lifted his cup to take a sip. In one quick motion, Delta slapped it from his hand, sending it to the floor where it shattered, the crash splintering through the quiet apartment. Surprise flashed across Mr. Hadrian's face, but only for a moment.

"I suggest you clean that up, Ms. Fox," he said, his tone glacial.

Delta matched his tone. "And I suggest you tell me who Susan is, Mr. Hadrian, or I'll be breaking a lot more than your teacup."

"You ungrateful little brat. Did you just threaten me?"

Delta looked down at the pieces of smashed cup. Nothing in Mr. Hadrian's little domain was ever broken or out-of-place. And now, there was the teacup. And her. "Akeno loved you, Mr. Hadrian. He loved you like a father. Like a hero."

"Which is exactly why I warned him away from the job when I found out about it, but apparently he wasn't looking for my advice."

"Who's this?" Delta pulled the picture of Susan from her pocket and held it before him. "Who is this bitch?"

His slate gray eyes looked at the picture, then slowly rose to meet the bright blue of his student's. "She's my daughter."

There. The connection. The ugly, ugly connection. Delta dropped to the arm of the couch, staring across at the man she once would've given her life for. "You owe me an explanation, Mr. Hadrian."

"No, Delta, it's you who owe me. Where would you be if I hadn't taken you in? You'd be some pathetic outcast begging for change, or maybe a street whore selling her body to make ends meet. That is, if you had lived this long. I told you to drop this matter, to take the money and disappear. Like Akeno, however, you seem to want to make your own mistakes."

"You knew she was going to use him?"

"Of course, I knew. It's what she does. But you don't know the circumstances of the situation."

"Then let's get this sickening exercise over with, shall we?" Delta said. "Explain them to me, and I swear you'll never see me again."

Mr. Hadrian lowered his eyes to his book, then gradually closed it and set it on the table with infuriating slowness. It was a biography of Marlene Dietrich. Mr. Hadrian, a movie star fan? He must've caught something in her expression because he said softly, "Not everybody in the business is scum. Recent experience should've taught you that much."

"Recent experience has taught me people aren't what they seem," she answered pointedly.

He briefly closed his eyes, a sign of concession—or preparation, for when he opened them, he started in. "Years before you were born, I formed a partnership with a female charlatan by the name of Xia Chang. She was a temptress, able to talk people out of their cash and secrets like the devil, and with exotic looks that drove even sensible men to make the stupidest of mistakes. The arrangement we had was that she would find her way into the homes of the rich and powerful, gathering the information I needed to do my work. A very profitable partnership, while it lasted."

"What happened?"

"Xia and I became…involved. A foolish thing for me to do, considering I knew full well what a snake she was, but at the time, I thought I could tame her. In fairness to myself, I believe she did care for me, at least as much as someone like her could, and so when she said she was pregnant, I was content to marry her."

Delta listened in amazement. She had never suspected her

mentor of having a family. To her and Akeno, he had always seemed like a rock of dispassionate strength, unbound to anyone or anything save his students. "How come you never told me about her? Why didn't you train her?"

Mr. Hadrian raised his hand, motioning her to silence. "Even before Susan was born, things were falling apart between Xia and myself. Knowing how manipulative she was, I feared I'd been trapped, and that our child would be a tool she could use to control me. I balked at that, and two months after my daughter came into this world, I left them."

Delta felt her insides shatter. "You left them? You abandoned them?"

"I sent money, enough for them to enjoy a reasonable living, but I wanted no part of their lives. It was the best choice I could have made, considering the mistake of getting involved with her in the first place. At any rate, after several years, Xia contacted me. She wanted me to train Susan in the discipline of cat burglary, while she taught her the arts of seduction and trickery. I suppose she had it in her mind that Susan could be a prodigy of crime. I warily agreed, and she came to study with me."

He paused for a moment, and when he continued, there was a distant quality to his voice. "She was beautiful, Delta. As striking as Xia. She was hardworking and eager to learn, and I found myself caring for her, just as I came to care about Akeno and yourself a few years later."

He didn't look at her when he said this, his first declaration of affection. Delta understood. She couldn't tell Brian how wonderful he made her feel, even after all they'd shared.

"I suppose everything could have worked out if it wasn't for my wife. No sooner had the girl found a place in my heart than her mother began to coax favors out of me. A little more money, the use of my contacts, minor jobs, each request getting more and more involved. It was only after two years that I finally realized what was going on. Xia and Susan were controlling me. Together, they were subtly pulling my strings, working in concert to make me their puppet."

"How old was she?" Delta asked.

"She was twelve when I finally realized what was happening. She'd learnt well from her mother, and become just as devious. Perhaps, even more so."

Twelve. Delta knew that age well. Too goddamn well. "So what did you do?"

"I did the only thing I could do. I turned her out. She went back to her mother, and I made it clear I never wanted to hear from either of them again. Xia contacted me several times after that, feeding me lines about how distraught Susan was, how she was growing bitter and sadistic, but I ignored her. She was poison, Delta, and my daughter was just as venomous."

"But she was only twelve," Delta said.

Mr. Hadrian nodded, but said nothing more.

"Why didn't you tell Akeno when she seduced him?"

He raised his eyes to her, and for perhaps the first time in all the years she'd known him, his face revealed himself—bitter, sad, heartbroken. "Do you really think it would have made a difference, Delta? If I'd told him, he'd have gone to her and she would've had her own version, and who do you think he'd have believed?" His mouth tightened. "Hasn't it been said that there is no greater fool than one in love? That's why I taught you to avoid the state at all costs, Delta."

She lowered her eyes. Perhaps it was her silence or her hunched posture that caught Mr. Hadrian's attention. His next words were as if he'd read her mind. "But you've already gone and done it, haven't you?"

She jerked, but he waved his hand dismissively. "I know. He's different from all the rest. He's good and kind, and he loves you because he looked you in the eye when he said it."

"He didn't say that he loved me," Delta cut in.

Mr. Hadrian threw up his hands in mock defense. "Well, at least, he's honest, then. For God's sake, girl, do you really still believe in such fairy tales?"

Mr. Hadrian didn't wait for an answer, but sighed, and taking a key from his pocket, went to a nearby cabinet. Unlocking a drawer, he withdrew a large manila envelope and handed it to her.

"Here's what's left of your money, Delta. Take it and run. Don't tell anyone where you're going. Not me, not him, not anyone. This world is a pitiless place, and it will bring you nothing but tears and pain if you let it. It's up to you to save yourself."

She took the envelope and shoved it under her arm, then got to her feet and headed for the door, blinking back a sudden rush of tears. She opened it, then paused. "You know I still plan to bring her down."

He inclined his head. "May the best thief win."

It sounded like a blessing of sorts. She swallowed. "Goodbye, Mr. Hadrian."

She had to wait for his answer but when it came she knew he meant it. "Goodbye, Delta," he said. "Take care."

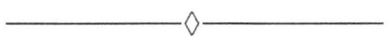

The meeting lasted way longer than Brian had anticipated, the executives grilling him on how he'd handle every part of the project, and fussing over the company's record. Then they'd started in on his life, what kind of jobs he'd taken, what motivated him, where he saw himself in five years and other stupid bullshit that was none of their business. He'd finally snapped and told them point blank that Cause & FX's record stood for itself, and if they wanted to use someone else that was fine by him. They had all stared, mouths agape, except for the showrunner—a big high-and-mighty with a baked-on tan, who told Brian they'd be in touch and then up and left.

True to form, Ursula fumed on the elevator ride down. As soon as he was in the lobby, he tried the hotel number. No answer. Delta should be back by now. She'd refused to carry a phone or any electronic device because she could be tracked. Yeah, better to worry the shit out of him.

"It's that hitch-hiker, isn't it?"

He'd filled Ursula in on the basics of Delta's situation, and she'd agreed that turning Delta into the police would be tantamount to signing her death warrant, and was willing to accept that she wasn't guilty of the murder the Yakuza were hunting her for, but she didn't in any way approve of his getting attached to her.

"Criminals are opportunists, Brian," she lectured him as they'd walked across the studio parking lot, her immaculate English giving way to the heavy Austrian accent that crept in every time she was upset. "Ven I first came to America I did counseling work in the vimen's prisons, and I never once met a prisoner who vas sincere. All of them vanted me to write a letter to the varden or the parole board or the child protection people about how good vey vere, vile in the meantime vey hadn't changed vays at all.

"You've got a kind soul, Brian, but sometimes it blinds you to the evil in this vorld. I think you did the right thing helping that voman, but to put your life on the line for her, that's idiotic."

Brian thought he'd try Gina next. Maybe Delta had checked in with her, not wanting to disturb him in a meeting.

"Hey, Gina. You get a call from the hotel this afternoon?"

From the corner of his eye, he saw Ursula throw up her arms.

"No, sorry, I didn't. You want me to call her room?"

"No, I already tried but she's not there, or she's not picking up or—" he stopped, not wanting to contemplate what the third 'or' might be.

"Or maybe," Ursula shouted, "maybe she is committing identity theft, racking up your credit cards, who knows, robbing a bank! Maybe she's doing exactly what she told you she does for a living—steal!"

From his cell phone came squawking. "Put her on!" Gina ordered him." Put her on!"

Brian handed over the phone and for the next few minutes, the two women tore into each other. Christ, if they'd been in the same room, they'd be rolling on the floor in a full-out catfight. He soon plucked the phone from Ursula.

"Gina. It's Brian. Enough." He pointed at Ursula. "You, too." The nun folded her arms across her chest and thinned her mouth.

Gina wasn't so obedient. "Look, listen to me for thirty seconds and then I'll let you be, okay?"

Brian sagged against his car door. "Shoot."

"I want to say that I've waited to see the old Brian for a long time now. This past while you've lost that whole maverick risk-taker fuck-the-naysayers attitude that made this place what it is. Delta brought that back to you. Don't let her slip away, okay?"

"You met her, Gina. If she wants to slip away, she's gone."

"She'll be back."

He remembered her naked underneath him, her curled into him while she told him her story. "Then I'd better head over to the hotel."

Ursula let loose an exasperated roar and strode off to her car.

Gina's hoot shot into his ear. "I win. In your face, Attila! I so win!"

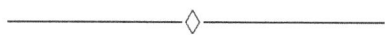

It was going on 7:30 when he arrived back at his room, at once swearing to shake the living daylights out of Delta when he got hold of her and just wanting her to be there. He slid his card into the reader and pushed open the door. Damn, it was dark. No Delta. He went to flick on the light but was grabbed and took a powerful blow to the stomach.

Winded, Brian swung at his assailant, but his attacker took his arm and flipped Brian onto the floor. Lights blazed on, and Brian stared up at the assassin he'd tangled with just the day before.

The Yakuza leveled a silenced pistol at him. "Where is she?"

Brian sat up slowly, to buy time and because he was in pain. But he was also relieved. Wherever Delta was, it wasn't with the Yakuza. "Go to hell."

The big man kicked Brian in the crotch with his steel-toed shoe. Pain, unbelievable fucking pain. Brian writhed, clutching his balls.

"Where is she?" came the same flat voice.

Brian gripped the side of the bed and struggled to his knees. He looked up at the big fucker and didn't reply.

"Answer me, Mr. Chanse, and you'll live. You know very well it's not you I'm after. Make me beat it out of you and I'll kill you. It's as simple as that."

"You're after the wrong person," Brian wheezed. "She didn't kill that boy, and neither did her partner."

The assassin squared his shoulders. "Then, who did?"

Brian slumped against the bed. "We don't know, we're trying to figure it out. That's why she came back to L.A. in the first place. To find out why you people were after her. Whoever shot your boss's son set her up to take the blame. I can even prove it."

"How?"

Brian gave a chin lift to the file on the table. "Take a look at the police report. The woman that pulled the trigger was a crack shot. Delta doesn't even carry a gun. Akeno had the combination for the safe, but where did he get it? Do you really think some maid would know what it was? Plus, Delta was on the other side of the country when all this went down. If you'd bothered talking to her neighbors or employer, you would have known that. She hadn't even talked to Akeno in almost two years."

The killer wasn't interrupting him, so Brian pushed on. "And why was the kid at the office in the middle of the night? Does it make sense that expert thieves would have made so much noise that he heard them through a closed door? And Delta. Think about how easy it was to find her. Why would've she stayed in Myrtle Beach if she knew you were after her? I mean, just *think* about it."

The hitman seemed to be doing just that, contemplating Brian for a long immobile moment. "Suppose you're telling the truth," he finally conceded. "What's your connection to Fox? Why are you helping her?"

"Because…." Brian trailed off. Christ.

"Because what?"

The truth was the only thing that made sense. He looked the killer in the eye. "Because I love her."

The gunman gave Brian a look approaching pity, then with a flick of his thumb, he clicked on the pistol's safety and slid it into the shoulder holster beneath his jacket. "I already looked at the report, saw what you saw, so here's the deal, Mr. Chanse. Find the killer for me by midnight tomorrow, along with hard proof, and I'll let you and Ms. Fox live. Don't, and not only will I kill both of you when I find you again, but I'm also going to pay a visit to that pink-haired receptionist."

What the—? "Gina has nothing to do with this."

"She led me off Ms. Fox's trail when I first visited your company. She booked this hotel room for you. I'd say that makes her involved, so consider it extra incentive. Believe me, I've hunted people far tougher and smarter than you, and not one has ever escaped me."

Bruised balls and no gun. He was in no position to bargain. "How do we reach you?"

"I've got your cell number." The corner of his mouth curled at Brian's groan. "My name's Kannon. Kannon Takahama. And I won't be far away, Mr. Chanse."

With that, the Yakuza soldier exited the room and Brian, giving into the pain, let himself roll to the floor.

Love her or not, the second, the fucking second, Delta showed up, he was going to kill her.

CHAPTER 12
TWELVE

DELTA WAS IN a daze as she got out of the taxi at the hotel, the emotional rollercoaster of the past several hours making her lightheaded and queasy. God, she looked forward to seeing Brian again. She stepped to the door, then froze. Wasn't that Gina's car parked ahead?

Why would Gina be here? Brian wouldn't bring her to the hotel to talk business. Brian and Gina weren't—? *He's different from all the rest. He's good and kind, and he loves you…*

"Get out of my head, Mr. Hadrian," she muttered. No. Something was going on, and whatever it was, couldn't possib-ly be good.

Before she'd even finished her thought, she rounded the hotel front to the side, her attention zeroing in on the fourth floor window of their room. No real run-up but the staffer car angle-parked should work. At once she took off in a full sprint, ran up onto the car roof and leapt. Her fingertips caught the bottom of a windowsill, and pulling herself upwards, she planted her feet on the six-inch sill and jumped again, repeating the process till she reached the fourth floor. Hanging there a moment to catch her breath, she cautiously raised herself to peek inside.

Brian was lying on the bed, a pillow under his head, dressed in just the top half of a business suit, his face red and contorted, and his crotch covered by an ice pack. Beside him sat Gina, biting her lip as she put away a medical kit. Thank God. Brian was—they were alive. Supporting herself on one hand, she knocked on the glass.

Surprised looks were quickly followed by Gina opening up the window as far as it would go. The space wasn't much, but Delta wiggled through it like an eel. "What happened?" she asked breathlessly as soon as she touched the floor.

"That big angry killer guy kicked him in the nuts," replied Gina before Brian had a chance to answer. "Pretty bad swelling and a couple of stitches. His balls are literally blue. And like this." She spread her hands wide in demonstration.

Brian blew out his breath. "Thanks for that, Gina. A couple of hours ago when I got in, that Mr. Kannon Takahama was here to greet me. He wanted to know where you were, and seeing as I couldn't help him out with that, he got kind of annoyed with me. By the way, it was good you had sex with me earlier, because I don't think I have the parts for it anymore."

Delta shot an embarrassed look at Gina. "Brian—"

"Oh yeah, because it never occurred to my sex-obsessed brain that the two of you weren't going at it like rabbits here," Gina said. "How about I stand way over here"—she leaned against the wall, which only made Delta remember what happened there—"and give you some privacy while you lay a big fat juicy welcome kiss on him."

"I don't really need—"

"You might not need to but look at the poor boy. Wounded, broken, all in the name of defending your life against the baddie."

Brian didn't move, stared up at the ceiling. Gina made 'get-on-with-it' circling of her hands. Very carefully, Delta crawled across the bed and knelt beside Brian. He was still staring up but there was his mouth with that little upturn. Brat. But God, she was so happy he was alive and almost well.

He turned to her and said, "You know, early this morning, I dreamed about you climbing the wall into the hotel room. And here you are, making it come true."

"Oh, gag me with a spoon! Shut him up."

Delta didn't need any more encouragement. She bent her head and kissed him, long and soft, and giving to him all she couldn't say. And he gave back, his mouth soaking up all the sadness and tension of her day. She could kiss him straight through till morning.

Gina made a noise. "Okay, this is too sexually frustrating. Time's up."

Delta went to straighten but Brian's hand was firm on the back of her head. "What took you so long?" he murmured.

She couldn't talk about Mr. Hadrian right now. "Later, okay?"

His green eyes narrowed but his hand eased and she sat up. "So…uh…" Delta said, looking to carry on as if the kiss hadn't happened. "…don't take this the wrong way, but how are you still alive?"

"I managed to persuade him that it wasn't you that killed the kid, so he's granted us till tomorrow night to find the murderer. If we don't, then he's going to kill you, me, and Gina."

"Gina?" Delta swung her head to her. "But she didn't do anything!"

Gina shrugged. "Well, I wouldn't say that exactly. There

was this one time in Bangkok when this transsexual tried to rob me, but she didn't know I had a switchblade in my purse, so—"

Flat on his back, Brian ordered, "Shut it, Gina." And she did.

Delta felt her lungs tighten, her heart pound. *Get a grip.* She had to be calm and concentrate on the task at hand. "Okay, I pretty much know who did it. And how, and why. The question is how to prove it."

"Except I don't think I can stand right now, let alone walk," Brian said, wincing as he gingerly adjusted the ice pack.

Delta heard a throat cleared, and looked to see pink-haired Gina flash a grin. "Guess we girls better come up with a plan then, huh?"

Gina had had some pretty awesome experiences at Venice Beach, but only during the day. At night, with the crowds and vendors gone, the place looked like something from a bad horror movie. As for the people that remained, it was enough to make a solid girl like her believe in zombies.

She'd phoned Xia Hadrian as soon as Delta had filled her in on Susan's background, weaseling an appointment for that very evening. It wasn't much, especially when compared to scaling walls or taking one for the team in the gonads, but she was sure she could play her part in the plan—keeping the fortuneteller busy while the cat burglar did her stuff.

Delta, she discovered on the drive to Venice, wasn't one for small talk, which wasn't good because Gina needed to talk like fruit flies needed to die. When they reached the parking lot

175

that bordered the area, Gina gave it one more shot but focused on the task at hand. "Okay, my appointment is in ten minutes, and it's for a half-hour. I'll try to draw things out as long as I can. Do you need me for anything else?"

Delta was scanning the area, probably looking for stuff that wouldn't occur to her in a million years. "No," Delta answered. Then her amazing blue eyes focused on Gina. "If things go sideways, run to the car and get the hell out of here. Don't come looking for me. I'll find my way back."

She said it low and even, and then she gave a sweet smile. "Don't worry. You'll do fine."

That smile, those eyes, the ninja attitude. Sheesh. No wonder Brian had fallen hard.

Gina headed directly for the beach as Delta followed at a distance. By the time she reached the boardwalk, the thief had slipped away like a shadow. Yep, just little old Gina alone on the boardwalk with the zombies. But hell, nothing could be more dangerous than the man that had given them the ultimatum. He'd seemed so delicious, but his attitude was enough to turn her off chocolate forever.

Reaching the psychic center, Gina rapped at the door. She heard a woman's voice bidding her to wait, and then a moment later The Woman Known as Xia drew back the bolt and opened the door.

"Ah, hello, my child," she smiled politely. "You must be Susan's friend, Karen."

"Yep, that's right. Pleasure to meet you, Ms. Hadrian." Gina took her hand and pumped it. She decided to go for the Ultra-Friendly-Girl-Next-Door act because it came naturally. "Susan told me all about the amazing reading you did for her and when her friend Tom didn't want to go, well, I said more psychic goodness for me!"

"Do call me Xia, my child," the old woman replied, extracing her hand from Gina's grip and ushering her inside. When she locked the door behind them, Gina felt like the gates of a dungeon were being slammed shut. "Come in and make yourself at home. Would you like some ginger root tea?"

Gina didn't, but she went for it anyway to buy Delta more minutes. It appeared to work. Xia produced the cup of tea with the precision of a chemist preparing a deadly formula. She carried it to a small table draped in purple velvet where they took seats across from each other.

"So, Karen-my-child, you mentioned on the phone that you had a problem you required urgent advice on. Please, do tell me what it is."

Gina paused to conjure up the story she'd hastily prepared for the woman. She wasn't God's gift to the acting world, but hopefully she wouldn't need an Oscar-winning performance to fool the old charlatan. "Well, recently my uncle passed away, and he left me a whole ton of money. His house, his boat, his Rolling Stones memorabilia. I even got his cat Sparky, which was kind of weird seeing as he had her stuffed last year."

The old woman's eyes cast about, obviously searching for something to say. "Oh, my…my condolences. He sounds like he was very fond of you."

"We were real close, but the problem now is that my whole family is bugging me for money. I don't know how to handle it, and I was hoping there was some way of reaching my uncle and getting his advice. You know, like with one of those Ouija boards or something?"

"Ah, indeed there is, Karen, but such communications are not always easy. It may take several visits to establish contact with those who have passed on, but if you have patience and faith I can assure you of success."

177

Yeah, right, Gina thought. She'd *deserve* an Oscar if she could keep up this gullibility act the whole half-hour. She opened her eyes wide in her best attempt at appreciative wonder. "Oh, that's fantastic, Xia. How do we start?"

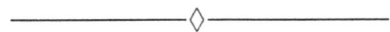

Delta, in the meantime, had scaled the building right next to Xia's, leapt the gap between the two, and was now skirting the edge of the roof looking for ways inside. The large windows facing the ocean were the obvious choice if nobody was home, but the lights were on and music was playing, and anyway, the lack of any overhang would make her easy to spot were she to clamber down.

Other options? A small bathroom window facing the back alley, two bedroom windows fitted with security bars, and, of course, the front and back doors. The dark bathroom it was. Delta gripped the edge of the roof and slowly lowered herself down so that her toes rested on the window's narrow frame. She hooked one hand over the top edge, and then was hanging off of the half-inch rim of metal.

With her free hand, she tried sliding the window open, but as expected, it was locked. From her back pocket she removed a box cutter, one of the two tools she'd bought on the way to Venice. Carefully she ran the blade along the rubber molding around the glass, returned the box cutter to her pocket and produced a small folding knife. With this thicker blade, she gently wedged the top of the glass free, and once the knife was pocketed, she took hold of the glass and tugged it free of the frame. She set it on the edge of the roof, then slipped her body though the tiny opening in one fluid motion.

Her eyes already well-acclimatized to the darkness, Delta

surveyed the bathroom. It was both much cleaner and more opulent than the building's exterior suggested, its marble counter crowded with expensive cosmetics and perfumes. The female Hadrians were doing well to afford a spiffy biffy. She got on her hands and knees to peer under the door into the lighted room beyond. The place wasn't terribly big, but expensively furnished with posh antiques. She couldn't see footprints in the carpet, but judging from its cleanliness, Ms. Hadrian and her daughter were far better housekeepers than the downstairs suggested. There were no telltale dog hairs, but then again, it looked freshly vacuumed.

Delta stood and took a moment to let out a long slow breath. Okay, this was where things got a little tricky.

She turned the door handle with infinite slowness, then with equal care opened the door two inches. The living room was empty, though she couldn't see into the adjoining areas. In one unbroken motion, she slipped past the door and dropped behind the cover of a large leather couch, crawling its length to better observe the kitchen, her eyes correcting to the increased light.

Seated there at a table, her back to Delta, was Susan. The woman was dressed in a black silk bathrobe snaked with a red dragon, and was reading her iPad, sipping from a martini glass, and by all signs was oblivious to Delta's presence. Hatred, a hard dark force she'd not experienced since Judge Hall, flared in Delta. *I'll get you, bitch. I'll get you.*

But now was not the time. She crept back and out from behind the couch and to a door leading to another room.

She silently opened and closed it behind her, pausing a beat to adjust to the darkness again. She was in a bedroom, neat and pretty as the rest of the house, but it wasn't the furnishings that caught her eye. Lying on the bed was a huge pit bull, its light snoring audible now that the door muffled the music. Delta watched its nose for any signs of twitching, but the beast seemed sound asleep. For now.

She should get out. Searching a place with the owner awake and a dog known for tearing off limbs one leap away was suicidal, but unless she found something fast, the Yakuza would make suicide redundant.

There was a large wardrobe and dresser in the room, as well as an ornate desk, and Delta began sorting through their contents. Both the wardrobe and dresser contained a range of fashionable garments, as well as some of studded leather that left no doubt about Susan's proclivities. She found linen, lingerie, jewelry and a small collection of rare coins, but nothing of real interest. Giving the dog a wary glance, Delta moved on to the desk, and opening the first drawer, immediately found a small precision handgun.

Whether this was the weapon that killed Matsuda's son there was no way of telling, but it was of the same caliber, and was exactly the kind of firearm a professional would use— light, concealable and accurate. Whatever the case, it wasn't useful as evidence. Susan's fingerprints were probably burnt away, too, and even if this gun was used in the murder, that didn't mean she pulled the trigger.

The drawer also contained a bankbook, which proved of more interest. Delta's cursory examination of the margin notes showed that Susan had been cashing personal checks from a lot of different people, some of which she recognized from *The Sweet Pepper* membership. It bore closer examination later, and pocketing it, Delta continued.

The other drawers contained such uninteresting items as stationery and tax records and old receipts, and Delta was about to dismiss them when one caught her eye. It was from a security company, and pulling it out she saw it was for the installation of a concealed safe a week before the Matsuda burglary. This is what she'd been looking for. If the safe contained what she thought it did, it would be proof positive that Susan was behind the crime.

Delta folded the paper, slipped it into her pocket with the bankbook, and was closing the drawer when the music stopped. She heard Susan enter the bathroom. Time to clear out. Fast.

She slipped into the living room, locking the bedroom door shut as she did, exactly as Susan rushed out of the bathroom, her eyes widening on Delta, and both of them froze in their tracks.

Delta was the first to find her tongue. "Nice set-up you got here, Suzie. Almost as nice as your dad's."

Susan's immaculate face contorted into a mask of vicious hatred. "You cunt," she spat. "You're never getting out of here alive."

The woman charged Delta, leaping with a jump kick, but Delta was the slightest bit faster, and dodged the blow. Susan's foot punched through the drywall, and in the moment it took to free herself, Delta bolted past her into the bathroom where she slammed the door shut and locked it.

Outside, Susan screamed in frustration as she found the door to her bedroom also locked, and Delta clambered out the window and up onto the roof. Running its length, she jumped to the next building, then the next and the next, only stopping at an alley too wide to cross. A few seconds later found her sliding down an access ladder, a smile on her face as she ran for the parking lot where Gina's car was.

———————◇———————

Gina looked upwards as the sound of shattering drywall, slamming doors, screamed curses and a barking dog echoed through the ceiling. "Uh..."

Xia looked surprised by the ruckus as well, but then her dark eyes snapped to Gina. "So you're a diversion, are you?" she said, her calm, celestial tone becoming all witch-y. "I knew you were bullshitting me, but I didn't know why. But now you're going to tell me who sent you here, aren't you?" Gina stood, raising her hands. "Yeah, well, I'll be going now. No need to show me out."

Xia had other ideas. From out of nowhere, she conjured a small silver revolver which she leveled at Gina. "Oh, you're not leaving yet, *Karen*. Who sent you? Hadrian? Or is that Fox who's upstairs right now, hmm?"

Gina had come from a tough family—a family that wasn't exactly on the right side of the law—and, as a result, she'd learned to take care of herself. In a flash, she grabbed the edge of the table and flipped it up, toppling the con woman from her chair.

The gun went off, blowing a small hole in the ceiling, but already Gina was bolting from the room. Reaching the door, she twisted the deadbolt, but as she turned the doorknob, there came a scrabbling of paws and rabid barking from the back room. Outside, she slammed the door shut and ran for her life, straight back to the car where she prayed Delta was waiting.

She was halfway there, when she glanced back to spy a huge pit bull hurtling after her, its lips drawn in a snarl of unholy fury. She had a can of mace in her purse, but given the size and ferocity of the canine, all it would do was piss the animal off even more.

But at least she wasn't alone. In the distance she spotted Delta. She was wrapping what looked like an old beach blanket around her arm as she sprinted towards Gina.

"Dog!" Gina shouted. "Big dog!"

"I'll take care of it!" Delta yelled back. "Just get the car."

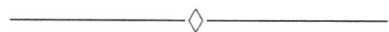

Delta and Gina rushed past each other in opposite directions, then Delta skidded to a halt as the huge canine redirected its bloodlust onto her. She held up her blanket-wrapped arm, her chin tucked down and her body angled to twist the instant it took hold. She couldn't let it knock her over. With its weight, if it got on top of her, her throat would be torn out. This beast wouldn't be as restrained as the police dog who'd dragged her down at Judge Hall's. This time her life depended on a different outcome.

The pit bull leaped, sinking its teeth into the blanket, and even as prepared as she was, the impact almost sent Delta sprawling. She managed to stay on her feet, engaged in a deadly tug-of-war, circling the dog as it yanked on her arm, pulling herself back and forth not hard enough to break free, but forcing the animal continually off-balance so that it couldn't use its full strength to topple her.

From the corner of her eye, she spotted Gina reaching the car, starting the ignition while still shutting the door. Roaring out of the parking spot, rubber burning, she cut across the road, the car riding up over the curb to where Delta was under attack, screeching to a halt beside her. The passenger door was thrown open. "Play time's over, girl!"

With a strong yank, Delta jerked the dog off its feet, and wiggling her arm free of the blanket, she threw it over the dog's head and made a break for the car. The confused pit bull chomped rabidly at the empty cloth, then realizing its prey was

183

escaping, tore after her. Swinging shut the door, Delta caught the dog across the side of the head, knocking it aside by the narrowest of margins. Planting her foot on the accelerator, Gina fishtailed away, leaving Susan's hell hound to bound fruitlessly after them.

Delta glanced over at Gina who looked okay, other than the fact her arms were in a locked position on the wheel, and they were tearing down the road at double the speed limit.

"Slow down, Gina. Don't want the cops pulling us over."

Gina eased off, her arms sagged and she turned to Delta. She snapped back to full tension. "Ohmigod, Delta. The dog got you."

Delta's arm was covered in blood, but judging from the pain, she'd suffered worse. "It's okay. Got any paper towels? I don't want to bleed on the seats. A real pain to get out." She opened the glove compartment, stared at the contents, glanced over at Gina who almost, almost looked embarrassed, and then quietly closed it.

Gina recovered first. "Check under the seat."

Delta gingerly did so and found only paper towels, thank God.

"Are you sure you don't want to go to the hospital?"

Delta gave a little smile. "Get real. This isn't anything you can't patch with the med kit. After stitching up Brian's balls, this ought to be easy."

Gina laughed and winced at the same time. "I don't know, Delta. You're bleeding pretty bad."

"Trust me, it's nothing," Delta reassured her. "None of the bites are deep. It only looks terrible because there are lots of them."

Gina mouthed that last bit in disbelief. "I owe you my life, Delta. As soon as I heard the commotion upstairs I made a break for it, and I had hardly got out the door, when they set that dog loose. I don't know what I would have done if he'd caught up with me."

"She." Delta corrected. "At least we're not the only tough bitches on the streets tonight."

Gina laughed again. She had a great laugh, Delta decided. It rolled and rippled and grabbed hold of the craziness of life. She and Brian were the best two people to happen to her in years. And both stood to be taken from her. Her throat began to swell with emotion.

"I found something," she said quickly, before the lump got any larger.

It was like telling Gina she had a secret. "What, what? Tell me, tell me!"

"Let's wait, and I'll tell you and Brian at the same time."

"Not fair. I did all the work," Gina muttered and sulked for all of a block before chattering about the evening's escapades. Delta leaned back and inserted appropriate noises, and worried alone about whether she'd found enough to save them all.

Back in the hotel room, Gina sewed another stitch into Delta's arm. Delta could feel each poke and tug but she kept her face blank because it was good practice and because Brian looked as if it were him getting the needle.

"You sure you're okay?" he said.

"You sure you don't need a hearing aid? For the hundredth time, yes."

He sank back in his chair, scraping a hand over his jaw. God, she really wished he wouldn't worry so much. It wasn't necessary.

Delta pulled in a deep lungful of air, picked up a bottle of disinfectant, and quickly poured it over her arm. Okay, that stung. Brian and Gina grimaced with her as the chemical did its work.

After a moment, Delta relaxed, and slowly began wrapping a long roll of gauze around her wounds. She could feel their eyes on her and said, "How about we catch a few hours sleep then get a printout of *The Sweet Pepper* client list and compare it to Susan's bank book. I think I'm getting a pretty good idea of what's going on now. The only question is how she's connected to the Matsudas."

"Feel like bouncing your theory off us?" Brian said, his question more like an order. He was pissed about something. What, she had no idea.

Delta had already explained to him about Susan's background prior to the appointment with Mrs. Hadrian, but he had a right to know. "Susan's mother used to be a seductress. She'd infiltrate people's homes, collect information for Mr. Hadrian, and then split the take with him after he'd robbed them blind. Susan was trained to do both those jobs, which is probably why she's a member of an upscale swinger's club."

Brian nodded. "The club provides her with a great supply of rich people to seduce and rob."

"Well, at least they got something for their money," said Gina.

Brian shot her another of his withering glances and Delta hurried on. "What I suspect is that someone close to Matsuda hired her to kill the gangster's son. By passing herself off as a maid, she suckered Akeno into doing the burglary. She didn't need his help to do the job, only to pin the murder on him— and me. No doubt she got at least part of the money that was taken."

"I get it," Brian said. "That way she not only got away clean with the murder and the theft, but she also got to take out her resentment against you and Akeno. In a way it was the perfect revenge on her father."

Delta jabbed a safety pin into the bandage and patted the finished product. "That's the gist of it, but there's still some things we need to find out. Susan's bank book shows a lot of checks from members of *The Sweet Pepper*. I'm hoping that those names'll connect us with the Matsuda family. Then there's what happened to Akeno in Miami. With luck, Morgan can get that to us before time runs out, and the police file should also give us a clearer picture of how it all happened, and who it was that wanted Matsuda's son dead in the first place."

Brian growled in obvious frustration. "That killer's calling tomorrow night, which is the earliest we're getting anything from Morgan. We won't have enough time."

Exactly what Delta feared but she didn't want to show it. Brian looked worried enough. "We'll bargain for more time. We've got new intel, plus...plus he owes me one."

"The man that's trying to kill you owes you a favor?" Gina said incredulously. "How does that work?"

Delta snuck a look at Brian. She chose to focus on Gina's friendly face. "The last time he tried to nail me I got his gun off him. I could have blown him away right then."

"But... you let him go?" Brian asked.

Delta got busy tidying up the medical supplies. "I'm not a killer, Brian. I'm not even a true criminal in the sense that Susan and her mother are. My work might not have been totally legal, but it wasn't totally illegal either, and the only time I ever really broke the law was when I was working on the sly for the cops."

"I know you're not a criminal. I just meant…well, the guy was trying to *kill* you. Shooting him would have been self-defense."

Delta turned to him. "Maybe, but it would also have blown any chance of getting the Yakuza bounty off my head. Sooner or later one of their assassins would have tracked me down. And…" she hesitated. "It was too hard to pull that trigger even if he would have done it to me in a heartbeat. He's trained. I'm not."

His face softened a little, and he seemed about to speak when Gina cut in, "Which reminds me we don't even know how he found you two here. Does he have the phones tapped? I turned off the GPS thingy on my phone, too."

"Not likely with all the security you have. Probably just has feelers out for us."

Gina scrunched up her face. "Feelers?"

Delta paused, thinking of an example. "Remember, Brian, how you hired those street kids to keep an eye out for me? Well, there are people in this town who can do something similar, but on a much wider scale. Someone here at the hotel probably recognized us. Could have been the valet, or the concierge, or maybe one of the cleaning staff. You only have to think about how small some of their paychecks are to see why they'd rat on us."

"So you knew we might not be secure here?" Brian said, distinctly accusatory.

God, what was his problem? She was trying to save him worry and trouble. She'd done nothing wrong. "Here's a newsflash, Brian—we're not secure anywhere. I told you that early on in the game, and I haven't had the time to educate you on all the ins and outs of the L.A. underworld. I'm trying my best to get us out of the mess we're in, so if you want to belly-ache about it, go do it someplace else."

Brian stared back. "I suppose you're right," he said, sounding as if she weren't. "We're both tired. We should get at least a little sleep, especially with the blood you've lost."

"You make it sound like I took a knife to the gut. Quit being so dramatic."

There was an odd silence. "You make it sound like I'm not allowed to care."

Huh? "You can care if you want."

All of the tension he'd been giving off since her and Gina had gotten back was nothing to the anger that pulsed off him right now.

"Oh, would you look at the time?" Gina caught up her purse, a huge pink thing with brass hoops. "Sorry I can't sleep with you two tonight. Don't be too disappointed. I'll call tomorrow."

And she was out of the door like a shot. Brian hadn't shifted. "Delta, I'm going to assume you made those comments because you didn't know any better, and you didn't mean to be a bitch."

Delta tightened at the last word. "I'm not a bitch. I don't want you worrying for no reason."

Brian opened his mouth, closed it, and repeated that twice more before he eased ever so slowly back in his chair. "How about you come over here and very, very carefully sit in my lap?"

The man was all over the place but Delta thought it best to comply. As soon as she was positioned, he cupped one hand on her butt and inserted the other hand under her cami to cup her breast. "There. I can't strangle you if my hands are otherwise occupied."

"Look, Brian, I think—"

"I worry. The second that door shut on you and Gina tonight, I worried. I laid on the bed, sick with worry. I turned the T.V. on and off a million fucking times. The time got close to when you two should be back, I sat in the chair and concentrated on the door and listened. Listened to the elevator open and shut, listened to people walk not quite to the door, listened to people walk past the door. Listened and waited.

"And then finally—finally—I hear Gina and before I can get up she's running in straight for the med kit, saying how everything's okay and—I swear, Delta, I actually felt my heart stop—and then you walk in, fucking blood all over you, and I go to you and do you remember what you said?"

Delta did and she squirmed, realizing now how it might sound given the context. "I said, 'Don't touch me. You'll get blood on your shirt.'"

"And then I have to sit in this chair some more while Gina pokes holes in your skin and tells me how you went ten rounds with a fucking pit bull and then you tell me Susan attacked you and when I dare ask you more than once if you're okay, what do you say?"

Delta couldn't look him in the eye. To his ear, she whispered, "'Don't worry.'"

His hands gave her body parts a firm squeeze, and his voice pitched low and soft. "I've dodged bullets, got in high-speed chases, nearly got blown up, got kicked in the balls. None of it compared to being forced to wait for you to come back to me."

She tried to look him in the eye, but got as far as his mouth. His jaw was stubbly like the first time she'd ever seen him. He hadn't known her name but he'd taken care of her. She'd put it down to his nature, and it was true—he'd take care of lost puppies, too. But he hadn't needed to keep caring for her. That had been his choice, his gift to her. And she hadn't treated it with respect, instead she'd made him feel it wasn't important. She hadn't meant to, just as he said, because the last thing she'd deliberately do was anything to hurt him. It was that thought that made her raise her eyes to his.

"I'm sorry, Brian. I'm sorry."

The tense line along his jaw eased, and, bit by bit, the corner of his mouth quirked up. "You going to show me how sorry you are?"

For a long while she did with her mouth and hands, until his head fell back against the chair. "When we get through this, we're taking a long vacation," he said.

"The last one you took didn't end so well."

He twisted his head to look at her chest where he'd worked one breast out of her cami. "Ended just fine."

He looked so contented, she hated to burst his bubble but better now than later. "Brian, I'm wanted, remember? Means I can't travel out of the country, means I have to dodge police all the time, means I can't use hospitals, means I'm cash only. Means that when you're with me you're all those things, too."

"Isn't that a little extreme?"

"No. It isn't. Right now, you're aiding and abetting, hiding a fugitive. If I'm caught, you're going down, too."

It didn't seem to register. He reached over, fixed her cami back into place. "We'll work something out, Delta. I haven't come this far with you to back away from a fight."

It wasn't any use arguing with him. He'd got something in that stubborn head of his and that was that. She'd have to deal with this herself.

CHAPTER

13

THIRTEEN

DELTA CLICKED AWAY at the Cause and FX laptop Gina had brought over the night before, her eyes, dry and itchy, fixed on the screen. Whether it was the adrenaline rush of the break-in, the throbbing ache of the dog bites or Brian's industrial-decibel snoring, she hadn't slept a wink. So she'd slipped from her spot tucked alongside Brian, dressed, brewed a pot of coffee and begun the job of comparing the files from *The Sweet Pepper* to the information from Susan Chang's bankbook.

Two hours into it, and so far no connection between Susan and Matsuda. Susan's notes in the bankbook were cryptic initials and calculations that could be deciphered if she could match them to members, which meant systematically going through the membership list to find out who the various couples were. The evidence didn't have to stand up in a court of law, only convince the Yakuza, but she had to be dead certain who the traitor in Matsuda's camp was. If she made a mistake, it would be fatal. The search was slow-going, and other than a few of the more prominent swingers—actors, musicians, executives and lawyers—she'd already skipped over dozens of names as her web searches drew blanks. Here she was at the 'R's, and still absolutely nothing.

She poured the dregs from the pot into her cup and swallowed a mouthful of lukewarm coffee gritty with grounds. The bedside clock said 5:42. The call from the black ball-buster would come at midnight that evening, so that left eighteen hours. Eighteen hours for her to get them all free or clear or—. No, she wasn't going there. Death was not an option. Mr. Hadrian had drummed into her and Akeno to plan the exit before ever entering. Somewhere in this database was everyone's exit, she just had to find it.

And then what? The question had fizzed and banged about her brain since her conversation with Brian last night. She could go back to Myrtle Beach, but for what? The Yakuza had killed her poor dogs, and her sudden disappearance meant her alias was blown, which meant her job would be gone and her house put up for rent. Her barebones life meant there weren't even any significant possessions to go and recover, save for the money she had concealed behind a false panel. In the two years she'd been there, she'd made no real friends, keeping her own company in the same style as Mr. Hadrian.

She indulged in a look at the rumbling mound of Brian. God, he was such a—*boy*. Chased one adrenaline-fueled adventure after the other, damned the consequences, acted on faith that it would all work out in the end. The man had no exit plan. Yet, it was *her* that he worried about.

He'd never understand they had no future together. She'd tried to explain it to him. As long as there was a warrant out for her arrest, she couldn't have any kind of legitimate life. Being together would start out as inconvenient, and soon grow intolerable. Since meeting Brian a week ago, she no longer wanted to be the Delta Fox that she had been. She wanted to be safe, she wanted to love Brian, and most of all, she wanted to be free.

The monitor went blank. Delta had spent too long away from it. There was work to do, loved ones to save. She'd save herself later.

She moved on to the S's. No matches for Robert and Gale Sandworth. John and Beverly Sapper were owners of a sleazy but legit adult movie company. Next was Jeanelle Saramond, one of the few single members of the club. Delta typed in her name, and was surprised to see several hits come up on her. Selecting one, Delta read, and suddenly she felt a rush of triumph.

"Gotcha," she whispered.

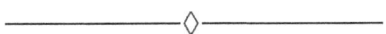

Brian woke to his phone playing Japanese anime pop music. Gina must've messed with it last night. Sometimes Ursula had a point about her. Eyes mostly closed, he fumbled for the phone, moaned as his balls shifted. The extra-strength ibuprofen had worn off. "Delta," he called out. "Wake up. Time to get our butts in gear."

His hand skimmed the sheets where she'd cuddled right beside him. He flung back the covers and sat up, his groin screaming at him. "Now where the hell are you?"

"Right here." He twisted to find Delta at the table, laptop open, chin in her hand, looking at him as if he were a slightly amusing sitcom. "You snore like a water buffalo with a sinus condition."

He fell back onto the bed. "How do you manage to hide in full view?"

"Helps that your eyes were closed. And," she said with

firm accusation, "that you didn't expect me to be here."

He opened an eye for that. "You're accusing me of not trusting a thief?"

"Look, I got your message last night about respecting your concern for me but you've got to believe me when I say I know what I'm doing."

Brian looked at her full-on. There were dark rings under her eyes, her knees were pulled up to her chin, and a fist tapped against her mouth. She was all balled-up energy.

He propped himself up on his elbows. "What's up, Delta?"

She launched from the chair onto the bed, landing cross-legged beside him. He was pretty sure he didn't feel the mattress shake at all. Sometimes, she really freaked him out. "Turns out Susan isn't the only one into the swinging scene. Looks like the Matsuda family has secrets."

"You mean the old man's a member of *The Sweet Pepper*?"

"No, but Ms. Jeanelle Saramond is."

"Who's she?"

"Matsuda's wife. She's registered under her maiden name, but I recognized her first name from the police report. I did a little digging on the Internet and found an article about the Matsuda wedding. It was a big event in Tokyo a few years back."

"So, this Jeanelle hired Susan to kill her stepson? That explains how Akeno wound up with the safe combination and access codes."

"Yep." This time, he did feel her bounce, right in his sore testicles. "Now, ask me about all the money Susan's been getting from the club members."

Brian stuffed a pillow behind his head and leaned back.

195

"So, Delta, what did you make of all the money Susan's been getting from the other club members?"

"Blackmail. The checks are coming at regular intervals and always for the same amounts. I calculated she's pulling in about forty grand a year between them all, and that's not counting the people who are paying in cash. I've recovered evidence from blackmailers before, and this amount barely ranks. The Matsuda break-in was her big take."

"She decided to graduate from thief to blackmailer to assassin. That's quite the criminal career she's got going there."

This time, Brian braced himself when she gave another bounce. "That's not all the news I have. Morgan's message has changed again. Looks like for once we've gotten a break."

"Great. So, now what?"

"Nothing we can do during the day but tonight I'd like to meet with Morgan. I can do the trick with the radios and binoculars again, but at another site."

"Why? What do we need from him other than the Miami files? We already have the scoop on Susan."

"I need to talk to him about something else." She pointed at him. "Don't look at me like that. This is a personal matter. It's got nothing to do with the situation we're in."

"Then, why didn't you talk to him about it the first time you met?"

Delta threw him an uncompromising look, and Brian relented. "Okay, okay, have it your way. I'll take you wherever you want, but don't expect me to be happy about it."

There was a moment of rocky silence, and then she slid a look to his midsection. "How are you doing?"

"Sore."

She frowned. "Still?"

196

What the—? "Imagine getting a boot to the clit. How would you feel twelve hours later?"

She shrugged. "Couldn't be any worse than giving birth, and most women are on their feet like two hours later."

"I'm not most women." And before he could correct the stupidity of that remark, she keeled over sideways onto the bed and was giggling like a madwoman, making the mattress jiggle. He whacked her one with a pillow.

"I'm going to work."

She sobered herself somewhat. "Are you well enough?"

"I can get ice packs there." He levered himself off the bed and headed to the shower, trying not to walk bowlegged. From the sputter and snort behind him, he hadn't succeeded. "And respect," he shot over his shoulder.

He closed the bathroom door with enough firmness to convey a message. Peals of her laughter broke through. Truth was he didn't mind her laughter, even if it was at his expense. It must be all that tension letting loose. She never stopped thinking or doing, never slept right, and now she'd snapped. It was the most beautiful sound he'd ever heard. Well, second to her orgasms. He could not wait for this business to be over so he could take her someplace where he could hear a lot more of both. Made it almost worth having blue balls. He touched them with compassion. Emphasis on 'almost'.

Jeanelle Matsuda pulled her Mercedes into the parking lot of the shopping center, her teeth gritted in fear and anger. At the very core of her arrangement with Susan Chang was that the thief *never* call her once the job was done, and especially not at her home. If her husband were to gain even the slightest inkling of the role she'd played in his son's death, he'd be worse than merciless. For such betrayal he'd see to it that Jeanelle had the most indescribably horrific demise his sadistic mind could conjure—and he could conjure quite a bit.

Yet the stupid woman had done what she'd been explicitly told not to do. Jeanelle had ended last evening's call quickly, saying she'd phone Susan back in the morning, and had been awake half the night fretting over it. Fortunately, she hadn't been shopping since her stepson's death, and so had managed to get out of the house on that pretext. She didn't dare use her cell in the event that her husband's security people were monitoring it, and could only pray that nobody had intercepted Susan's call.

In the mall, she strode directly to the public phones, punching in Susan's number. God help the stupid bitch if she didn't have a good reason for phoning, she thought, as the line started ringing.

"*Venice Beach Psychic Center*," Susan answered, her voice high-pitched with stress.

"What the hell is going on that you need to put my neck on the line?" Jeanelle hissed.

"I could ask you the same thing!" Susan snapped back. "You promised me Fox would be dead by now. I even leaked her address to your husband's people. Who do you have hunting her, the fucking boy scouts?"

Jeanelle's grip on the receiver tightened until her knuckles whitened. "You're calling me about *that*? You stupid girl, what difference does it make? Fox doesn't know a thing about what's going on, so who cares if she runs around a bit before they nail her?"

"Well, I guess I got kind of concerned when she broke into my fucking apartment last night! You said she'd be dead within a day of Akeno, and now two weeks later, she's climbing through my goddamn window! How the hell did she even know I was involved?"

The bottom fell out of Jeanelle's stomach. Fuck. "I thought your place was secure! What did she find?"

"Nothing damaging, from what I can tell, but the very fact that she was here means she must be piecing together what happened. I told you she was friendly with the cops, and they're probably helping her! I swear, you get rid of her or I'll make sure you regret it. I'm not going down for this alone."

Jeanelle's back stiffened at the threat, but she bit back a retort. Now was the time for a level head. Kannon would finish the job soon, and she was in a position to put pressure on him. "I'll do what I can, and I'll contact you as soon as I'm able. Meanwhile, sit tight and *don't* phone me again. You understand?"

"What I understand is that unless Fox is dead within twenty-four hours I'm going to have to leave L.A. and go into hiding. You think a million is going to last me the rest of my life? You think I want to live being hunted like some fucking animal?"

"You won't be. Just do as I say and wait for my call."

The woman began to say something else but Jeanelle hung up on her, leaning against the phone to calm her pounding heart. Settling herself with considerable effort, she picked up the phone again and dialed Kannon's number.

"Hello, Mr. Takahama," she greeted him when he answered. "I'm phoning to get an update."

As always, Kannon's voice was cold as a dead fish. "Where are you calling from? This isn't your cell or home number."

"I believe you have more pressing concerns."

"I stand by the estimate I gave you earlier, Mrs. Matsuda. You can tell your husband that the matter will be dealt with very shortly. Of that, I'm extremely confident."

"I should warn you that my husband is running out of patience. He's displeased with your slow progress and is prepared to dismiss you and your men if you don't get results soon. I hope you're not expecting to be forgiven any more slip-ups."

"I could repeat myself," Kannon replied, "but that would probably annoy both of us."

Arrogant bastard, but there was little else she could say. Kannon never had responded well to threats. "Call us as soon as you're successful." She emphasized the last word, and reached to disconnect.

An instant before getting there, she heard the dial tone.

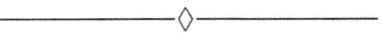

Brian flipped through the Miami report on Akeno's murder, then dropped it onto the passenger seat. He'd been waiting for Delta for almost half an hour now, and anxiety was making him twitchy. The detective had delivered the file as promised, and hadn't offered any protest at being frisked and driven to an unscheduled meeting with her, so it was unlikely that he would be trying to make an arrest. Still....

Damn, he wished that she would let him know what was ticking in that brain of hers. He couldn't ever imagine ruling her life, or ever wanting to for that matter, but every time she left him out in the cold, it gnawed at him. Gnawed because he worried about her, but more to the point because it meant that she didn't need his help. And the fact of that matter was that he needed her to need him.

All he could think about was getting her back to the safe walls of their hotel room. They'd have to go through the file, and he'd felt his stomach clench at the gory photos of Akeno's body. Seeing them would be brutal on Delta, and as tough as she was, he knew that what she'd need tonight was comforting. And he'd give it to her.

At last, he spotted her coming down the sidewalk. Something was wrong. No, not wrong. Different. She had always looked confident, but in a guarded, edgy sort of way. Now, she seemed somehow more open, softer, as if she'd finally dropped that chip on her shoulder. Something happened with Morgan, and despite how well she looked, it pissed him off that he didn't know, and wouldn't be told, what it was.

He tossed the file into the back seat, got out and opened the passenger door for her. She gave him a huge smile before sliding in, but by the time he sat down next to her, it was gone. She had the file on her lap, and was already rifling through it.

He eyed her as he started the car. "You sure you don't want to hold off on that till we get back to the hotel?"

Her eyes didn't leave the papers. "It's okay. I can read while you drive."

Brian sighed, but left her to it. It wasn't going to be a long trip anyway, and the photos were at the back. Maybe they'd be at the hotel before she got to them.

There was silence as Brian negotiated the Friday night traffic, and he was thinking she wasn't going to tell him anything when she spoke. "It says here that Akeno checked into the motel a week before he was killed. He was using a high-quality forged Canadian passport under the name Edward Ho, but they were able to trace him back to Los Angeles by checking where he'd flown in from. It goes on to mention that he didn't check in alone, but that his 'wife', Sandra Ho, was with him. One of the bellhops remembered her well enough to give the cops a description, and it matches Susan perfectly."

Brian nodded, his eyes on the road.

"It also says that Akeno had a large parcel placed in the hotel's safe upon check-in, and that very early the next morning, Susan had it taken out again. Akeno spoke with the people at the front desk later that day, trying to locate her, and when he discovered that the package was gone, he was visibly upset. They offered to call the police, but he declined their assistance and left."

For several minutes she read on quietly, and when she did choose to speak again, he could hear her suppressed fury. "According to the hotel records the 'Do Not Disturb' sign was up on his room for several days after that, and he made no phone calls and only ordered a couple of small meals from room service. The first time the staff remember seeing him again was the morning that he was—k-killed." He could hear her swallow but true to form, Delta carried on. "He had a light breakfast in the hotel's restaurant, then left. He was shot down the block not two hours later. The gunman killed him at close range, and was described by different witnesses as being Black or Hispanic or Polynesian, but they all agreed he was dressed in a dark suit."

"Sounds like he went out for a walk and Takahama was waiting when he got back," Brian observed, turning into the parking lot of their hotel.

Delta didn't answer, nor did she say anything else till they had reached their room. Leaving the file on the table, she sat on the bed. Her shoulders sagged and eyes closed. Thank Christ she hadn't got to the photos. "It was a sad way for him to die," she said softly.

Brian crouched before her, gently taking her hands in his.

"If you want to talk about it, Delta, I'll listen."

She opened her eyes, looking at him. "We were best friends, Brian. We went on a lot of adventures in this city."

He squeezed her hand tenderly, encouraging her to continue, but she didn't. "It's okay," Delta said. "I know you're trying to help, but it's not something I want to talk about right now."

Shut out again. He was about to speak when the phone rang. Checking the bedside clock they watched the digits switch to twelve o'clock. Brian picked up.

"Brian Chanse here."

"Mr. Chanse." The assassin's voice was hard as stone.

"Yes, it's me."

"Do you have something useful?"

"Yes, we do. We need to meet, show you what we got. It'll convince you that Delta's not the person you should be hunting and, just as importantly, who you should be after."

There was a grunt. "Lobby. Now."

The line went dead.

CHAPTER
14
FOURTEEN

THE ELEVATOR DOORS opened to reveal Kannon Takahama and two henchmen standing in the small lounge area, faces as grim as their profession. Aside from them, the lobby was deserted, and Delta and Brian stepped out into a palpable silence. The henchmen moved forward to frisk them both, by hand and then with bug detectors, before the assassin gestured to a couch. Once they were seated, he did the same, easing into a large armchair across from them as his two men flanked him.

He appraised Brian, then turned his cold gaze on Delta. "Convince me."

Of the long line of situations Brian had seen Delta operate in, none gave him a greater rush of pure admiration than as he watched her lay out their case to the Yakuza. In a light, efficient voice and with steady hands, as if she were his personal assistant briefing him on a sticky piece of company business, she covered the table with the police reports, membership files, pictures and miscellaneous documents. She explained the process of her investigation with Brian, and how they had pieced together the resulting evidence. Her presentation held as little conjecture as possible.

The man listened, examined the documents handed to him with clinical interest. In fairly short order, Delta came to the conclusion of her story, and they waited for him to render his judgment.

There was a long silence as Kannon studied the lineup on the table, and only after several minutes did he speak. "You've convinced me, Ms. Fox, that I need to add Ms. Chang to my list. You have not convinced me that Mrs. Matsuda was behind this. As for the matter of your guilt, that's immaterial."

"What do you mean, 'immaterial'?" Brian asked. "Isn't your job to take revenge on the right person?"

"What matters is not whether Ms. Fox is guilty, but what my employer's opinion is."

"If that's so, then why haven't you killed us yet?" Delta asked.

"Because I happen to hate Mrs. Matsuda, and would greatly enjoy the opportunity to see her suffer."

There was no mistaking the iron punch behind those softly spoken words. He laid it out squarely for them. "You have linked Ms. Chang to the murder. Do the same with Mrs. Matsuda, and her husband will likely retract his order to kill you. I don't have unlimited time, so you'll have to come up with something fast."

Delta nodded, as if this was a totally reasonable response, and Brian could see how in the L.A. underworld it was. Matsuda's objective was revenge. He didn't care who *didn't* kill his son. He wanted to punish the people who *did*. Convincing Kannon of Delta's innocence was only the first step. Now they had to convince Matsuda himself with rock solid evidence. Only then could they hope to avoid becoming a blast point for the gangster's rage. Even if Delta was granted the opportunity to go through all the circumstantial evidence with the crime lord, piecing together the mosaic of deception and betrayal for his edification, why wouldn't the old shogun just wipe her out for good measure? He sounded more than happy to take a shotgun approach to nailing his son's assassin. All that had come out of this meeting was a short reprieve in their sentence.

Then, to Brian's surprise and relief, Delta said "I understand, and I believe I know a way in which I can get that kind of proof. It may require a small amount of your aid, however."

The assassin's face remained expressionless. "What's your idea?"

"I'll need a little time to think through the details, but I could present a plan to you in the morning. Would that be acceptable?"

The man to whom she'd once shown mercy gave her a dark look, then nodded. "I'll come to your room at seven tomorrow morning."

Their strange meeting concluded, the assassin exited through the hotel front doors, leaving his two thugs to escort Delta and Brian to their room. Brian waited until they were inside before speaking. "Well, we're still alive. That's good. So, what's the plan?"

Delta collapsed into a chair. "I don't have one."

Brian felt winded. She'd lied and gotten away with it. For once, he was grateful for her deception. "Well, then," he said, "we'd better hurry up and come up with one or we're not going to be having a very pleasant morning."

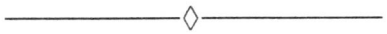

Susan Chang stared at her bedroom ceiling, hot with

206

hatred. She had lived in her mother's apartment for most of her life, and was used to the noises of Venice Beach at night. The distant shouts of rowdy drunks. The occasional roar of a muscle car as it raced down Pacific Avenue. The rattle of shopping carts as the homeless scavenged the path out front for bottles and cans. But on nights such as this, when her fears and losses clawed at her mind, each sound triggered another ugly memory.

She hated so many so much. The hypocrites at *The Sweet Pepper* who preached openness and freedom, then paid her to keep her mouth shut about their sex lives. Her father who rejected her despite her obvious talents, leaving her training forever unfinished. Akeno, for all the guilt he'd left in her heart, where it ate at her whenever she remembered his trusting face. But most of all she hated Delta Fox. The thief who'd stolen her father from her. The replacement who had stepped in to fill the void in his life while she was left to feel empty and broken and unworthy.

Hate fueled her revenge, made her feel powerful and complete. It had given her the strength through her adult life to plot against her father and his students. It would have been perfect if Fox was killed at Myrtle Beach, and she added the incompetent assassins to the list of those she despised.

It was almost three in the morning when she tamped down her emotions enough to let sleep come, and just past three when the phone at her bedside rang, jarring a bark from the pit bull at the foot of her bed.

"Shut up," Susan mumbled, prodding the dog lightly with her foot as she fumbled for the phone. "Hello?"

"Good morning, Susan. This is Delta."

Susan shot upright in bed. The hate flared and Susan breathed deep to bring it under control. And then to show the

207

bitch she couldn't be intimidated, she held on for a few more beats before she answered. "What do you want?"

"Money. Specifically the money Akeno and you stole from Matsuda."

She was guessing, trying to blackmail her. "No idea what you're talking about."

"Try looking in that hidden safe you had installed. That ought to jog your memory."

Susan's eyes shot to the bedroom armoire. How the hell did her nemesis know so much? "You're crazy," she responded.

"Not really. Because of you I'm on the run from the Yakuza, and it would be handy to have a few hundred thousand extra. You'll give it to me or I'm going to make sure they wind up on your tail as well."

"And how do you think you're going to do that, bitch?"

"I happen to have a report on the police investigation into Akeno's death," Delta continued calmly. "Seems the hotel staff remembered you pretty well, what with you taking the money out of their safe while he was sleeping."

Susan laughed, but even she could hear the edge of fear in it. "You're joking. That could be anyone."

"It could be, but I also have a picture of Akeno and you together at *The Sweet Pepper*, and the date and number of the flight Akeno took to Miami, and if I'm guessing right you were on it, too. Perhaps under the name Sandra Ho. But then, you probably didn't even bother using a fake I.D., did you? I mean, why go to the trouble when you didn't think anyone would connect you to the murder? You still think I'm kidding around?"

Hatred and fear exploded through Susan. "You black-mailing little—"

"You're not one to talk about that, Susan," Delta interrupted. "I know all about the people you've got your hooks into. You're a thief, you're a blackmailer and you're a murderer. I know all your secrets, and unless you want the whole world to know too, you'll shut up and do exactly what I tell you...."

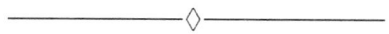

Their wakeup call came at six in the morning, but the phone only had a chance to ring once before Brian stifled it. Rolling over, he looked into Delta's bright blue eyes, which too had just opened.

"Good morning." She smiled, running a cool hand over his chest.

"Good morning," he replied, reaching for her breasts. "Looks like today's the big day."

He half-expected her to stretch and jump out of bed. Hell, he'd half-expected her not to still be in bed. Instead she cuddled right tight against him, fitting a warm breast snugly into his hand. "You know, Brian, even if this is my last day, I couldn't think of a better way to wake up."

He gave her breast a light squeeze. "I like the words, hate the meaning. Today isn't going to be your last, Delta."

"I don't think so either, but we're not in the clear yet."

His face must've shown his unease because she carried on in her light, practical way. "It's just that nothing is for sure. It never is. But we did the best we could, you and me both, and if that isn't good enough, then it's nobody's fault."

Where was this coming from? Shifting to his elbow, Brian looked squarely down at her. "Delta, why are you talking like that? The plan we came up with is going to work. Hell, even the bastard they hired to kill you is willing to help you out. Once all this is over, you and me will have all the time in the world."

Delta lowered her eyes for a moment, then raised them again in a blaze of blue. "Brian... all my life I've fantasized about meeting someone like you, and for the fact that it happened at all, I'm grateful. You're a good man, and you deserve everything life's given you."

He made to reply but she stilled his lips with her fingertips. "I'll shut up now, but I just wanted you to know how I felt. Okay?"

Brian kissed the hand, then bent to kiss her mouth. "Okay, Delta." Let her think whatever. At the end of the day, they'd come up with a plan. They always did.

Over the next hour, the two showered and dressed, and Brian recognized the build-up in himself of the same focused energy that came when he prepared for a stunt. It was an altered state, one of calm and anticipation, not a dismissal of the danger but attuning to it. And from the set of Delta's face, she was having the same experience. True adrenaline partners.

At one minute past seven, there was a knock at the door, and Brian answered it to admit the gunman.

"You're finally here," Brian said, before the other could speak. "Sleeping in while we've already been hard at work on our kickass plan."

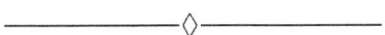

Saturday morning found Jeanelle leaning against the sill of her bedroom window, puffing on a cigarette as she surveyed the view of the Santa Monica Mountains. Her husband didn't care for her smoking, repulsed by the smell it left in her clothes and hair and mouth, so she had quit soon after meeting him. This morning, with the old dragon still in bed and unlikely to rise for a few more hours, she had decided to risk the brief indulgence for the sake of her nerves.

Two days ago she only mildly cared as to when Kannon killed Fox, his failure to do so a reason to provoke his pride. Now the issue burned like a branding iron. Every moment that the thief was out there was torture, and she had to work to keep her uncertainty from blossoming into panic. She'd planned Kei's murder so carefully, it was inconceivable—it was unfair—that the scheme should come apart when she was so close to success, yet that was exactly what was happening.

There was a quiet tap at the door, and cursing under her breath, Jeanelle flicked the cigarette away and hurried to answer it. The knocking hadn't woken Hiro, and the last thing she needed was him being disturbed.

It was one of the maids, eyes lowered in subservience, a sealed envelope in her outstretched hand.

"What's that?" Jeanelle hissed.

"Excuse me, ma'am. A man delivered this to the front gate a few minutes ago for you. He said it was urgent."

Jeanelle snatched away the envelope. "Go."

The maid bowed, and scurried off.

Glancing quickly at her sleeping husband, Jeanelle stole out of the bedroom and rushed down the stairs to the privacy of the library. There, she tore open the blank envelope. Inside was a picture of Susan and Akeno, taken at *The Sweet Pepper*, and a photocopy of a partial list of the club membership with her name highlighted. Her breath catching in her throat, Jeanelle pulled her attention to the neatly printed note.

Meet me at noon today outside the main entrance of Griffith Observatory. Don't be late. – DF.

Jeanelle checked the library clock. 9:53. What was she going to do? She could call Kannon and direct him to the site, but how was she going to explain how she'd come by the information? She couldn't just ignore it. The next letter could be addressed to her husband, and as Fox had obviously uncovered the plot, it would serve as her death warrant. The fact that Fox hadn't done that already could mean only one thing—blackmail.

Feeling faint and nauseous, Jeanelle sat down in an armchair, wracking her brain for a way out of this nightmare. Susan might be able to kill the bitch. She was more than proficient with a gun, but then again Fox no doubt knew this as well. The maid had said a man had delivered the letter, which meant the thief had backup. She might even have her own hired guns.

Kannon had assured her that Fox would be eliminated within a few days, so perhaps all she needed to do was stall. If the thief didn't realize how close the assassin was on her trail, the matter could resolve itself without having to pay so much as a dime.

But what if it was a trap? If Fox was working with the police, perhaps in return for clemency on the charges she was already wanted for, the picture and note might just be a ploy to lure her into incriminating herself. It seemed no matter what she did, she risked putting herself in harm's way.

There was only one thing to do. She had to get in contact with Susan and see if between the two of them, they couldn't finish off their mutual enemy once and for all.

Returning to the bedroom, Jeanelle dressed faster than she had in years, stealing out again without waking her husband. A couple of minutes later, she was pulling out of the front gate, and driving her Mercedes directly to the nearest payphone, she dialed Susan's number.

The phone rang several times before at last a somewhat elderly voice answered. The mother.

"I need to speak to Susan. It's important."

"I'm afraid she's away on business this morning. Who, may I ask, is calling?"

Jeanelle slammed down the receiver. "Useless biddy." She'd have to arrange another meeting as soon as possible and enlist Susan's aid then. Like it or not she was on her own, and getting back into her car, drove to Griffith Park.

The weekend having arrived, the place was crowded, not just with tourists but locals, all enjoying the beautiful green expanse of meadows and forest in the very center of Los Angeles. Though it wasn't even noon, it proved difficult to find a parking spot anywhere near the observatory, and she had to circle several times before spotting one.

She steamed towards the Art Deco façade of the building, pushing her way through a throng of milling tourists before halting in her tracks. There, standing by the door, was Susan.

"What the hell are you doing here?" Jeanelle demanded, marching up to her.

Susan's eyes widened. "What the—? I could ask you the same thing!"

The two women looked in sudden dismay at one another, realizing they'd been summoned by the very same person. Before they could react, she was coming up the steps towards them.

"Hello there, ladies. Beautiful day, huh?"

Both women regarded Delta with all the affection nor-mally reserved for a poisonous viper. "What game are you playing here, Fox?" Susan growled.

"No game. I just wanted to have you both here so I

wouldn't have to explain things twice. Each of you has lots of money, and you're both going to start making payments to me. I was thinking ten grand a month, the first payment being today. I believe you brought along the cash, Susan?"

Her eyes burning with hate, Susan pulled a thick envelope from her pocket, handing it to Delta.

Jeanelle looked Fox up and down as the thief opened the envelope and inspected its contents. She was as small as Susan, and while fit, was hardly threatening. How such a creature could have eluded a hunter like Kannon boggled her mind. Nevertheless, there was no choice but to deal with her, at least for now. "I'm afraid there's no way I could make any payment to you today, Ms. Fox. My husband controls the money in our household, and I don't get anywhere near that amount as an allowance."

Delta looked at her in mock sorrow. "Gee, that is a problem, isn't it? I guess you'll just have to pay in jewelry. One of those diamonds on your fingers will cover off this month. I'll let you pick which one."

"But these are gifts," Jeanelle protested.

Delta responded with a contemptuous laugh. "And you thanked the man by having his son blown away. You give me one of those rings now, or both you and Chang here are going to get a taste of what my life's been like lately."

"But I just paid you!" Susan gasped.

"Is it my fault the two of you are tied into this together? Either you both pay or you both die. One way I get cash, the other I get revenge, and while I'd prefer the former, I'll settle for the latter."

Jeanelle's hand clenched at the sheer audacity of the little bitch.

"Just give her the ring, Jean," Susan snapped, scanning

the crowd. "I don't want to spend all day here."

Setting her jaw, Jeanelle twisted off a penny-sized diamond from her finger, dropping it into Delta's outstretched palm.

"Thanks," Delta said, as if the payment were nothing. "Starting exactly four weeks from today, at exactly the same time, the two of you are going to be coming back to this spot and handing over ten grand to an associate of mine. Fail to pay, and I'll make sure Matsuda hears the truth. My man will be here for fifteen minutes only, so being late is going to be a life and death decision."

"If you live till then," Susan snarled.

Delta shrugged. "If I die, even if it's from choking on a bread roll, my man will make sure the police know the whole story. Both the cops and the Japanese mafia will come a-knocking, and take it from me, that's not somewhere you want to go. Better hope I stay real healthy."

She tucked the money down the front of her cami and slipped the ring onto her middle finger, wiggling her hand so the facets flashed and sparkled. "Pretty, huh? Now ladies, I'm going to go. I want you two to stay here for at least five minutes, then you're free to leave." Without another word, she turned her back on the women, trotted down the front steps, and cut to the parking lot as if she didn't have a care in the world.

The two women waited in silence, checking the time every thirty seconds. Not three minutes had passed when Jeanelle's patience ran out. "This is ridiculous. I can't stand around here all day."

"You can see why I wanted her dead," Susan said. her dark eyes having traced Delta like crosshairs until her enemy had vanished from view.

Jeanelle rubbed the empty spot on her finger. "You'll get your wish. One of my husband's men is close to catching her. He's one of the best manhunters in the world. She won't last long."

"Maybe not, but that won't stop the guy she's working with from blackmailing us after she's dead. It's wishful thinking that this is going to end anytime soon. You can trust me on that."

The woman was right, but Jeanelle was determined not to worry about it until she had to. She headed back to her car, not caring what Susan did. The ring was just a trinket compared to what she'd have at her fingertips soon enough. Hiro was old, and the death of his son had struck him a blow that was already visibly sapping his vitality. Without an heir, all his wealth would go to her, and with it, she could have all that she deserved without ever having to debase herself again.

Approaching her car, she noticed it was leaning oddly, and coming around to the driver's side of it, she saw why. A rear tire was completely flat. Fox had made sure she wasn't going to be tailed. Jeanelle pulled out her phone to call roadside assistance. She was beginning to dislike Fox almost as much as Susan did.

CHAPTER 15
FIFTEEN

JEANELLE GUNNED PAST the security gate of her home, ignoring the expressionless guards. She swung to a stop before the front doors (someone would park the Merc in the garage later), but no sooner had she set foot on the threshold than it swung open to reveal Kannon.

Jeanelle froze, but it only took a second for her to recover. "What are you doing here? Who let you in?"

The assassin ignored her questions. "I came to report that I caught Fox. She won't be troubling your husband anymore."

"What?" Jeanelle asked, stunned by the sudden news. "You mean she's dead?"

Kannon showed her nothing. "You know my profession, Mrs. Matsuda."

A wave of relief flowed though Jeanelle, and she couldn't help but smile. The timing was miraculous, and as much as she disliked the hitman, she was grateful to him at that moment. "Congratulations."

His deadpan expression showed that he cared nothing for her praise. "I just gave the news to your husband. He's in his office."

"Well then, if you'll excuse me I'll go and see him."

His next words stopped her. "Terrible thing to lose someone you love."

There was something in his voice that made her turn back. "I suppose it is."

"A man would give up his life for someone he loved. He'd certainly never forget them."

This was about his wife. When she'd died, he'd been crushed. He'd recovered in time, but Kannon was still weak when it came to his daughter. What was her name again? Oh yes, Zoe.

"And how is Zoe doing? I remember she took it so hard when her mother died." She didn't even try to sound as if she cared.

"Doing well. Your husband has agreed to fund her education. I'm grateful for his generosity."

"Well, well, look at that. Kannon Takahama has a soft side."

"We all have vulnerabilities. Like the man you hired to arrange the car accident. He talked just to make the pain stop."

Jeanelle remembered the man she'd hired. She couldn't imagine what Kannon had done to make him beg for mercy. A chill rippled her skin, raising goose bumps on her bare arms. Never mind. Kannon couldn't touch her.

"You best be very careful with your accusations, Mr. Takahama. You work for my husband. You need my husband. And that means you need me." She spun on her heel, for once, *for once* cutting him off before he was done.

She knocked at the office door and immediately heard her husband beckon her inside. She entered and her heart stopped.

It was Delta Fox. She was seated on the other side of the desk from her husband, and in the chair beside her was a man, likely the one the little bitch was working with.

One of her husband's guards slid a chair over beside Delta, and Hiro flicked his hand for her to sit. Her heart had restarted and now pounded in her chest.

"Hiro…who are these people?"

"Sit."

Obediently she moved to the vacant chair. No sooner was she seated than Kannon entered, closed the door behind him and took a position directly behind Delta. So, this was it. Fox had made up a story in a last ditch effort to save herself. But she knew Hiro. She knew that out of pride he'd not want to find his own wife guilty. He'd not want to see the truth.

Her husband rested a hand on a neat stack of pictures and documents. Police evidence about Kei's death. "Where were you just now?"

"I went out for a drive, that's all. I've been cooped up in this house for days. Please, Hiro, what's all this about?"

"Did you go to Griffith Park this morning?"

"No. I went to the mall."

"Did you meet Miss Fox today?"

It was her word against the bitch's. "No. Why would I?"

Hiro looked up at Kannon. "You're certain it was her?"

"Yes, sir. I had a clear view through my binoculars, and my men identified her as well."

Jeanelle swallowed sudden bile. "He's lying! He's hated me since the day he met me! He didn't like taking orders from a white woman, so he's trying to turn you against me!"

"We also took photos," Kannon added.

Hiro's cold eyes shifted from Kannon to her. He opened a top drawer and held up the ring she'd given Delta at the park. "How do you explain this?"

Jeanelle knew it would be pointless denying the ring

belonged to her. Like all of Hiro's gifts of jewelry, it was a custom piece. "That's…that's my ring!"

His voice rumbled like distant thunder. "I know it's yours. I'm asking why you gave it to Miss Fox."

"She…she must have stolen it! I haven't worn it in awhile. I didn't know it was missing. Please, Hiro, you know how much I adore you. What lies have these thieves and murderers been telling?"

Fox's man cleared his throat quietly, drawing the crime lord's attention.

"Sir, if you call your provider for roadside assistance, you'll find that your wife's car had a tire changed out by the Griffith Observatory this morning."

The little bitch slanted her a look. "I suppose I stole your Mercedes, too."

Jeanelle knew they had her. She couldn't win on reason. She threw herself at her husband, her hands gripping his arm, the tears streaming down her cheeks not all fake. "All right, so I was there! I gave her the ring. They were blackmailing me, Hiro! They said that they would frame me for Kei's death if I didn't pay them, and now they're doing it anyway! You must know that I could never do such a thing. I loved Kei as if he were my own son. You remember how we used to go out—"

Hiro closed his hands into fists, his arm muscles cording under her hands, fury in his eyes as they locked on her. "Why did Kei come to this office that night, Jeanelle?"

"Why are you asking me? He must have heard the thieves!"

He gestured at the office door. "That's an inch and a half thick. What was he doing up in the middle of the night? What did you do with him when you two went out together? Fuck? Is that why he came here? To meet you?"

"No! We went to movies. We went shopping." Desperately Jeanelle pointed at Fox. "This bitch killed Kei, and now she's trying to destroy me too! This is Fox's doing. She's the liar. She was Akeno's partner. Everybody knows—"

Hiro raised his hand, silencing her in mid-sentence. Slowly his piercing gaze moved from her to Kannon, on to Delta's man, and then finally settled on Delta. "You've accused my wife of murder and betrayal, Miss Fox. What do you have to say for yourself?"

Jeanelle loathed the bitch but now as she watched, she experienced another vicious emotion. Jealousy. For Delta stretched out her hand and her man took it. A bold yet simple declaration of love and all that love gave—strength, purpose and always, always, victory. Kannon had had that once, and she'd taken it from him. And now Fox had it, and in the pit of her heart, Jeanelle knew that because of it, she'd lost.

Fox looked the man Jeanelle most feared straight in the eye, her voice as firm as iron. "I say that you're a smart enough man to know a lie when you hear it. Akeno robbed you, Susan murdered your son, but it was your wife that orchestrated both crimes. I'm the one that revealed this, and in return, I ask for nothing more than my life, and that of my partner's."

Her husband folded his hands on the desk. He closed his eyes, and slowly the seconds ticked by. The whole world seemed to be holding its breath as he sat there, motionless as a boulder, and after what seemed an eternity, he spoke. "It was not any of you that brought misfortune upon me," he said quietly. "I was the one that allowed an enemy into my home. I alone failed my son."

Opening his eyes, he looked at Delta. "You did what you did to save your own skin, thief. I owe you nothing, nor do you owe me. Now get out of my home."

Delta and her man stood and walked calmly to the office door.

"Hiro, no!" Jeanelle cried, her world collapsing.

"Don't cry," he said softly. "You have no reason to cry... yet."

Brian closed the office door, muffling Jeanelle's scream of pure terror. Hands joined, they walked down the stairs and out of the house, not pausing until they were inside his car a block away. Relief and exhilaration swept through him, and he gave a fierce whoop of joy.

"Delta, you did it! You did it!" He gave her a hard, smacking kiss.

Delta gave it right back at him. "*We* did it, Brian. I'd be roadkill on a New Mexican highway if you hadn't happened along."

Christ, this was one sweet moment. He rubbed her cheekbone with his thumb. "Well, roadkill, life's strange, isn't it? You know, I've never been more scared in my whole life in the time leading up to that meeting."

"Yeah, well, nothing like the threat of death to crank up the adrenaline level," she said, quick and bright.

Brian knew damn well she was deflecting him, so this time when he kissed her he made it long and slow, something there was no getting around. "It wasn't my death that frightened me," he whispered against her lips. "It was yours, Delta. I honestly don't know what I would've done if anything had happened to you. I don't think you realize how much—"

"Don't." She pulled back. "Listen, Brian. I know we need

to talk about things, the future and that, but right now, I just need to get out of this place. Okay?"

Brian studied her. Her face had lost its freshness, and lines of strain pulled across her forehead. Something was troubling her, and he tried to quell the worry that automatically rose up in him whenever she was in distress. "Okay."

They drove in silence, and then as a strip mall came into sight, Delta asked him to pull in so she could use a payphone. His cell phone was in his pocket, but he didn't offer it to her, and he didn't ask her what it was about. No point. Maybe, eventually, she'd come to trust him enough. Maybe she'd come to realize that life wasn't meant to be lived alone. Meanwhile, he'd wait. He now had the luxury of time. He swung into the parking lot and pulled up by a phone booth, and she was out before he'd come to a proper stop. She kept her back to him during the call, which lasted no more than a couple of minutes, then she was beside him in the car again.

"I need you to drive me to one last place," she said quickly, her gaze fixed on the windshield. "It's a coffee shop in the downtown."

"Okay."

That got a reaction. She threw him a swift glance. "You're not going to ask me what it's about?"

"Would you tell me if I did?"

That earned him a smile. "I see your point."

His fingers curled over her strong yet fine-boned hand. "You know you could tell me if you wanted to, right?"

She gave his hand a hard squeeze and nestled it against her thigh. He pulled out of the mall, and their ride continued. As they approached the heavy traffic of the downtown, Delta's grip tightened. What the hell? Brian pulled up outside the coffee shop behind a nondescript blue Chevy, and was about to ask Delta what was the matter when the doors of the car ahead opened. Two men emerged, the one on the passenger side was Detective Morgan.

"It's a trap!" Brian swore and made to swing the car back out into traffic, but Delta wrapped her hand around his wrist.

"No, Brian. It's not." Her voice was quiet and steady. He stared into her bright, blue eyes and then back at the men who were now leaning against the car, discreetly giving them space.

"Brian. I'm turning myself in." Her voice had that deliberately calm tone that doctors used when breaking bad news to their patients.

Brian's mind reeled. His whole being reeled. He'd spent the drive, daydreaming about their future, about the things that they could do together, about hunting for a place to live together, about spending entire weekends practically living in bed, and in the blink of an eye, all that was gone because she'd made other plans.

"That's what the conversation last night with Morgan was all about, wasn't it? You lied to me! You said that it had nothing to do with us."

Delta didn't back down. "I didn't lie. I said it has nothing to do with our situation with Akeno and the Yakuza. This has to do with Judge Hall. It has to do with what happened way before we even met."

"That's bullshit and you know it. This has everything to do with us. Otherwise, you'd have had the guts to tell me upfront. Instead you trick me into actually taking you right where you want to go. So, what have you got planned for the farewell scene? A handshake?"

"Nothing," she mumbled. "I had nothing planned."

He couldn't let it go. He couldn't let *her* go. "This is insane!"

She shook her head. "Brian, please. I want you to under-stand. Please listen. Please."

He stared out the window. Morgan's partner looked pointedly at his watch, and Brian returned with a rude gesture. Morgan tilted his head to the coffee shop, and the two detectives disappeared inside.

Delta talked. "Just a few days ago, I could have died and no one would've missed me. I've no family, and with Akeno dead and Mr. Hadrian out of my life, no friends. But, since meeting you, I've been needed. I've mattered. I've belonged some place and to someone. Despite everything, I was happy. You were the best thing that ever happened in my life."

Her use of the past tense was like a punch to the gut, and despite his better judgment, he hit back. "So, what the hell happened?"

Delta carried on. "It was exactly because of that, that I'm giving myself up. Brian, I've spent my whole life running and hiding. I made a living sneaking into places where I didn't belong and taking things that weren't mine. I've never been a member of anything because people will ask what I do and then I'd have to lie. The past two years, I worked a normal enough job, but I was always looking over my shoulder. I couldn't risk involving myself in anything personal. Then the Yakuza came knocking on the door, and I was right back to square one, by myself on the streets.

"But now, Brian, I have the chance to do it right. I've always tried to cover my debts, and now there's one I have to pay—to myself. I owe myself the right to a normal life. Do you understand, Brian?"

Sure, he understood. Good, old Brian, he thought bitterly. Make sure everyone else's needs were taken care of first. "And what about the debt you owe me? That you owe us?"

Delta looked genuinely confused. "I don't understand."

Brian snorted. "No, I don't suppose you would. Don't you have any consideration for what this is going to do to me? Is it all over between us? Is that what you want?"

"What exactly did you have in mind, Brian?" she shot back. "We couldn't travel safely. I couldn't get any kind of respectable job. You couldn't take me out to parties. I couldn't open a joint account with you. I'd still have to lead a hidden life. The best we'd have would be no better than an affair. I want a relationship with a future. If I go to prison, if I pay my dues, then that's what I'll get. A future."

"So, what are you saying? That you're doing this for us?"

"No, Brian. I already said I'm doing this for me. It's just that for there to be an 'us', first there has to be a 'me'."

Brian leaned back against the headrest, suddenly and utterly weary. He turned to look at her. He took in her incredible sky blue eyes, her smooth skin so susceptible to blushes, that wild gingery hair with its original blond glints. He'd given his heart to this woman, and she was handing it back to him. She didn't need him anymore. She was planning to create a life of her own, and there was nothing he could do to change it.

His mouth worked. He had to try twice, and even on the third attempt, it came out hoarse. "Goodbye, Delta."

She gave a small, tender, brave smile. "Goodbye, Brian."

He closed his eyes, willing her to leave before he broke down. So he didn't see that when she opened the door, she turned to him one last time, and mouthed 'I love you'.

He only heard the slamming of the door.

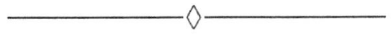

In the far recesses of his mind, Brian heard the urgent whisperings of a female voice and felt a relentless patting of his face. He turned his head away to escape its insistence, and a pain shot through his skull. His mouth was dry, his whole body felt hot and sore. The Yakuza had gotten him in the end, he thought, and were torturing him. What had they done to Delta? He moaned, "Delta?"

"Brian. It's Gina. Get up. Quick, before Ursula finds you like this. She'll skin you alive. You know I'm not joking." She was pushing under his shoulders to lever him up into a sitting position on the lunchroom cot.

The shifting sent a sudden wave of nausea through him and he collapsed back, pinning Gina underneath. She squeaked and squirmed out, and looked down at him in fear and pity and helplessness. That was when Ursula entered.

Ursula, precise and immaculate in her gray office dress, stopped just inside the door, and he imagined what she was seeing. Him lying on the bare mattress of the cot, stripped down to his boxers, a fifth of whiskey tucked against his side, his clothes strewn about, beer cans, all empty, littered over the tables and counter.

Through woozy vision, he watched Ursula pick her way across and stand over his stretched form. "Pathetic. Absolutely pathetic."

Gina spoke above him. "I've been trying to get him up for the past half-hour but no luck. He's just going to have to sleep it off, I guess."

"Sleep!" Ursula barked, causing Brian to jerk in agony. "Sleep! It's nearly eight o'clock on a Monday morning. If he wanted to sleep, he should have done it on the weekend. This sort of nonsense will not be tolerated." She strode over to the blinds and snapped them open, the bright morning sunshine cutting a piercing swath over Brian's face. He moaned and went into the fetal position, his arms wrapping protectively over his head. She strode back, and gripping him under his shoulders, hauled him upright in one, swift motion. Brian let out a low noise of anguish, and made retching noises. Gina cast about, and spotting the empty duffel bag, got it there in the nick of time.

She looked away, grimacing, until Brian was done. She zipped up the bag. "As soon as you're sober again, I'm asking for a raise."

Ursula returned with a pitcher of water. "Stand aside." And without hesitating, tossed the ice cold contents of it over Brian's head.

Brian yelped, and Ursula gave a small smile of satisfaction. "There. Better."

Between attending to company duties and redirecting phone calls and prying eyes from the lunchroom, it took the two women nearly an hour to bring their employer to full working consciousness, and another half-hour to get him in the shower and properly clothed. Although his body was now more or less resurrected, his emotions were as still as much in a turmoil as they had been when he'd driven to Cause & FX late Saturday night. He'd intended only to sleep, to escape the heartache of Delta for a little while. But then in the lunchroom, he'd spied the company liquor cabinet, and even then he'd planned to throw back only a single glass of whiskey. The mess and the pounding headache on Monday morning were the hell his good intentions had led to.

He lowered himself with infinite slowness into his office chair and stared at the papers on his desk. He swallowed a slug of black coffee and stared at the papers again. Christ, how was he going to get through the day? And the one after that? The days stretched out bleak and empty before him, just as they had before he'd met Delta. Except now it was worse, because now there were the memories of her. Of her scaling that wall, facing the Yakuza, smiling up at him their last morning together…

There was a quick knock and before he could answer it, in came Ursula and Gina. He groaned. What cruel and unusual punishment were they going to inflict on him now?

Ursula took the chair directly opposite from him and Gina perched herself on the corner of his desk. "Gina's got the intern on the front desk," Ursula said, "and you and I are officially taking a teleconference call and will be done in forty-five minutes. That's the time we've got to clear up this situation."

He opened his mouth to tell them to mind their own business, but then he saw their expressions. Gina and Ursula, who'd argue with each other over the color of the sky, were both looking at him with genuine worry and sympathy. Slowly, haltingly, he told them of the previous day's events, ending with Delta turning herself over to Detective Morgan.

"And so that's that," he finished, glancing from one to the other. Their initial looks of concern had redrawn themselves into ones of downright disapproval.

Gina stared wide-eyed at him. "You just left her there? By herself?"

"She didn't ask me to go with her," Brian protested, but even as he said it, he knew it sounded weak.

"Does she have legal representation?" Ursula demanded.

"No, I don't think so. I mean, I don't know. She handed herself over to them. Do you even need a lawyer for that?"

Ursula leaned forward, pinning him with her best Mother Superior look. "Are you telling me that she turned herself in without first engaging the services of a qualified lawyer?"

"Er…yeah."

"And that you've done nothing to assist her while she's being detained? Indeed, quite the opposite, you deliberately turned yourself into a drunken, filthy mess and left her alone in the prison system, which let me assure you, is not the most pleasant place to be. You," Ursula drew herself up even straighter, "ought to be ashamed of yourself."

Brian slid a look over to Gina. Her lips were pulled into the same thin, steely line as Ursula's. "She saved your life. She saved mine," Gina said not as harshly. "She still needs your help."

Ursula threw up her hands. "She's proud and stubborn. Are you looking for a perfect woman or one you can love?"

Gina stared at Ursula. "Wow, Ursa Major. That's like— romantic. Maybe there's hope for you yet."

Brian dropped his head into his hands. "You're saying I've been a jerk."

"Yes!" they said in unison.

His head still hurt, but not as badly, because now he understood. Yes, he'd been a jerk. He should've stayed with her instead of going off on a drunken bender. He'd tell her that the minute he saw her again. He'd tell her more, too. Once, he dealt with a few things here.

He turned to Ursula. "All right, then. Get in touch with a damn good lawyer and have him or her get in contact with Delta immediately."

He switched to Gina. "Find out where Delta is at right now, and see if you can pay her a visit. She could probably do with the company."

Ursula and Gina jumped to do his bidding. As Gina closed the door, Brian called her back in. "When you see

Delta, could you tell her that I'll be by later to see her?"

Gina grinned. "Already had it covered."

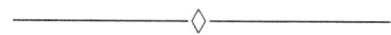

When the husky female guard led her to the visiting room that afternoon, it was all Delta could do to keep walking to the table where Brian sat. The corner of his mouth gave the ol' upturn as she slid into the chair across from him, and his eyes were soft with worry.

"Are you okay?" he said gently.

She nodded, but said nothing.

He cleared his throat. "I want to apologize for my behavior the other day. I was selfish and cruel. This can't be easy for you, and the last thing you needed was for me to bail out on you."

Delta bit her lip. "It's okay." The truth was that she'd never felt so utterly alone. Though Morgan had advised her what would happen when she turned herself in, she still wasn't prepared. Not for her small bag of possessions to be confiscated, her clothes replaced with the pumpkin jumpsuit, everything that had made her Delta Fox taken from her. She was put into a holding cell with three other women with trash mouths and trashed faces. She'd kept telling herself: *I'm not them. I've broken the law and I'm going to pay for it just like them, but I'm not them.* Then, another inner, ruthless voice would cut in: *If you're not them, who are you, Delta Fox? Because you aren't anyone on the outside, either. You are no one and you have no one.* She spent the nights on the cot with its stink of countless bodies, and pretended to sleep and tried not to think of Brian.

But here he was sitting in front of her, apologizing. Why

did he always have to be such a nice guy?

"Good of you to come by." She kept her voice even.

He gave her a long, thoughtful look. "You're angry with me."

"I am not."

"Well, you should be. I admit I was at you." He paused, then held up a hand, whether to stop himself or Delta from speaking, she wasn't sure. "Never mind. We don't have all day, and there are other, simpler, matters to clear up. First, Gina tells me that you refused bail. I know you can afford to post it, Delta. What was the reasoning there?"

She avoided his eyes, running her fingers around an old coffee ring on the table. He reached across and took her hand.

"No touching!" The guard barked.

Brian pulled back. "Come on, Delta. Talk to me."

She felt her face grow hot. "One of the conditions was that I had to provide my home address."

"Ah. I plan to get my own place very soon, but until then, I'm sure you'll be able to stay with Gina. So how about—"

"I can't impose on Gina," Delta protested.

"She has a great hairy dog and a great hairy cat and a great hairy hamster. And a girlfriend, too. You'll love it there. Now, as I was saying, in the meanwhile, you need to talk to a lawyer. Ursula has lined one up for you, and having worked in the prison system, she knows how to pick them. This one will be coming by later and will arrange the bail for you, okay?"

Delta squirmed in her chair. "But, Brian, I don't really need one. I'm planning to plead guilty, anyway. I don't want this to go to trial. I just want to serve my time and get on with my life."

Brian leaned across the table, his green eyes boring into hers. "Do you want that life to begin in ten months or ten years?"

"I've turned myself in for a nonviolent crime. They're going to go easy," Delta snapped. "Are we finished? You're only here because Gina and Ursula bullied you into it."

"Is that what you think?"

"Yes."

"Actually," he smiled sheepishly, "you're right."

His glib admission riled her. "Well, since you've done your duty, why don't you head on home?"

"Sure," Brian said equably. "It's not like I don't know where to find you. That'll be the one upside of your stint behind bars—knowing where you are at all times."

The ugliness of her surroundings and the uncertainty of her future and, above all, the loss of Brian swelled and broke inside Delta in a torrent of anger and hurt. "What? The upsides? Do you know what it's like being crammed in a cell with druggies and pushers, to have them look at you as if you're trash, because at least they've got a husband or a boyfriend or a girlfriend or a kid. At least, they've got somebody."

She felt tears rush up and she clamped her mouth tight to get control. *Come on*, Delta, she scolded herself, *do the right thing*. "Go, please."

"No. I did that on Saturday, and it hurt like hell, so I'm not doing it again. Look, when you told me what you planned to do, I think I could've handled it if I'd known ahead of time, if it was a decision we'd discussed and arrived at together. But when you didn't tell me I felt that you were trying to shut me out of your life, and Delta, I want to be part of it. I want to be the part that sees you through this. And after you come through it, and I know you will, I want to be that part that wakes up beside you every morning and that goes house-hunting together and makes plans. Do you know what I'm saying, Delta?

"I love you."

She couldn't have felt more stunned, couldn't have felt as if her life had changed more than at this moment. And when she spoke it was a kind of death-bed confession she made." No one in my life…has ever told me that…not my—not anyone."

His eyes held hers. "So, you don't think it's true?"

"I think it's rotten timing."

"You don't think it's going to last."

"Don't think it can."

Brian's eyes still held hers, their one point of contact. "This is what you don't get, Delta, and you really, really need to understand, okay?"

She nodded because that was all she could manage.

"You got that I worry about you, and you did your best not to give me cause. So now I'll tell you what you need to do." He leaned as close as the cold table allowed, and very slowly said, "You need to accept it.

"Use my love. You need to wear it when you're cold. Turn it on when the room's too quiet. Read it when you're bored. Pop it back when you're sick. Call it when you're in trouble."

"Marcia used you," she reminded him.

Brian shook his head. "My short time with you has shown me that I didn't give it to her willingly. I begrudged it. That wasn't fair to either of us. With you, it's another world."

"I-I don't know that I will use your l—it right."

"It won't break."

She softly voiced her real fear. "I might wear it out. And it's—my only one."

"You'd be surprised. Gina's pretty stuck on you. And

Ursula told me on my way out to drop her name at admin. Apparently the guards will see to it you're not bothered. If Ursula gives her name to a cause, believe me, it means something. And then there's my family. Do you know I've got seventeen nieces and nephews?"

Delta shook her head.

"Yep. Gina keeps their birthdays on a spreadsheet. There'll be a few among them who'll think it's awesome my girlfriend climbs buildings without slinging webs."

She gasped. "I don't think—"

"Take it, Delta. Take mine, take it all."

She swallowed. "I've nothing to give in return."

"Nothing at all?"

She knew what he wanted. He knew how to love somebody. She'd get it wrong, she didn't know how to love. "You don't want my love. It's small. And hard. And poky."

Brian sat back in his chair. It was the farthest he'd been from her since coming into the room. "Like a burr," he said. "Your love."

"Guess so."

"Your love sticks to everything, won't let go and can't be ignored."

"Yeah, okay."

She didn't mean it, the words just slipped out, but his head gave a warning tilt. "Okay, okay, I just meant that you're right. My—it's what you say it is. I don't want—"

"I'll take it."

She froze, her mouth open.

"No telling when something small and poky will come in handy."

Her mouth clamped shut but there was no stopping the tears this time. They burst from her in great hiccuping gulps.

Brian went for his front pocket and instantly the guard started towards him. The guard she'd forgotten all about. She'd never, never forgotten where everyone was in a room at all times. She was falling apart.

"It's just tissue." Brian smiled at Delta. "Gina made me pack them."

The guard held out her hand, and Brian passed the tissues over. In turn, the guard dropped them in front of Delta, except for one. She took it, wiped her wet eyes and her nose, and then returned to her position at the door.

Delta wiped and blew until there was a pile in front of her. "I'm not usually like this," she finally said.

Brian grinned. "Yeah. I've noticed."

She smiled back, completely stumped for words.

"Does this mean you'll see the lawyer this afternoon?"

"Yes."

"And that you'll come house-hunting with me and my mom?"

"Yes."

"And will you promise to obey me in all matters from now on?"

Her smile grew wide. "Go to hell, Brian."

He laughed and leaning across, and without the guard's objection, kissed each of her wet cheeks and then her warm, salty mouth. "Spoken," he whispered, "like a woman in love."

EPILOGUE

One year later

DELTA SIGNED FOR her belongings, then carried the cardboard box into the change room, intent on ditching the bright orange jumpsuit she'd donned for the past eleven months. She'd never considered herself fashion conscious, but she swore to Gina during one of their visits that once she got out she'd never wear a speck of orange again. Gina had shown up the next time with bright orange hair and a track suit in the same atrocious color. "It's my sympathy outfit. Y'know, like when people shave their heads for cancer patients."

It had also been Gina who'd come nearly two months ago with two huge shopping bags stuffed with clothes from which Delta could choose her 'Freedom Day' outfit. "Honey, I'll have to return the rest before Ursula sees the credit card bill. Her heart ain't what it used to be." She'd settled on a short, blue, sleeveless dress, and it was into this that she now changed. She examined her reflection in the mirror. Her blonde hair had grown back in, wisping around her neck. She experimented with tucking strands behind her ears and then with raking them forward. Never mind, what was she doing wasting her time in this prison bathroom when she should be beating a path out of here?

Not that her incarceration had been the grueling experience she'd expected. First, it hadn't turned out to be as long as she'd thought. Ursula had retained a lawyer as tough-minded as her, and very competent. He'd advised Delta to plead guilty to unlawful entry, but since she had willingly turned herself in, he managed to get the charges regarding her escape dropped. Better yet, he had cleared her of the crime of burglary, as Judge Hall had never reported anything actually stolen from his home. As a result, her time behind bars had been reduced by more than half, and being a model prisoner, she was paroled as early as possible. She'd be on probation for a couple of years, but after serving her time, that was nothing.

And the actual serving of the sentence hadn't been without its bright spots. Although Morgan wasn't interested in confessing his role in the Hall case, his sister was the prison's head of security, and had ensured that Delta was given every privilege possible without raising the ire of her fellow inmates. She had wound up working as a tutor in the facility's literacy program while earning her high school equivalency, and so had spent as much time in the classroom and library as in her cell.

Her educational pursuits had met with Ursula's approval. She had come to visit as often as Gina had, although the tenor of the conversation couldn't have been more different. While Gina's chatter was just that—light and gossipy and totally escapist—Ursula focused on matters of career and health and security. Delta had come to depend on those two women more than she'd ever thought possible.

And the two women that had endangered her life—

Jeanelle and Susan—had also paid their dues. That winter, Kannon had caught up with Susan at a small town in rural North Dakota. She was found frozen solid in the back alley of a cheap motel, apparently having jumped out a window only to be gunned down by the assassin as soon as her feet had touched the ground.

As for Jeanelle, the police hadn't located her until a week ago, when a couple of geologists had discovered her remains in the Sonoran Desert. The papers had been sketchy, but according to one report, she'd been stripped naked and staked out under the sun atop a nest of fire ants. Death couldn't have come more painfully.

Delta folded the despised jumpsuit, and under the escort of a guard, carried it down to the warden's office. The woman was a heavy-set, cynical chain smoker who barely gave her a glance when she entered. "Ready?"

"Yes, ma'am."

She waved a beefy hand at the line of papers on her desk. "Sign beside the 'X's."

Delta sat on the chair opposite and, balancing her box of belongings on her lap, she began signing them all quickly, not paying the slightest attention to what they were about. As she did, the warden asked, "What are your plans for the future?"

She shot the woman a sly look. "Waiting for me outside as we speak."

The warden smiled. "Wouldn't be the same plan that kept clogging our mail office for your entire stay?"

Delta laid a protective hand on the box. "The very same."

When she was done, the warden scrawled her own signature on them, shoved them into a file, and gave a curt nod. "You're free to go."

Delta shot to her feet. "Thank you, ma'am."

"Go on, get out. And don't ever come back, y'hear?"

Delta beamed at her. "Yes, ma'am!" And was gone.

She burst through the front doors and into the wide, outside world.

Free, at last.

Brian was there, leaning against a fast car. "Hi there, beautiful. Need a lift?" She grinned at him, sauntering over till their lips met. The kiss was long and soft and cool, like drinking from an oasis. And when it ended, they stayed in the circle of each other's arms.

"That depends," she answered. "Where you headed?"

"Palm Springs."

Delta raised an eyebrow. "Palm Springs?"

"Yeah, the company's finally got some downtime after a crazy schedule and the shooting wrapped up on the show last week, so we're good to go."

"Your show?"

"That's the one."

Brian had become the star of his own program, *Adrenaline Junkie*. While trying to land a contract, he had caught the eye of an executive who pushed the idea of a show about an extreme stunt guy. Delta had watched the pilot in a special screening with Brian and the warden. It had come with more warnings than a box of explosives, and had Brian outrunning lit dynamite. Delta told him it was dumb to risk his life for no good reason, and then she read in the credits that Brian was donating his salary to his newfound charity for homeless kids. And her heart had experienced its own kind of explosion.

"You're dating a Hollywood star, you know?" he said now, his knuckles stroking her cheek.

His tone was joking, but Delta heard the question in it. The show had aired a couple of months ago, and with Brian's looks and natural charm, it hadn't taken much for every wannabe to come crawling out of the woodwork. Gina had told her that she was fielding as many calls from groupies as from legitimate callers for company business.

"A gay Hollywood star. How does that work?" To deflect interest, Brian had arranged to be caught going into a well-known gay bar with one of Gina's friends. The plan had backfired because he now had a following among both women and men who wanted him to be their best friend.

Brian cupped her face. "I don't know, but I need you to believe that it will."

She met his gaze. "Seeing how I spent a year in prison so I could be with you, I'm not about to blow it on my first day out just because there are thousands who want to be where I am right now. That's dumb. Fact is, I want the world to see what a great person you are. I think I can share." She thought about that. "Except weekends and nights."

Brian gave that good ol' boy smile that curled her toes and always made her face go hot. And he kept smiling, his arms returning to her waist and his back shifting against the car, pulling her closer. The sun speared her eyes and sizzled her shoulders. If he kept this up, she'd combust.

"Brian, I'm hot. Let's get in the car and go."

He threw back his head and laughed, and then eyed the box on the car roof. "Is that all you have for clothes?"

She grinned. "Actually, I'm wearing my whole wardrobe. Only just enough space in the box for one hundred and two love letters."

His eyes went wide. "No kidding. Is that how many I sent?" She nodded. "And you kept them all?" She nodded again, her face on fire.

He tightened his hold. "And how many times did I visit?"

241

"Only twenty-two times." She tried to look suspicious. "Apparently, you were away on several so-called business trips."

"A grand scheme to send you even more letters." Brian's eyes shone on Delta with such open tenderness that it made her feel unaccountably proud yet shy. A year ago in her heart of hearts she hadn't dared to expect him to be here with her now. But he'd stuck by her in the time leading up to the sentencing, going so far as to take her house-hunting. He insisted on calling their cozy place in Santa Monica "our place", even though she'd never lived there. It was after the sentencing when she secretly feared his commitment to her would fade. It wasn't that she thought him fickle or weak-willed. It was that she'd thought herself not deserving of his love and loyalty. But every time she'd grown depressed, there would be another letter or postcard from him, and sometimes he'd pop in for a surprise visit. She'd come to trust his love for her, and she, in turn, had become freer in expressing her own love for him.

Brian took the box of letters and tossed it into the back seat, keeping one arm around her. "Christ, I've missed you, Delta. And loved you every minute of every day," he whispered. His hands began to roam her body, palming her back and buttocks, coming back up her sides and grazing her breasts. Delta leaned into his urgent massage, pressing her lips against the base of his neck. She felt Brian hard against her belly, and began to lay a string of kisses up his neck and across his jawline. He turned and settled his mouth on hers, drawing her into a long, very thorough kiss. He finally eased away.

"Delta. Car. In." He lifted her up a few inches and with their fronts stuck together carried her around the car to the passenger door and deposited her inside.

As he drove away from the grey gates of the prison, she

asked, "So, what's the plan?"

"Seeing as you've been cooped up for so long I figured we deserved a vacation. Thought we'd start in Palm Springs, maybe take a road trip up to Vegas, then keep heading north till we reach Wyoming. You've met my mom but the rest of my family is absolutely dying to meet you. Don't worry, I've already cleared it with the parole officer."

She stared at him in amazement. "Brian, are you serious?" She knew all about his family: his four brothers, two sisters, and now eighteen nieces and nephews. She couldn't help feeling a little intimidated at the prospect of meeting his clan, especially considering....

"Uh, Brian, do they all know that your girlfriend is an ex-con?"

"Yep."

"With no job prospects, no cash and whose worldly possessions fit into an oversized shoebox?"

"Yep. I don't care so they don't, either."

As simple as that. If you wanted something you went for it. And it still amazed her that he wanted her. Yeah, he was good to everybody but he *wanted* her.

She unsnapped her belt and tugged at where his shirt tucked into his jeans.

He groaned. "You're three hours ahead of schedule."

"Three hours?" She began working the buttons.

"Yes," he said quite firmly. "I've scheduled 'Get Naked' sessions throughout the trip, and the first one is not until we reach the bed & breakfast in Palm Springs."

Her fingers kept busy. "And how many of these sessions have you scheduled?"

"One every six to eight hours. Like taking a painkiller."

She paused. "At that rate, how are we ever going to get

anywhere?"

He gave an exaggerated sigh. "I know. It's a hectic schedule, especially considering that we have to get to my folks' by the twenty-first."

He left the explanation hanging and Delta obligingly played along. "And why the twenty-first?"

He swerved the car to the shoulder and leaning over, dropped open the glove compartment. Inside was a jeweler's box which he opened to reveal a single, stupidly large, diamond solitaire engagement ring. "Because that," he said softly, "is when our wedding is going to be."

He poised the ring above her finger. "Can I put it on?"

She must've said 'yes' or nodded or something because he slid it on, a perfect fit.

She kissed him, hard and hungrily, but pulled back enough to ask, "You scheduled in my full and complete answer?"

Undoing her seatbelt he slid her onto his lap, laying his seat back as he did. "No, but we'll make it work somehow. We always do."

THE
END

BONUS!

Take a peek inside Delta's letter box with these love notes from Brian:

OCTOBER 31

Dear Delta,

Do you know how hard it is to write a love letter with Ursula and Gina yapping in the hallway? Gina came to work today in a gray suit, white shirt, sensible shoes. Hair dyed gray (looked more blue). The works. Check the date above for an explanation. Ursula didn't figure it out until the guys in the back told her. She'd actually complimented Gina on the outfit.

Gina brought candy for me to hand out at the house tonight. I don't know if anyone will show. Wish you were with me to hand it out. I saw a cute little French maid outfit complete with a duster. The cat burglar outfit I gave a pass. Didn't seem you.

Hugs and licks,
Brian

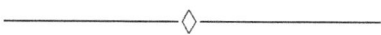

NOVEMBER 2

Dear Delta,

I was right. No one came to the house. Strangely, the candy is gone, and I don't feel so well.

Groaning and moaning (also because I'm missing you),
Brian

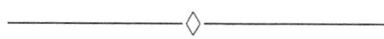

DECEMBER 25

Dear Delta,

Actually it's Boxing Day. Two in the morning. Just wanted you to know that I had the best Christmas Day ever. I've put all the gifts back. Your ipad's on your side of the bed. I printed off the photo of us together, and the orange of your jumpsuit goes okay with the frame. Really. You can't see the orange for the blue of your eyes.

I know you thought I was lying when I said that it was the best Christmas Day ever but it was. I was where I belonged and where I felt needed. I love you, woman. Next Christmas, I'm planning for you to wake up covered in presents. But don't tell anyone. I want it to be a surprise.

Love,
Santa Brian

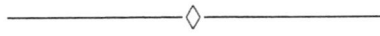

JANUARY 1

Dear Delta,

Outside there are fireworks and you're not here to see them with me. These holidays are hell. All I want to do is work and not let up until the summer when you are released. When *we're* released. My New Year's resolution is to change every thought from 'I wish you were here' to 'Next year, you'll see this/be here/laugh at this, too. These letters are the only way I can make you part of my world.

Here's to making our own fireworks,

Brian

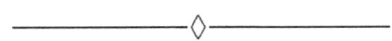

MARCH 4

Dear Delta,

You would not believe what the producers want me to do for the show. Zipline across some waterfall in Hawaii while wrestling out of a straitjacket. They ought to be put in one. They first thought of strapping a monkey to my chest but they didn't want the animal activists on their case. But it's okay if I do it, because I'm intelligent enough to sign a consent form. I haven't told Mom. She's always said I was born with a danger symbol on my butt. I'm thinking of you naked with labels. 'Handle with extreme care' across your boobs. 'This end up' across your butt and 'Slippery when wet' with an arrow pointing down on your lower belly.

Love,

Brian.

———————◊———————

MARCH 17

St. Patrick's Day. Gina came draped in green and went around pinching the butts of every non-greenie. Ursula made the cutest little squeak. Gina's keeping a spreadsheet of all my fan mail. You wouldn't believe what some of the women are willing to do, Delta. They want to 'co-star' with me. I had this policy that I'd answer every letter but I don't want to encourage them. I might be an adrenaline junkie but sheesh, taking up with them will take me down a dangerous road. Like a stormy New Mexican road where I pick up a hitchhiker....

Love from your biggest fan,

Brian who can't believe you think I'm tacky.

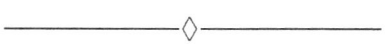

APRIL 4

Dear Delta,

I want you. I love you. I miss you. I need you. No cable reception here in the Rockies. I want you. I love you. I miss you. I need you. No cell reception either. I want you. I love you. I miss you, I need you. No idea where the mailbox is. I want, love, miss, need you. Not sure why I need to be a survivalist. I figure I can just raid the camera guys' stuff.

Slapping mosquitoes instead of your sweet ass,

Brian

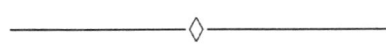

APRIL 17

Dear Delta,

Congratulations on getting your high school equivalency! Wish we could've celebrated properly but I got in a few good licks and squeezes. You know you got a job at Cause & FX anytime you want. Sexual harassment guaranteed.

Are you blushing?

Brian

MAY 11

Dear Delta,

Everything's quiet here in the trailer. It's a night shooting and there's nothing to do for anyone until later. Everyone's napping or grabbing a quick fuck with whoever they can. I'm here. I hate these times because it means I'm missing you. Hard to keep up the New Year's Resolution at times like these. And yeah, I know. We're almost home-free, you and me. Just 68 more sleeps to go. So close. But, I tell ya, my patience ran out long ago. The visits, the letters, they get me through but each time I see you, each time I have to say goodbye, it kills me. I write all these letters for the opening, you know. For the Dear Delta part. I've got to liking how I put those two words at the top and I got all this blankness below it. I know most of my letters have been short. Not letters, just notes. But I've become addicted to writing them. I'm a 'Dear Delta' junkie. For this past year, it's been the one true way of being with you. In some ways, it's been more important than the visits. The visits end up with me feeling so happy and so frustrated because you're right there and I can't touch you the way I want to. You and me talking over each other, trying to get it all out, and the goodbyes kill me every time.

But the letters. Every time I write them there's this feeling that comes over me. A peace, like everything is as it should be. I remember now when I first felt it. It was the night I picked you up and we're in that Santa Rosa motel. I'd got you warmed up and I'd dozed off beside you. I woke up. It was all quiet. The rain had stopped. No cars on the road. Nothing. And then clear as day, you said, 'Hello.' I thought you were awake, I leaned over and you were sleeping.

I said 'hello' back.

I woke up to you on the floor, hissing at me. And I thought it was a dream. But it wasn't. You can't fake this feeling.

I love you, Delta Fox.

Brian

THANK YOU

REVIEW REQUEST

Your opinion matters. Here's your chance to tell us and other readers what you think of *Fox Hunt*. Readers will get a better idea about what to expect, and we get valuable feedback about what you like and what you want.

Come to our website <u>S. M. Stelmack: Cars, Guns, Skin and Sunsets</u> and sign up on our email list at <u>S. M. Stelmack Pillow Talk</u>. Sign-up means we'll periodically send you exclusive stuff, like love letters and research findings, and we'll alert you to our upcoming releases.

We are on Goodreads! Come to our author page at <u>S. M. Stelmack</u>.

Want more? Please read on for excerpts from our forthcoming novels. First off, is an excerpt from *Gina Takes Bangkok*, our next offering in *The Femme Vendettas* series. Release date is September, 2013! Then, there's the opening to

Undertow, the first in our urban horror romance series, *The UnderCity Chronicles*, available now!

All of these excerpts are also available over at our website, too..

Family's everything.
Everything's gone to hell.

GINA TAKES
THE FEMME VENDETTAS #2
BANGKOK

S. M. STELMACK

CHAPTER ONE

GINA THWACKED THROUGH the racks at The Lime Salamander, her favorite store in all of Los Angeles. She came here often, so often that the owner had slipped off to do some banking, leaving her alone to mind the place. Small, simple, and filled with retro clothing, it was her number one hunting ground when she needed A Find.

Most people—and all men—shopped with something particular in mind. Gina viewed that approach as terribly limiting because, like kindergartners and bubble gum soda, what you wanted wasn't always what was best for you. She preferred to think of shopping as an experience in which she would let the universe guide her purchases, so she only shopped when she felt the urge. Never mind that the urges came with nymphomaniac regularity.

A slight cosmic shudder passed through her as her hand brushed a hangar. She tugged it out. A thigh-high creation in red with gold slashes. Wowza. She had shoes, bags, bracelets and boas to accessorize this beauty. Then—whoosh—the feeling vanished.

What the—? Seemed like she and the universe were out

of sync, and if so, she had a pretty good idea why.

Yesterday, on the other side of the world, her father had celebrated sixty-five years of staying alive, and being a dutiful and loving daughter, she'd phoned to wish him a happy birthday. Her step-mother had answered, saying that he'd gone fishing. Her father had spent nearly a quarter-century in Thai waters and had never fished. The millisecond the call ended she was in the grips of a mega-urge. So today, right after work, she'd hit the store.

Now a solid hour later and nothing. She should go but leaving empty-handed was not the way things worked. She wove among the racks, her wanderings edging her to the front. That's when the tingles started again, hot and heavy, pulling her to a rack close to the window. The tingles swelled into a near orgasmic sensation of A Truly Amazing Find aimed at one G-spot on a rack. There. She swept it out and held it aloft.

A black dress with elbow-length sleeves, a hemline at the knee and a neckline at the collar bone. No slits and no buttons.

The universe wanted her to buy a boardroom basic? This could not be for the best.

She looked at the price tag on the destiny dress. One hundred and twenty bucks! That was all her cash. Really?

Her body thrummed and warmed in a kind of afterglow.

Okay, something was seriously out-of-whack.

Tossing the dress over her shoulder in a fireman's hold, she slipped her pink bag from her arm, rummaging for her money clip. Where was it? She shouldn't carry all this crap. After all, it had been months since she'd used the mace. Tucking a shank of her black-and-purple locks behind her ear, she set the purse on the floor to better get at it. Engrossed, she didn't notice the car hurtling toward the store until it smashed through the front window.

The explosion of masonry, glass and ceiling tiles threw Gina against a rack and she fell to the floor in a tangle of clothing. She laid there, stunned. Not five feet away, the mangled hood of the car sizzled and steamed. Whoever was inside had to be hurting. She struggled to her feet, secured her purse and wobbled to the driver's door, just in time to get smacked hard across the chest as it swung open, knocking her back on her butt.

A young Asian female, blood zigzagging from a gash on her forehead, staggered out and, eyes full of fear, looked over her shoulder. Picking herself up for a second time, Gina followed the girl's gaze outside to where an unmarked van had screeched to a stop in the center of the street. The driver, clearly not cop material, drew a powerful handgun from his jacket as he got out.

This would be a good time to run.

Taking the girl's arm, Gina pointed through the wreckage. "Come on! There's an exit at the back."

The two of them sprinted through the stock room, rushing out the back door to the alley. The young woman made to continue running, but Gina pivoted her towards the dumpster. "Get in there and hide!" She boosted the girl, forgetting that Asian females were made of bamboo, and with a squeal and windmilling of arms, the girl fell inside with a crunch of cardboard.

From her bag, Gina pulled out a little piece of insurance she always carried with her. With a flick of her wrist, she extended the pink-handled telescopic truncheon her father had mailed to her three Christmases ago, and positioned herself by the door.

The gunman burst out, and with a samurai cry, Gina swung her baton at his wrist. There was a snap of bone as the titanium tip scored a direct hit, and the man dropped his weapon, howling in pain. But Gina didn't let up. Whacking away at the thug for all she was worth, Gina struck him across the face and head once, twice, three times, until he dropped to the ground, twitching and bleeding.

Panting for breath, Gina snagged the man's gun from the pavement and was about to make a citizen's arrest when she heard the roar of a motorcycle. Her attacker had backup, and it was headed right for her. With a yelp, she yanked open the door just as the bullets started flying, and slamming it shut behind her, clicked the deadbolt into place. She backed up, keeping her gun aimed and ready. The motorcycle squealed to a halt outside, and, a heartbeat later, someone pulled violently at the door.

Gina fired, putting a bullet hole neatly through the center of it, and waited. Hopefully that ought to be enough of a deterrent. The seconds ticked by and all was silent, then the girl cried out.

"Aw, dammit." What part of 'hide' didn't she understand? Tiptoeing to the door, Gina peeked out the bullet hole, but could see squat. She snapped back the deadbolt and opened up, gun at the ready.

The girl stood in the dumpster, apparently unharmed, but her two attackers weren't so lucky. The clubbed one was lying very still, dark blood pooling around his head, and the other was spread-eagled, her shot having pierced the door and struck him straight through the heart.

She'd killed. Again. And well. Like she was meant for the life. Dizziness tilted and blurred everything around her. No. She couldn't lose it. Not this time.

Gina looked at the gun, shaking in her hand, then at the teenager. "Don't worry, you're safe. We've done nothing wrong. The cops will be here any minute."

The girl shook her head, her straight black hair whipping about as she climbed out of the dumpster. "No! I need to find Gina Zaffini. Please, do you know her?"

Gina blinked in surprise. "I'm Gina, but how did you—?"

"Yes! I'm Tasanee. Your father and mine are friends, and they're both in big danger! I have to get back to Bangkok."

"Tasanee?" Alak Montri's daughter. She hadn't seen her god-sister in ten years, but given the kind of business their fathers were in, the last thing she could afford to do was get the police involved. She steered them over to the motorcycle. "Get on and let's get out of here. You can fill me in when we get somewhere safe."

"Oh thank you, Ms. Zaffini! Thank you."

"Don't sweat it. Just hold on tight, and call me Gina. We're sisters after all."

With Tasanee perched behind her, Gina took off down the alley. They were a mile away when she remembered the god-awful dress. Oh well. It'd been a narrow escape in more ways than one.

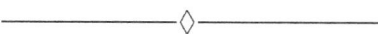

John Wakai resisted racing for the phone the second it rang. There was nothing he wanted more than to return to the serenity of order, to have his inner state reflect his Bangkok penthouse—clean, simple, and of unimpeachable quality. This call would determine if the control that had slipped from his grasp was his once again. If his plans, as rushed as they'd been, had worked.

Rolling his wheelchair to the coffee table, he picked up his smartphone. He breathed out, and with the voice of a Zen master, answered, "Is it done?"

"No. We're in trouble." His sister squeaked, her tone somewhere between rage and panic.

"How bad?"

She wavered close to hysteria. "The men I had working for me...they weren't able to finish the job."

"She got away?"

"Yes. No. I mean they won't be able to finish the job. Ever."

This could *not* be happening. "I thought you said they were right on her tail."

"They were. I don't know what happened. One minute they had her, the next they were both dead. I can't believe they came recommended."

Dammit. He'd thought he was privy to all of Montri's secrets, but his former boss had kept an ace up his sleeve. Someone watching over his daughter. Someone dangerous enough to protect her from even his sister's vicious associates.

"I have no idea where she went to. How do I find her now?"

"You can't," he answered with forced calm. "Whatever happened I'm sure she'll be back in Bangkok soon enough, and that means we have a challenge. A very serious challenge."

"So the plan failed?" she asked. He bet she was scraping her chiseled nails down her face. She always self-injured when anxious.

"No," he assured her. "And I'll make sure it doesn't. I'm not going to let anyone harm you." And of course he wouldn't, even as disturbed as she was. How could he, with all she meant to him? After everything and everyone he'd sacrificed to protect her. "You did the best you could. Come home, Victoria.

Catch the first flight you can, and meanwhile I'll sort this out."

He ended the call. As suddenly as the threat to her had developed, he'd masterminded a plan tight with checks, balances and contingencies to keep her safe. Now thanks to the incompetence of a pair of mercenaries it was unraveling.

Two years ago a man named Erawan Boontan—not an especially smart individual, but still a very feared and dangerous one—had attempted a similar power play against Montri. The coup might have even succeeded had his boss not retained the legendary assassin, Kannon Takahama, to punish the usurper's audacity. At first, Erawan hadn't worried—after all, he had many friends and supporters, and was no stranger to violence. Two months later he, and all who had collaborated with him, were dead. Kannon wasn't just a man. He was a force of nature.

But nature could be tamed. All he needed to do was find the girl and capture her, as he'd done with her father. With her prisoner, he'd easily control Montri, and even an enemy as relentless as the assassin would be brought to heel.

Resting the phone on the arm of his wheelchair, he closed his eyes. His meditation was short-lived. Though the number was blocked, Wakai knew who it was. His plan would never have worked without so formidable an ally, yet such pacts were a double-edged sword. Displeased friends could be far more dangerous than enemies. Especially friends such as these.

"Get her?" said a deep, cold voice, thick with a rural Cambodian accent.

"No. She had some security I didn't know about," replied Wakai, with studied firmness. "Killed the useless gunmen Victoria hired. Apparently they came recommended by some idiot."

"*I* recommended them."

Wakai had insulted him. Worse, he'd made it sound as if Victoria had insulted him, too. Now more than ever he couldn't afford to show any fear.

The man was angry now, the kind of anger that got people brutally murdered. Or much, much worse. "We couldn't have made this any easier for you! With the girl, we could have taken the city in one stroke!"

Arrogant psychopath. How convenient to forget that it had been his knowledge and strategy that had afforded them such a quick and decisive victory, albeit an incomplete one. "I said I'd take care of her and I will, but it's going to take a little more time."

"You're so smart you're stupid" came the scathing reply. "Kannon's tracking you down right now, and his boss has friends in every corner of the city. Sooner or later, he's going to come knocking at our door with who knows how many others, and you're going to wind up getting tossed off that fancy penthouse of yours, just like Erawan."

Wakai grimaced. Back then he'd still had use of his legs. Had been there when the assassin had thrown Erawan to his death—with one hand.

"You have one week to solve this problem. After that, there's no word for the kind of punishment you'll receive."

Punishment? After all he'd just done for them? His new partners were quickly becoming as hazardous as his former boss, but it made no sense to reason with monsters like them. He'd find some way to get a muzzle on the mad dog. Until then, he gave the only answer he could. "Consider it dealt with."

The line went dead, and Wakai released a loud curse. No way to zen his way back to peace now. Seven days was all he had to put out the fire his sister's vices had started. Fail, and it would explode into an inferno.

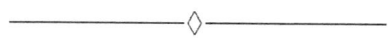

Kannon was running out of time, but not as fast as Jarun who he had tied to a chair in the stock room of the man's own grocery store. Taking the cigarette from his mouth, Kannon stubbed it out on the prisoner's forehead, eliciting a shrill cry of pain as it hissed against flesh. He relight the cigarette and took a puff. "I'm starting to get annoyed with you. Tell me where my boss is."

"For the last time, I don't know," Jarun spat, blood trickling down his sweat-slicked face. "And even if I did, you'd just kill me the second I told you."

There was every reason for his prisoner to believe that. After all, Jarun had never shown any mercy to those who he'd brought to the back of his shop. The man was an enforcer. A fighter. A torturer. One look at his hands, knuckles enlarged and calloused, told that story.

"You help Wakai kidnap Mr. Montri, murder his lieutenants and hunt his daughter. The question is not whether you're going to die. It's how unpleasant I'm going to make that process. Now tell me what I want to know."

The man gritted his teeth in stubborn determination. "Fuck you."

Behind Kannon, the door opened to admit his apprentice, Ryota. The tall, wiry man nodded to his boss, his expression a mask of cold indifference. He held up a phone. "I have a few numbers that might be leads, and he has a message on his voicemail. Other than that, the place is empty. No sign of where they're keeping the boss."

Kannon removed his cigarette and held the burning tip

close to one of his prisoner's eyes. "Where is he?"

Jarun clamped his mouth shut, as he struggled at his bonds.

Kannon growled. "You think you know how to torture? Compared to me you're an amateur. By the time I'm done with this cancer stick you'll curse your father for not pulling out of that ten-baht whore you called a mother. Now. For the last time. Where is—?"

His cell buzzed. Not breaking eye contact with Jarun, he pulled it from his suit jacket. "You better pray this is good news."

He stepped away to take the call.

"Kannon?"

Tasanee. "Where are you?"

"I'm in Los Angeles. I got away from the apartment like you told me to, but somehow Wakai's men still found me. They would have had me for sure except Gina saved me. She killed them, and we're at this workshop, and—"

"Slow down. What did you say? Who killed them?"

He heard the phone being handed to another person. "Hi, Kannon. Remember me?"

Part of what made him such an expert manhunter was that he rarely forgot a face. Or a voice. And though it had been three years since their last run-in, the receptionist he'd completely failed to intimidate was fixed in his memory. "The pink-haired woman."

Of all the people in the world, she was Vincenzo Zaffini's daughter?

"Actually my hair's black-and-purple now, but it's awful sweet of you to remember. We're at the same place you blew up on your last visit," she rattled on. "I couldn't believe it when Tasanee told me who she was, and who Montri had hired as muscle. You really should step up your security, y'know? Next time I might not be around to do your job for you."

Her squirrel chattering grated. "Put Tasanee back on."

"Fine," she said, "but don't expect me to bail you out again with that attitude." A moment later, Tasanee was back.

"Kannon, I'm at this place called—"

"I know where you are. The people there are...associates of mine." He looked at his watch and scowled. "I'll be there tomorrow night. Stay where you are and who you're with." He added what he knew the girl needed to hear. "You're safe now."

"That's what Gina keeps saying."

Gratitude mixed with his irritation, and the two didn't sit well. "She's right. Don't call anyone else."

"Kannon? Is...is my dad okay?"

No way was he saying otherwise when he couldn't be there for her. "He's good. Don't worry."

Her breath blew out. "Thank you, Kannon. Thank you so much."

His jaw tensed with emotion, but looking at Jarun, he kept his voice even. "I'll be there soon."

Kannon slid away his phone, and withdrawing his silenced pistol, strolled over to his captive. "Tasanee's safe. Seems like you're getting less useful all the time."

"I don't want to die," the man said, his body dripping blood and sweat. "But I can't tell you what I don't know."

Kannon pressed the gun up against Jarun's chin. "What's the access number for your voice mail?"

Jarun let it go. "3579."

In one lightning stroke, Kannon pistol-whipped the man, knocking him out. He wouldn't kill him. Not yet, at least. He was an old friend of Wakai's, and might still be of some good.

265

Ryota retrieved Jarun's voice mail, and with the click of a button, played the message on speaker.

"Jarun." It was Wakai. "I need you to come and talk to Montri. Victoria screwed up the job and I have to get as much information as I can on who's protecting his daughter. I'll send someone around first thing tomorrow to pick you up. He'll be there at seven." The man who'd betrayed his boss, the man Kannon had bowed to as a superior, softened his voice. "You're the only one I can trust anymore, Jarun. I know what you think of all this, but I know you'll stand by me. I know I can count on you."

Kannon regarded Jarun's slumped form. "Ryota, if they get Tasanee everything's lost, so I have to fetch her. Keep Jarun alive, and when that driver comes by in the morning, take him, too."

"Couldn't he lead us back to where they're keeping the boss?"

Ryota was twenty-four, young enough to be Kannon's son. A good man. An excellent student. But if Kannon did his job well, he'd turn Ryota into a hard, calculating killer. Someone who recognized the naiveté of that question.

"Not without Jarun," Kannon explained. "Even if he did, we're not equipped to stage a rescue. Besides, Wakai will move our boss as soon as the chauffeur doesn't return. No. You hold them. Soon as I'm back with Tasanee, we'll pick up from here."

"So…she's okay?" Ryota asked tentatively, and Kannon realized he'd not told him. "Yes. In Los Angeles. She's with Mr. Zaffini's daughter."

His assistant's eyes widened with surprise. "I know they're friends of the boss, but what if it's a trap? Can we trust her?"

Kannon remembered a pair of light brown eyes, fearless and full of life. "This is no trap."

It was past midnight when Kannon pulled up at the special effects company, the full moon shining down on the building. The lobby was lit, and another room on the same level. Outside security lights at the corners showed nothing. Good. Maybe this visit would go smoother than his last one. Back then, he'd been hunting the woman he'd believed to be another assassin, though as it had turned out she was merely a thief wrongly accused of murder. That said, the place was an unwelcome reminder of the only time he'd been bested. Delta Fox had not only got him flat on his back, but taken his gun. Had she been a real killer, his story would have been over. It seemed fate had decided that he'd come knocking here again.

He didn't get the chance. As he reached for the buzzer, the door swung wide and he was confronted by a thin older woman in a severe gray suit, her countenance like a constipated drill sergeant's.

"So," she said in a heavy Austrian accent, inspecting him like he was a new recruit, "you're the one responsible for the explosion."

Kannon looked beyond her as he entered. Leaning against the receptionist's desk with smirks on their faces was the little blonde thief, Delta Fox, and judging by their matching wedding rings, her husband, Brian Chanse. They looked like your ordinary, genial California couple. Until you crossed them. The gray suit shoved a sheet of paper in his face.

It was a bill for all the damage Kannon had caused, when one of his bullets had missed Fox and instead, hit a locker full of explosives. The blast had trashed the company's back bay, and according to the bottom line, bolded and underlined, caused a high five figures in damage.

Kannon looked to Chanse. "No insurance?"

"It's the principle of the matter," the female commandant answered before her boss could. "If you were any kind of man, you'd take responsibility."

He brought the full weight of his regard on the woman, the same look that made most slink away. She sucked in her breath, her face flushed, but stood her ground. With employees like this, Chanse could set up his own enforcement racket. Chanse cleared his throat. "If it's any consolation, I didn't have Ursula charge you for my car. I figure I had a hand in it getting damaged, seeing as I'm the one that ran *you* off the road."

Although Kannon had a distinct memory of his boot connecting with a tender part of Chanse's anatomy, he didn't care to continue the conversation, especially since he couldn't see Tasanee anywhere. Or the Zaffini woman, for that matter.

"Funny," Kannon responded, his tone making it clear that it was anything but. "Where's the girl?"

Fox pointed down the hallway. "This way. In Brian's office. Tasanee was lucky Gina was there. She had to kill two men." She pinned him with her bright blue eyes. "So far no cops have come calling, but you owe her, Kannon."

He knew that. Two women, two lectures. And two more females to go yet. He needed another cigarette.

Tasanee sat on a chair getting her long black hair braided. Gina, frowning and smiling, in concentration and pride, had the same look his wife had had when fixing their daughter's hair so many years ago. Tasanee rushed into his arms. He returned her hug, then brushed the hair from the bandage on

268

her forehead. "You said you were okay," he said.

"A bit of storefront came through the windshield when she crashed," Gina said, perching on top of her boss's desk. Her long legs dangled down forever, and Kannon had to force his eyes upwards. She wore tall white boots with platform heels, a short dress splotchy with pink and yellow blossoms. It was to this flower child that he was forced to say, "I'm indebted to you, Miss Zaffini."

Fox, Chanse and Ursula had all filed in behind him, and Fox made a surprised noise. "Hang on. Zaffini? I knew that was your last name, but Gina, after what you did today, it takes on a whole new meaning. Do you mean Zaffini as in the Miami Zaffinis?"

Gina shrugged. "Yeah. My father was a made man, but I kind of took a different path in life."

"Okay, I'll bite," said Chanse, leaning against the office wall. "Who are they?"

"Italian Mafia," Fox supplied. "One of the last traditional crime families."

"And here I assumed she was as harmless as she is incompetent," Ursula said.

Gina brightened under the insult. "Don't beat yourself up about it. Menopausal women often experience lapses in judgment." The older woman made choking noises, and Gina carried on to the room at large, "We liked to think of ourselves as the American mafia. Sounded more patriotic that way. Not that there's really any of the family left anymore. My dad's about the only one who's not dead or serving a life sentence, and that's because he took off for Thailand."

"Thailand?" asked Fox. "So what's the connection there?"

Gina played with a red hair clip, snapping it open and

shut like jaws. "Well, after my mom died, he got together with a Thai hooker, and when the FBI got too close they took me to live in Bangkok. Anyway, my dad met Tasanee's dad there and the two became friends. Only now it looks like there's been some trouble." She looked squarely at Kannon.

No point delaying it. He turned to Tasanee, taking her by the shoulders. Not knowing he was doing it, he looked to Gina Zaffini. And just like that, she slipped off the desk and stood close, so close she could've wrapped her arms around the both of them. She didn't, of course. Still, for whatever reason, it made what he had to say easier. "Tasanee, I'm afraid there's more than trouble. Your father...he's been kidnapped. He's being held hostage."

Tasanee froze. Only her lips moved. "What...how? When?"

"One of your father's bodyguards managed to get a call off to me saying they were under attack. That's when I phoned and told you to get out of your apartment. Your father's lieutenants were targeted as well, so we're wiped out."

Tasanee went pale and under his hands, he felt her slump. He realized his mistake. "Not all of us. Ryota's fine, too."

It was as if he'd pumped air into her. She straightened, expanded and concentrated. "But who could have done something like that?"

"It was your father's top lieutenant, John Wakai. He betrayed us, and now he's trying to control the city. That's why he wants you. He knows your safety is the only thing that could ever make your father bend, and if your father bends then so will the gangs who follow him."

Tasanee was nineteen, still a girl in many ways, but she was also the daughter of a major crime lord. She bit hard on her lip and gave a quick nod. "I see."

Kannon released her. "Don't worry. I'll get him back. But right now I have to make some arrangements with our… friends here, okay?"

With Ursula left to tend to Tasanee, the rest of them stepped out into the hall.

"You're not in any position to protect her if Wakai's men track her here," Kannon said. "I'm taking her back to Bangkok."

"I'm going too," said Gina.

He might owe her a debt, but she wasn't going to be dictating the terms. "No, you're not."

Gina crossed her arms over her chest. "First of all Tasanee's my god-sister. That makes her part of my family, and that makes this personal. Everybody in Bangkok knows Alak Montri and my dad are best friends, so if this douchebag takes over his organization, the first thing he'll do is strip my father of everything he owns. I'm sure you're tough as nails, Kannon, but you need some serious backing and you don't have time to screw around. Kun pôot paa-sǎa tai bpen mǎi?"

"What?" he replied, irritated.

"I asked if you spoke Thai, and you just answered my question. How do you expect to track down this guy quickly without some help?"

"I've got people."

"People you can trust?" she shot back. "With Wakai in charge, don't you think at least some of your guys might switch sides?"

Kannon made a deliberate pass over her appearance. "I don't think you're cut out for the kind of work that needs doing."

"I knocked off the two killers they sent after her." She said it like a statement of fact but he saw the whites of the eyes widening, the tensing of lines around them, the determined focus. Killing them had shook her. He had a sudden idiotic urge to take her by the shoulders and tell her, as he'd told Tasanee, that everything was going to be okay.

He stiffened. Not his place. And not a place he wanted, either.

Those clothes, that hair, that attitude. She didn't take her job as a receptionist seriously because she didn't need to—she came from a world of privilege, even if it was an *under*world. There she stood, like a purple-haired cat that had eaten his canary, and he had to take it.

She poked him in the chest. "Give me all the dirty looks you want. I'm the one that saved Tasanee's life, and I've got the connections to rescue your boss. I know Bangkok, speak fluent Thai, and with that bastard threatening my family this fight is as much mine than yours. I'm coming to help you, and that's that. You owe me and this is what I want as payback."

The happily married couple had silently listened to the exchange, arms looped around each other, but now Fox contributed. "I don't think that's how debts work. You're supposed to get something in return."

"I do. A trip to Thailand with my own personal body-guard who scares the skin off everybody." Gina glanced around. "Present company excepted."

Kannon grimaced. Fox and Chanse had both got the better of him at some point, the Witch of Finance couldn't be cowed, and Gina, being a Zaffini, had probably never feared anyone in her life. Other than the days he had with his daughter, it had been a long, long time since he'd been in a place where no one was terrified of him.

A pair of honey brown eyes were fixed on him in bratty defiance.

"Call your father and let him know we're coming."

She blinked. "I already did."

Chanse snorted. "Man, welcome to my world. Women ask permission, then do whatever the hell they want."

Kannon knew it only too well, but played it out anyway. "But it'll be your father's decision. If he says so, you go back to Los Angeles. Agreed?"

"Kao jai láew."

That was it. He was getting language lessons. "Which means?"

"We've got a deal. Now if you'll all excuse me, I'm off to pack." She cut away, back down the hall to the lobby. "Wish me luck," she called over her shoulder. "Too many clothes, too little room. I'll be a mess before it's done."

Kannon observed the swing of her body and knew it was all talk.

WANT TO READ IT?
If you're on Goodreads, here's the link to adding
*Gina Takes Bangko*k to your bookshelf.

www.goodreads.com/book/show/17566767-gina-takes-bangkok

UNDERTOW

THE UNDERCITY CHRONICLES

The City is deeper than they know.

S.M. STELMACK

PRoLoGUE

Lindsay desperately wanted to hold Jack's hand. Her breath came fast and shallow, and her every muscle had stiffened into near rigor mortis. And still the elevator dropped beneath the city streets, down into the dark guts of New York, its metal lattice floor the only barrier between her and the shadowy depths below.

She wasn't about to admit her fear of heights to Jack. Sure she had a crush on him, as bad as any fifteen-year-old could have, and would've considered herself the luckiest girl in the world to hold hands with him. Yet, she also knew he hung out with her because she could keep up with him. To confess her vulnerabilities now would make her no better than all the other girls, and she was determined that he would remember her as someone exceptional.

Sam Cole, Jack's father, gave her a lopsided smile. "This crate's on the slow side, but we'll be there in a minute. That hardhat fit okay, Lindsay?"

She managed a nod, and the oversized yellow helmet slipped over her eyes.

The other side of his smile shot up. "Good. I'm glad Jack invited you. Another couple of weeks and we'd be finished down here. Not many people ever get to see the real underground."

As if on cue, the elevator reached the bottom, making Lindsay's already queasy stomach lurch.

"You okay?" Jack asked.

Great, she probably looked like the vomit she was trying to keep down. "Yeah. I'm–I'm a little nervous of heights."

His golden eyes shone. "So I noticed." He looked down. Her hand had his in a death grip.

Lindsay gasped and let go, her face burning. "Oh, jeez. Sorry. I didn't even realize that I...sorry."

She hurried off the elevator—and stepped into a fresh hell. The subway tunnel was dark and filthy and reeked of grime and oil, and she could feel claustrophobia begin to crush her. The halogen lighting created a pool of civilization in which the workers called to each other, and there were the strong noises of steel striking steel and generators throbbing out energy. Beyond that, in the world Jack was going to take her, there was only darkness and silence. Yet he and his father looked content, as if this dank scene was a veritable wonderland.

Jack had used that very word when he was talking her into coming. A wonderland. She described it the same way to her parents, and to her brother, fifteen years her senior, and his wife around the dining room table. Her niece, two going on irrational, wanted to go right away, and when Lindsay explained that wonderland didn't mean Disneyland, she said it was okay, that Jack could lift her on his shoulders and take her to the playground there. Due to her gender, Seline adored Jack. Lindsay's mother melted when Jack came over and ate through the fridge and pantry, and Lindsay had the distinct feeling that it was Jack's charms had played a large part in her mother had giving her permission to go underground. Her father, being male, had only given the go-ahead once he knew Jack's father was going to be nearby. Then her brother, male and bossy beyond belief, had called up Jack's father to confirm the dos and don'ts. Gracie, her sis-in-law, had winced in sympathy. "You should see him with the babysitter. The poor girl is stiff with worry before we've even left, and then she's got an evening of Seline. I always give her an extra ten as stress pay."

Sometimes Lindsay envied the casual bachelor relationship between Jack and his father. Sam Cole was pretty laidback as far as parents went, and actively encouraged his son to explore the tunnels. He'd done the same thing in London when he was a boy, and was overjoyed that his only child shared his lifelong passion for places deep and dark.

"Be back within the hour, and no taking Lindsay off the track," he said. "I don't want to go searching for you again."

Jack laughed, sharing an in-joke with his father. "We'll be careful. Let's go, Linds."

He flicked on his helmet light and waited long enough for her to do the same before leading her down the tunnel, away from the swarm of tradesmen and engineers. Jack was always ready to chart unknown territory, and he wasn't one to check if anyone was following. He was always the first to take a dare, not to show off but because he couldn't resist a challenge. That she was his regular buddy filled her with pride. That he was leaving for Hong Kong in a month, and likely never coming back, filled her with a profound sadness.

Right now with him so real and solid beside her, Lindsay wasn't going to worry about the future. The immediate present was freaky enough. She could feel the darkness here. It had a kind of smothering thickness to it, so alien to anything on the surface.

"What's this about sending out a search party for you?"

she asked off-handedly, as if this was no different than walking the streets above.

"They did, but I made it back on my own and they got lost. In the end, I was part of the group that found them."

That was Jack. Total master of his surroundings. Lindsay looked about, her light cutting a pale swath over wet concrete walls, iron rails, graffiti. "Sounds like you know these tunnels pretty well."

"No, I've barely scratched the surface. One day I want to come back here and map the whole underground."

He wanted to come back. Okay, not to see her. Still, there was no way he wouldn't look her up. She squashed down her excitement. "How long do you think they'll take to map?"

Jack gave a short laugh. "A lifetime."

She stopped in her tracks. "You want to spend your life in tunnels? Don't you think that would get old after a while?"

"Not for me. Come on, I want you to meet someone."

"What?"

"There's this guy who lives down here. Name's Tim."

"Who the hell lives in a tunnel?"

"People with nowhere else to go, Linds," he said quietly and, to her ears, reproachfully. "Used to be a lawyer or judge or something. When the transit authority kicked him out of the tunnels, I got him a copy of the keys so he could get back in."

Lindsay wondered what the men in her family would say if they knew Jack was taking her to visit a bum. Or that he'd done something shady for that bum. Maybe she'd skip this part.

"Tim knows everything about the tunnels. My dad told me they've had people down here since the 50's. Tim says there were people underground before that. Way before. You wouldn't believe the stuff that goes on down here."

Lindsay looked over her shoulder, uneasily noticing how far they were getting from the work crew, and bumped into Jack, who'd stopped immediately ahead of her.

"Sorry…"

Jack didn't seem to notice, his gaze focused down the tunnel on some point beyond the beam of his helmet light.

"What is it?" she whispered.

"I thought I heard something up ahead. Like a yell or… something."

Lindsay strained to hear anything. Nothing but the faint dripping of water. "One of the workers?"

"No," he replied hesitantly. "They'd be wearing a light." He started forward again. She couldn't stop herself. She caught his arm.

"Shouldn't we go tell your dad?"

Jack kept his eyes on the darkness. "It's probably just Tim. He said he has nightmares sometimes. Sees things that aren't there. Come on. There's nothing to be afraid of."

Then why had his usual confident pace slowed? Wordlessly, she followed on Jack's heels down the tunnel for what seemed like a mile, each step taking them further into the gloom of the underworld until the lights behind them had almost faded to nothing. Cold crept over her, a vapor that twined about her limbs.

She was about to suggest again they return when Jack pivoted to face a small side passage that branched off the subway line. The opening didn't reach Lindsay's shoulders and was barely as wide as her body, and it was so obscured by pipes and cables that she never would have noticed it on her own.

"In here," he said, and crouching, disappeared inside.

Fear rooted her feet to the ground. Something was wrong

here. Very terribly wrong, and though she trusted Jack, her intuition screamed at her to run back to the safety of the surface, away from whatever lay beyond. But Jack was waiting for her, and she'd never abandon him even if she knew that disaster lay ahead. Especially then. She took a deep breath and followed.

She stayed right on his butt so she was beside him when the cramped passage emptied into a chamber the size of Lindsay's bedroom.

It was the smell that hit her first. Warm, metallic. Blood. Jack's hand clamped around hers, the beams from their helmets skittering about as they frantically scanned the room. Lindsay took in scattered newspapers and paperbacks, an overturned folding cot, pop bottles and a kerosene lantern.

Then Jack made a soft pained noise, and she turned so that her light ran alongside his. Blood was smeared along the wall by the entrance, left by hands that had clawed futilely at the concrete before being dragged off into the darkness.

"Oh my God," Jack whispered. "They're real."

CHAPTER ONE

Eighteen years later

Lindsay sat alone in Captain Monroe's small, drab office and tried not to be sick all over his desk, a mishap that might not have mattered much since it already looked as if raccoons had been set loose on it. The fluorescent lighting flickered, emitting that mosquito-like frequency as it prepared to burn out, though it wasn't loud enough to drown out the death rattle coming from the computer hard drive. On the printer sat a delicately balanced styrofoam cup of cold coffee, perched there like a bad deodorizer. She might've opened the window with its view over the slate gray waters of the Hudson River, except he doubted that would be appreciated given the freezing temperatures that had gripped the East coast during the past week.

Deep down she knew it wasn't her environment that was making her nauseous. It was why she had to be there. Her eyes drifted, as they did every time she visited, to the maps plastered on the walls. Faded from long years of use, they were, except for the one of the New York subway, all byzantine in their complexity. They depicted tunnels and sewers, air ducts and water mains, forgotten train lines and long-sealed garbage pits. There were maps of cable, gas and steam lines, each representing vast labyrinths buried deep beneath the streets, systems that joined and overlapped, multiplying their complexity.

If that were not enough, many of them were incomplete, inaccurate or both, rendering navigation in some sections of the city's bowels virtually impossible. She'd learned as much from several private investigators, all of whom had turned down her case.

After an eternity, Captain Monroe entered, steaming cup of coffee in hand, and sat across from her without a word of greeting. She bit back the urge to tell him about the precarious position of the abandoned cup. She wasn't here to regulate his coffee consumption.

"Thank you for seeing me, Captain," she said as evenly as she could. "Again."

He grunted, and began shuffling through the papers on his desk, clearly searching for something. "You here for an update?" His dismissive tone made it clear he wanted her out the door as quickly as possible.

She tried to keep the frustration out of her voice. "Yes. I'd like to know why nobody is searching for her."

Monroe examined a sheet, frowned, tossed it back and kept rooting around. Lindsay itched to jump in and make square corners and open spaces on his desk.

"Ms. Sterling, do you know how many miles of tunnels there are beneath New York?"

"No. I don't."

Monroe squinted at another scrap of paper. "Neither do I,

or anybody else. They run for hundreds of miles, and go down as deep as twelve stories. What I do know is how many men I have to patrol those tunnels, and that number is exactly thirty."

There was a stapled sheaf of papers suspended over the edge of the desk, and the way the Captain was bulldozing around it was going to slide off. "Nevertheless, it's your duty to search for missing persons."

He pinned her with a look no doubt reserved for punks and do-gooders. "I don't need you to remind me of my job. I've been on the force for thirty-four years. I know my responsibilities."

Clearly being nice wasn't going to work. "Then, why aren't you doing anything?"

"Ms. Sterling, how many times do I need to repeat myself before you get it? The people down there are not like the people up here. Most of them are drug addicts. Many have extreme psychological problems. Unless we get some kind of solid lead on this investigation, I'm not sending my men down in a blind search. It's too dangerous."

"But you're the police!"

The captain's face reddened in anger. "Last year we had an officer knifed to death down there. Another one was beaten so badly he'll never walk again, and do you know what he was beaten with? His own nightstick. And that's in subway and maintenance tunnels we regularly patrol, not in the lower levels. We'd need an army to conduct a thorough search, and—surprise, surprise—we don't have one. I explained this to your niece before she went down. She decided she knew better."

Lindsay sucked in her breath to snap back, and then slowly released it. If she was going to find Seline, she needed his cooperation, no matter how unwilling he might be to give it. She rescued the slipping report and set it safely on his desk. He peered at it, then snatched it up.

"Well, at least you found something that you were looking for," she commented with emphasis. "Look, I understand my niece was no great friend of the NYPD. I understand she was conducting her research despite your warnings, and despite *my* warnings, to be frank. I understand that you're undermanned and don't want to place your men in danger. But Captain, I can't just forget about her. There must be something we can do."

Monroe stared coldly across at her. She held it. "Ms. Sterling, I really don't think I can help you…" he began, but his eyes darted to a battered old Rolodex tucked against his computer. She pressed for the advantage.

"Please, Captain," she pleaded, "if you can think of anybody who could find her, anyone at all, I need to know."

Monroe stared back, setting his jaw as if weighing his options. "There is one guy," he said after a moment, though by his expression he was already regretting his words.

"Who is he?"

"His name is Jack Cole. Used to be a professor."

Lindsay froze, went as stiff as the bodies of the homeless that turned up every day now on the city's icy streets. "Did you say Jack Cole? Jack Andrew Cole?"

Monroe's hand hovered over the Rolodex. "You know him?"

"Yes," she replied, fond memories softening her initial shock. "We used to be best friends back in high school. I haven't seen him in"—she did the math—"eighteen years. He's a…a scientist?"

"Anthropologist. Expert in urban subcultures." Monroe set the Rolodex in front of him and began flipping. "Did a lot of work around the world. London, Paris, Rome, Moscow and here in New York. Nobody knows more about the underside of cities."

Lindsay shook her head in wonder. "That's the kind of work he always said he was going to do. He could find Seline, couldn't he?"

"If he wanted, though I doubt he will," Monroe said. "I guess you could say he's retired."

"Retired?" Lindsay echoed.

"About three years ago, Dr. Cole went missing in the underground during one of his expeditions. We searched for him as best we could. After a couple of weeks, we simply didn't have resources to keep it up. He was presumed dead, and that's the way things stayed till early last year when he finally surfaced."

"He spent two *years* underground? What happened to him?"

Monroe eyed one of the cards, then shook his head and kept flipping. "He didn't say."

"What do you mean he didn't say?" Lindsay asked. That wasn't the Jack she'd known. He would've popped up, those lion-like eyes of his bright with enthusiasm, and begun telling the world of his adventures.

"I'm saying he didn't say," Monroe growled. "End of story."

Not for her. She'd find him and he'd help her. He wouldn't let her down. She knew that much about him.

"Yeah, here it is." Monroe stopped at a card and began patting the papers in the hunt for a pen.

Lindsay produced her own pen and paper.

Monroe smirked as he jotted down the address. It was a few blocks from Gates Avenue, in Bed-Stuy. Though parts of

Bedford-Stuyvesant were wonderful places to live, featuring beautiful tree-lined rows of century-old brownstone homes and tight-knit communities, Gates Avenue was infamous for its poverty and crime rate. She didn't need to be a psychologist to see Monroe doubted that a professional white woman, dressed like she'd stepped off the pages of a fashion magazine, would dare set foot there.

"You have his phone number?"

"No," Monroe said flatly. "Now if you'll excuse me, I have a lot of work to do today."

Lindsay had the address memorized before she reached the door. As she was leaving, the captain called out to her.

"Make sure you go yourself."

She turned in the doorway. "I beg your pardon?"

"I said you'll need to go there yourself. Cole isn't likely to help you, Ms. Sterling. He definitely won't if you hire someone to go talk to him."

What did he take her for? Thirty years on the force and he hadn't figured out that appearances meant nothing. "I learned long ago that if I wanted anything done, I'd have to do it myself. Today you just reminded me of that."

At that precise moment, the fluorescent light burned out, leaving Monroe in twilight. It was her turn to smirk. "It's hell being left in the dark, isn't it?"

***

Seline woke to a sudden squeal, letting out one of her own as she bolted upright in the blackness, the sleeping bag provided by her captors twisting around her legs. She unzipped it, the opening of the nylon teeth sawing on her ears. She tried to determine the direction of the noise, or if there had been one, and not yet another hallucination. The chain that stretched from the thick collar around her throat to a concrete pillar clunked and scraped against the floor with her every move, messing with her ability to gauge sound. God, she hated the chain. Early on she'd measured it using her hands and estimated it to be fifteen feet long, not long enough to reach any of the walls in the tiled room, walls she knew existed because if she stretched her legs her feet barely brushed against them. She craved to have a wall at her back.

She sat cross-legged on the bag and breathed deeply, the smell of cold iron and stale air filling her, and willed her racing heart, the beats impossibly loud, to slow. It took longer each time the panic attacks hit, but she calmed herself enough to allow for rational thinking. She'd been down for about a week, though time was fast becoming a shredded concept in this world of perpetual night. She'd tried using the number of times she slept to gauge the passage of days, until she realized that the lack of light and noise made her sleep too often. Or maybe not. All she knew was that she was far from the surface, in the lowest levels of the tunnels, and that despite the silence that surrounded her, she wasn't alone.

She could only guess how many captors there were. She hadn't even gotten a glimpse of them before they'd pulled a sack over her head and dragged her through endless passages, her screams muffled. There were at least two of them to start with—one had held a knife at her throat while the other had bound her wrists behind her back. She now sensed that there were more. Many more.

"Hello?" she called, her voice echoing through the chamber. She always called out after waking. It was a way of establishing contact with her captors, of reaching out to possible rescuers, of proving her humanness. She'd heard somewhere that the best thing to do if kidnapped was to try and make friends with your captors. If they saw you as a person, as opposed to just a hostage, it made it harder for them to harm you.

"Hello?" she tried again. As usual there was no response, and it was the silence that made her more afraid than anything. She wished she'd listened to Lindsay, to that Jack Cole, to everybody. They all said the tunnels could kill. She'd gone down before, twelve times, and nothing had happened, not a whisper of anything. And then this. For the thousandth time she thought of Lindsay's story about when she and Jack went into the tunnels as teenagers. Was she going to be ripped apart like that poor man?

No. No. Against all odds she was alive. They would've killed her outright, if the stories were to be believed. Whoever or whatever was keeping her prisoner actually seemed intent on keeping her alive. She hadn't been beaten or raped. While she slept, the provided bedpan was emptied. A stringy meat stew, palatable after hunger had hollowed her out, was regularly provided along with a bottle of fresh water.

Only they hadn't uttered a single word to her.

"Listen," she called out, repeating once again her offer. "If you contact my sister, she'll ransom me. If you let her know that I'm alive, she'll pay for my release."

Silence.

"Her name is Lindsay Sterling," Seline continued. "You can reach her at Sterling Restorations. Or you can call her home." She rattled off the numbers.

Behind her she thought she heard the slightest rustle and twisted around.

Blackness.

"Please. I'm no threat to you. I'll go away and never

288

come back if that's what you want. I won't tell anyone about you, promise. Please let me go."

Silence.

"I only came down here to help. I'm not with the police. I'm not even a real social worker, just a student. I wanted to make the people who run this city realize that you're down here. To make them stop ignoring you."

Then, a sound. It came in hushed vibrations all around her, making her heart thump wildly. From every corner of the pitch-black chamber she could hear her keepers. Ever so quietly, they were laughing.

***

The street where Jack lived was all but deserted when Lindsay reached it, the rows of cheap shops and slum housing standing stiff and battered in the chill morning. A bunch of young men gathered around a junker turned as her Lexus cruised by, their expressions sullen and calculating. All seemed too cold to do more than look.

Jack's address turned out to be a dilapidated grocery store, its barred windows smashed and brick facade layered in crude graffiti. Pulling over to the curb, she double-checked the address. Had Monroe played some kind of cruel trick on her? Surely to God, Jack couldn't be living in a place barely fit for a rodent.

She locked her car and wondered if she would ever see it again. Oh well, that was why she paid the outrageous insurance premiums. You shouldn't have what you can't afford to lose. It's what her father had always said, and she'd made it her personal motto. She walked across the street and was about to step onto the curb when the heel on her right Blahnik got wedged in a pavement crack. She tugged with her foot, and nothing happened. The heel was sensible, a full inch across, and still this.

"Fine," she muttered. She unzipped the boot, slipped out her nyloned foot and hopped on the other as she began prying out the heel. From down the street, she heard the men snort in laughter.

Yes, she could afford to lose her six hundred dollar boots. Her pride was an entirely different matter. She was not going to meet an old high school friend with one shoe. Besides, it was freezing. She went at it again with renewed vigor.

The heel popped loose which sent her hopping madly about in all directions to keep her balance. The crowd laughed raucously, and Lindsay jammed her foot back into her boot, closed it with a most satisfying zip, and straightened. Then gasped.

She was looking up at the biggest black man she'd ever seen in all her New York life. He was a tree, a building, a mountain. He wore a knit hat, a parka that could've covered her car, and tundra boots that had to have been custom-made to fit him. A brown paper bag full of groceries hung from his bear paw of a hand with no more effort than she'd hold an empty envelope. Down the two-lane bridge of his nose, he looked at her with the mild disdain normally reserved for pigeons.

He took in her boots, her coat, her car, and no doubt, her skin color. "You lost?"

Lindsay tried for a friendly, brisk tone. "Not at all. I'm meeting a friend. He lives right here." She attempted to skirt around him. "I mustn't keep him waiting."

The giant pulled a face and narrowed his eyes. "Here? What's his name?"

She dropped the friendly and kept the brisk. "Why would I tell a stranger my friend's name?"

His eyes widened and apparently conceding the point, he stepped aside to let her pass.

"Thank you," she said. "Have a nice day."

She got past him and headed up to the rusted metal door of the shop. She tapped on it, then banged on it. Nothing. Aware that her every move was being watched, she tried the handle. It was unlocked—didn't, she realized, even have a lock. She glanced back to where the winterized wall of humanity stood watching her. He smiled, flashing a set of gold teeth, clearly not intending to walk on.

"Uh, looks like he left it open for me. Must be home, then."

His smile glittered. "Must be."

"I'll have to remind him not to leave his door open." She paused deliberately. "Who knows who might wander in?"

"Yeah. Good idea."

Lindsay didn't know what to do, so she pushed open the door and tried to close it quickly behind her. It took a couple of goes as the door didn't sit square with the frame. She waited, listening for the Yeti of Bedford to follow. Nothing happened, and she turned back to the shop's interior. Or what there was of it.

Crumbling white plaster exposed wires, and the floor was stripped straight to the plywood underlay. A patchwork of old linoleum tiles, mud-stained carpet rolls and cardboard trailed from the front door to a reinforced metal one at the rear.

"What the hell happened, Jack?" she said under her breath. She crossed the gutted store and knocked on the metal door.

No answer. Lindsay went straight to the door knob. It was

locked. She knocked again, harder this time. Behind her, the shop door crashed open and in came the giant.

"You ain't getting past that one," he said, nodding.

"Wha—?"

He strolled towards her, shifting his bag to one arm, while his hand dug around in the pocket of his parka. "Locked it on my way out." He pulled out a set of keys so full that they formed a stiff three-quarters arc and selected one.

He stepped forward and she stepped aside.

"You live here? Not Jack Cole, then?"

"That the name of the friend who's waiting for you?"

The game was up. She sighed. "Yeah, it is."

Again the man's mouth broke into an amused smile. "He'll be back soon. You want to, you can come down and wait." He moved sideways to hold the door open for her.

Lindsay tried not to look as scared as she was. What the hell had Monroe gotten her into? The cop had warned her to talk to Jack herself, but hadn't mentioned anything about his living in the basement of some abandoned building with Bigfoot. Perhaps it was a kind of test. After all, if she didn't have the guts to go down there, how could she expect others to face New York's real underground?

"Sure. Sounds good." Carefully she walked down the stairwell, him clumping behind her, filling the one escape route. They emerged into a clean, spartan apartment. No, not spartan. Spartan was its own kind of style. This was absence, the kind of deprivation found in a prison cell. There were no bookshelves, no television, no phone—not even a single picture on the cracked plaster walls. The only illumination was the weak beams of sunlight that fell through a pair of small street-level windows high on the back wall. Lindsay had no sense of Jack in the bleak apartment, nothing to make it seem as if this was where he belonged.

The black man kicked off his boots, carpeted the floor with his coat. "Sit down. He'll be back soon."

Her seating choices were two chairs, an uncomfortable-looking plastic one by a small formica kitchen table, and a worn mud-brown leather armchair pushed into the far corner. Lindsay crossed the room to take up the latter.

"So…my name's Lindsay."

The man took two cartons of eggs from the paper bag, placed one on the counter and the other in the rusted fridge. "That right?"

Lindsay was tired of being played with. "Yeah, that's right. Now could you stop with your I-know-something-you-don't-know game and act like a normal human being?"

His eyes positively gleamed. "Man, I can't wait for Jack to come back and see what I brought home."

"You make it sound as if I were a bargain at a garage sale."

He gave a soft hoot. "More than what Jack bargained for, I'll bet." He turned to the sink and began washing his hands under a sputtering tap. "Reggie," he tossed over his shoulder. "I'm Reggie."

"I take it you're a friend of Jack's

Reggie dried his hands on a towel that Lindsay wouldn't have washed her floor with and took a large frying pan from one of the small cupboards. "Yeah. Something like that."

Lindsay took in his familiarity with the place, and had to ask, "You and Jack are…roommates?"

"Yeah." Reggie scrunched his forehead in sudden thought. "You asking if I'm gay?"

The directness of his question threw her, and she reacted with her own bluntness. "I don't care if *you* are. I'm just wondering about Jack, is all."

Reggie let out a whoop of laughter, and he fell back against the ancient yellow fridge, rocking it and holding his gut. He chugged out a succession of long motor-like guffaws. "Oh, man, I can't wait. I can't wait." Gradually he subsided and began cracking eggs into the pan.

He was on his seventh when he theorized, "Might explain why he's so off women, but I doubt it."

Lindsay watched as Reggie broke all twelve eggs into the pan and proceeded to scramble them on a two-burner hot plate, his back to her.

"How do you know him?" Lindsay said, shedding her jacket and folding it over the back of the chair. The place wasn't as cold as it looked.

"How come you say you're a friend of Jack when you've never come around before?" he asked right back.

He had a point. "We were friends in high school, then he and his dad moved away, and I haven't seen him since. I didn't know until today that he was back in New York."

"You're here to say hello?"

Lindsay wasn't about to go into it with Reggie. "Yeah. Something like that."

He snorted at having his line thrown back at him. "I like you, girl." He shook his head. "I can't wait."

When the pan had heated to a steady hissing, he tipped half of the yellow globby contents onto a plate, and ate the rest out of the pan, staring off into space as if he were by himself.

"You live alone?" he suddenly asked.

This time Lindsay was prepared for Reggie's abruptness, maybe because he was a straight-shooter like her. "No. I have a niece."

He stopped chewing. He looked ready to ask another

question when the door at the top of the stairs opened. The light from the store above briefly cast a man's shadow down to the dim apartment. Gold teeth appeared in anticipation. "Must be him now."

Lindsay stood automatically. Her hand fluttered to her pale hair and she wished she'd thought to check herself in the mirror instead of watching Reggie shovel egg into his face.

Not that she was here to rekindle a high school crush, her ears tracking the descent of the booted footsteps. Still, there was no denying it. She was looking forward to seeing Jack Cole again.

WANT TO READ IT?
If you're on Goodreads, here's the link to adding
Undertow to your bookshelf.

www.goodreads.com/book/show/17564454-undertow

Also find there
Midnight Everlasting (The UnderCity Chronicles #2),
set for release in December, 2013.

www.goodreads.com/book/show/17831831-midnight-everlasting

ABOUT THE AUTHORS

S. M. STELMACK IS OUR pen name, short for Serge & Moira Stelmack.

We aim to give what we like in a story—gutsy men and women, high stakes and LOL lines. Serge is the storymaster who blasts out the beginning, middle and end. Moira comes behind, clucking and hemming, as the story undergoes countless rewrites till it meets our vision. She's also the media relations manager, senior editor, marketing VP, director of operations (domestic and foreign), comptroller and the one who makes sure that Serge has a steady supply of cola while he works.

We live with our two kids, and several other strange pets, in a land of wintertime sunshine and snow and summertime mud and mosquitoes. Actually, it's not that bad. The snakes in the local lake aren't venomous.

We really need to move.

Authors, Serge & Moira Stelmack
www.smstelmackauthor.com

www.ingramcontent.com/pod-product-compliance
Lightning Source LLC
Chambersburg PA
CBHW071252170626
46809CB00001B/179